* * * * * * * * * *

VIOLENT *Stars*

TOR BOOKS BY PHYLLIS GOTLIEB

Flesh and Gold
Violent Stars

✳ ✳ ✳ ✳ ✳ ✳ ✳ ✳ ✳ ✳

VIOLENT *Stars*

Phyllis Gotlieb

TOR®

A TOM DOHERTY ASSOCIATES BOOK
NEW YORK

VIOLENT STARS

Copyright © 1999 by Phyllis Gotlieb

Edited by David G. Hartwell

A Tor Book
Published by Tom Doherty Associates, Inc.
175 Fifth Avenue
New York, NY 10010

Tor Books on the World Wide Web:
http://www.tor.com

Tor® is a registered trademark of Tom Doherty Associates, Inc.

ISBN 0-312-86953-3

First Edition: May 1999

Printed in the United States of America

0 9 8 7 6 5 4 3 2 1

for Leo, Margaret, Jane
and eventually
Ethan, Oren, Rachel

* * * * * * * * *

VIOLENT *Stars*

PROLOGUE ✳

Khagodis: *Verona and Bullivant*

It was later on that the terrible beast came to take her, and later still that she found out it was called an Ix. It came after all the other upsets, and she was nearly asleep by then. Earlier she had just been lying there wishing she was dead.

The glastex dome had depolarized gradually as the light faded until it was clear under the night sky, and she could see a thousand brilliant stars blazing as only the sky of Khagodis displays them. So brilliant they hurt, and not one of them anywhere near her home sun.

No, it wasn't the stars that hurt, it was that flaming row. *You're some kind of father letting her drag me away without lifting one finger to stop her!*

How could I stop her when she had the right, Vronni?

Right? What right did she have more than you?

Somehow she had endured those three miserable years since her mother had pulled her half across the world and down the long roller-coaster ride to her own private hell, going into shrieking fits every other day, and even her happier laughter was hysterical. And he was far and unreachable in those offworld and exotic embassies—he'd just gone off like that, so how could he have cared?

Anybody with blue scales and three heads was more important to you than us!

And nobody to talk to, no one, not that unhappy woman in the cramped apartment in a tower like a sulking princess, where she had to be able to see all the walls and nobody leaving a shadow on the door without her knowing it. Only the smallest window for Verona to look through at the fellows in the street, rotten gangs of thugs her mother called them.

Vronni would have given an arm to ride a glittering moped with one of them, like those wild lumi-haired girls, pressed against a broad back flowing with muscles, all that speed and hot flesh. Even let them screw her. Just to be close to somebody.

But she had no way to get out with the armed guards in the corridors, all of them knowing her, muttering about spoiled brats and sniggering over her crazy mother. Life was just being crammed in there with glaring screens on every wall—they never showed anything but the doorways and halls outside—and her mother jumping at any movement on them.

And oh, the nights, the fearful nights! *She took all that drink and drugs to get away from whatever it was but she'd wake up in the middle of the night with the shakes, and crying, I used to go in and lie down beside her and rub her hands to warm them—they were so cold!—trying to comfort her. I tried and nothing ever helped!*

No friends, no family, not a brother or sister.

She—we couldn't have any more . . . and she didn't want them. You were her whole life.

The awful time her mother had lived through before she was born—as if she herself were guilty of it! *And she made herself MY whole life!*

And abruptly the woman had died. Clutched her head in her hands and shrieked.

Mother! Oh what is it, Mother! Running screaming to find her lying on the floor wrapped in a red and gold sari, dead just like that.

Then there was a great flap with all the armed guards yelling and police barking orders and setting at her with all these gnawing questions, until they decided it hadn't been murder, they thought it hadn't—didn't really know, maybe never would. Murder? By whom? What for?

However it had come about it was an aneurysm, they said, blown-out blood vessel in the brain, something else to do with that terrible time. And she, Vronni—a nickname she despised for the stupid name she loathed, Verona—orphaned and bewildered, had been fenced out of everything, afraid to ask a question, and left alone, finally, completely alone in that stark place waiting for him.

I came as soon as I heard, dear. I did.

He had been on their home world then, at Galactic Federation World Headquarters in Singapore, and came back to Toronto, an old leafy city centered with towers of pleated gold and sea-green glass. But not leafy like that in its outer reaches a hundred and twenty km north where the white apartment towers rode the stone hills like icons, like totems or the steles of Easter Island, and the reckless, useless young rode their mopeds in the pot-treed plazas.

But with him present at least there would be a funeral

and some remembrance. Sweating in black linen under the hot sun staring at the urn on the shelf in the Garden of Sleep, and a stranger muttering *I will fear no evil.*

His eyes were swollen and the words stumbled in his mouth. *I'll take care of you, Vronni.*

I don't want to leave here. She wanted to leave, but not with him. *Didn't Mother have any family at all here?*

She had a family, once....

Perhaps did still, but there was no room now for either mother or daughter, was that it?

I don't know, she'd never let me have any contact with them, and I have to leave for that world, it's where my work is—but Vronni, I really want you with me! I know it will be lonely, but it couldn't be as bad as it's been for you here.

A thousand stars hurling their time-wrapped light through the glastex dome, every one alien, on the first of— how many nights on this world Khagodis, before she saw her homely sun again?

There was a knock, and without waiting her father slid open the door and came in. The doorway was high and broad, not so much to suit the Khagodi who had built it as because they could not conceive of other beings not so tall and broad as they—lesser breeds, without the Law, maybe, from what she had heard of Khagodi snobbery.

Tom Bullivant was shorter than most Khagodi, but tall for an Earther, and pink-skinned in the daytime when you could see his complexion, with a bald head that had a perfect egg-shaped arch. "What is it?" she whispered.

He pushed back the door and regarded the girl-child in the starlight with her pale face. He saw her trembling in her misty-white nightsuit and then, as he touched the light switch, she became a thin fifteen-year-old with the remains of too much makeup smeared on her face, eyes red-rimmed with crying and black-circled from sullenness; from hunching over the trivvy smoking dope in the nights she had endured in the dark apartment, those three years, nights that were so long and dragging when they were not terrifying. Her long dark-gold hair had been curly when she was a small child; now it was hanging in a rough and tangled braid.

He pulled a chair over beside the bed, sat down and nerved himself to take her hands in his own. Hers were clammy and the nails were bitten down. She would have pulled away but he held on. "Vron ... you're far from home, because she died so suddenly and I had to bring you along to a new posting in a hurry, I can't help that, I know you feel friendless and alone here and there won't be much help for that, it'll be quite a while, but we can't keep having these awful fights over what you think happened."

"I don't know what happened, only that you made her unhappy, I don't know why. She never told me anything, nobody ever does, I'm not important enough."

"Oh Vron, that's really sill—no. If I go on like that we'll just find ourselves fighting the same old battle." His hands tightened on hers. "Your mother was the victim of a crime—a kidnapping—and an important witness. That's why everyone was crawling around her and you got pushed aside...."

"You could have helped her—and me too."

"The marriage got too binding on her. She said herself it was like another captivity. She wanted to be free."

"You had a say in what happened to your own daughter!"

His mouth was frozen in the act of answering, and in the moment of silence his hands tightened on hers.

She stared at him, seeing him suddenly from a new angle, more than one. "You're not saying and there's something wrong . . . your own daughter . . . I've always had this feeling. . . . Are you really my father? Are you? Say you're my father!"

He did not reassure her that she was suffering from a common childhood fantasy. He coughed. "I've been your father since you were an embryo—no, a fetus, six thirtydays Standard . . . plus fifteen years! What more can I say?"

She pulled her hands from his and at that moment heard a thud on the roof, a squawk and leathery flapping. She startled.

"It's just a lesser thouk, flying reptile, they don't have good sonar," he muttered almost apologetically. "The greater one stays down in the valleys."

"Do they?" *Who are you! Who am I? and what am I doing here?* She had no energy left to say this, scream this; she suddenly felt drained of anger, resentment, even fear. There was only a cold dull ache left. Alien sun, world—father!—blundering winged reptiles that banged into roofs in the dark. If only it were some Great Bird that would crash through and pluck her away, home, that comfortable embassy apartment in Singapore where they'd all three been together and she thought things had been quiet, where at least she didn't so much notice the guards with the infrared eyes.

She said dully, "I understand. When she married you she was already pregnant. Somewhere there's some man who really is my father."

"She refused to tell him she was pregnant, or tell anyone who he was. I know nothing about him. Her family were very strict colonial NewHavenites from New Southsea World, and when she was kidnapped they thought she was playing a trick, had run away, because she had always fought against their limits. The kidnappers were never caught, and she was let go finally, but her family still wouldn't believe her, and she did leave them then. It's what she told me. A part of her memory was destroyed by the trauma, and sometimes she was confused and changed the details, but—"

Verona had gone pale. "Did one of those kidnappers . . . make her pregnant with me?"

"No, no! I don't know when she became pregnant, before or after, the whole affair was kept out of the news, and she'd never say, but she told me she wasn't raped, because I asked her, and I know she wouldn't want to have a baby by somebody who treated her violently! She went through horrible experiences, but she survived for you, and even though that put a great burden on you it's a reason to remember her more gently. . . ."

He paused and looked at her searchingly. "Oh Vronni, I'm just a fellow who loved your mother so much, I could see what she had been, a bright spirited woman, and I so much wanted her to be restored, and help bring her back. I see her in you, I want to see her spirit more fearless in you, and I couldn't dream of having a daughter I loved more!" He stopped, abashed at himself because he was so used to weighing and measuring his words.

He had tried, too. Forcing herself, she thought back past that eternity of three years, to when they had been together. He had somehow kept her childhood just bearable. She had loved him, really. "You've always been good to us, I know you've done your best," she whispered.

"In this case it wasn't good enough, was it?" He kissed her forehead. "I don't even know who they are but I hate them, hate them," he whispered. "They made her hateful. Her marriage a captivity, and I not a good enough father for you." He left then, and when she found herself crying again it was for the sadness of her mother's loss, the hurt in this man who truly had been a father to her, and the hard fact that some savage minds had warped and then wanted to kill that harmless woman.

In a while a robot monitoring her deltas brought in a bowl of redleaf tea; it soothed her and she lay calm and almost content in the dim light. Beside her was the small brass night-table inlaid with blue Xirifor mother-of-pearl that she remembered from home in Singapore and sitting on it her own music box made by Lyhhrt crafters with the figure of an Orph woman playing an eighteen-pipe dugak. It was one of a series of eighteen "Alien Music Makers," and when the Lyhhrt discovered that the boxes were considered kitschy and tasteless they had stopped making them and destroyed the stock on hand; Verona's toy had become a rare artifact. She loved it, ugly or not. She touched its switch and the tiny squat woman set to pumping and hammering a faint and hideous music.

By now she was dipping in and out of sleep listening to this mild cacophony, thinking of herself somewhere on an even stranger world playing the dugak and belonging on the world, watching the blaze of its stars . . .

. . . and the black shape blotting half of them.

She surfaced at once and froze in terrified wakefulness, then heard the squawk and rustle, *It's that reptile, the lesser one. . . .*

There was a pop, and a hiss of escaping air (the oxygen capsule socketed behind her ear pinged on) and something bulged toward her that was dark, brilliant, full of blazing white eyes, flashing with spectrum colors, darting with jets of blackness, coming down on a line suspended like a monstrous insect. Lying frozen with terror, without ever having seen it or even heard of it she knew it, felt it, sensed it. It was what had been in the shadows, the horror haunting her mother for the dreadful fifteen years that had been almost half her lifetime, since Verona was born.

It was almost on her, reaching six limbs tipped with daggers of light, then her nose filled with an aching tang and everything went really black.

ONE ✳

Bullivant and Hawksworth

Bullivant came out in his morning robe, a black and white checked linen dashiki, and the valet, a squat but beautifully chromed robot, pulled his chair back for him and said, "Good morning Mister Bullivant sir here is a fresh egg for you."

"Thank you, Masterman," Bullivant said over his shoulder, and drew the chair forward on its casters. The sun was rising swiftly due east in this equatorial country, where the city of Burning Mountain supported the World Court and the World Galactic Federation Headquarters as well as an Interworld Court. The glastex enclosure of the small dining room let the brilliant blue light of the sky fall generously on broad ceramic pots of native Khagodi soils that held plants grown from Earth's seed, while outside beyond it the more exotic leaves and flowers of Khagodis pressed against the clear surface. The scene was very pretty and also very hot, and for each degree the sun rose in the heavens the rumbling of the coolers sharpened by a note.

Masterman presented a tray. The tiny glaur egg, a local product, had a delicate, green, yellow-speckled shell, but the colors looked glaring to Bullivant. He was suffering the headache of a powerful emotional hangover. "Call my daughter, please."

"Your daughter is not in her room sir nor in the Residence."

"What!" Bullivant had picked up a little spoon that seemed to have been made to fit the glaur eggshell, and now stared at his hand poised above the egg. Fear stabbed him and he put down the spoon. "Everything seemed to be going well when I left her." He did not expect Masterman to answer. He stood up. "Did no one see her go?"

"No doors were opened."

Bullivant regarded the robot. It had come with this office: the post was a new one opened only three years previous, and he had never had a robot under his personal command before, let alone a robot valet. He did not think this one was very intelligent. He pushed his chair back. "Call Secretary Hawksworth, Masterman."

"Secretary does not answer Mister Bullivant sir I will serve your egg." Before Bullivant could move the chromed claws reached out and grasped the egg. The spotted shell broke and pale yoke and white slipped through its cracks, falling in a ropy stream to the cloth below. It had not been cooked.

"Here is another egg for you sir," the robot said, and the claws of the other hand reached for Bullivant's head.

Bullivant grabbed the silver salver and chopped Masterman in the sensor complex. The robot coughed once and stopped. Smoke came from the grille of its voder. Bullivant ran past it and through the sitting room and the hall, doors were sliding open, a robot keeled over, crashing.

"Hawksworth! Where are you?"

The secretary, a thin man with black hair and a blue jaw, still wearing his nightsuit, was kneeling in the open doorway of his room with his hands up and his fingers crimped as if he had been trying to claw the door open. His eyes stared through Bullivant. "Hawks? What happened, man? Are you all right?"

Hawksworth said from the depth of his throat, "We have lost the bitch but we have the whelp. If you do not stop prosecuting and persecuting our people the whelp will suffer nine powers of six times what the bitch did." His arms fell and he shook his head like a dog and stared at Bullivant. "Ambassador? What happened? Have I gone mad?"

"Get up, Hawksworth! What were you raving about? Where's my daughter?"

"Isn't she here?"

"Oh my God, Hawks, go and sit down. I don't know what's going on!" Bullivant, running toward Verona's bedroom, found his hands clasping his own skull almost hard enough to break it. The door was locked. He pounded on it. "Vronni! Vronni!"

"It's sealed, sir." Hawksworth had come up behind him, limping from a night spent on his knees. "The indicator's turned red."

Bullivant swallowed. "The skylight must be broken."

"But she had an oxygen cap—and the sensors in her room would show a heartbeat on this indicator or any other kind of life, even—even in a decaying body."

"The way the system's working right now—"

"I've run these systems on three worlds, sir, long before I hired on with you. She's not in there, or we'd have heard alarms before the door sealed. I'll call Security."

Bullivant's housing unit was one of twenty in a loose cluster of seven or eight Embassy buildings linked by tunnels and airlocks for the different atmospheres of thirteen worlds. Security lived in a basement common to the whole complex, and Hawksworth pushed the red emergency button that summoned it. It gave the *ping!* that showed it was still working.

"I was afraid it was dead because the robots and doors were screwed," Bullivant muttered. "What happened here last night, Hawks?"

"I don't know! I went to bed and fell asleep, and next I knew I was on my knees babbling I don't know what."

Bullivant shuddered. "Something about, 'We have lost the bitch but we have the whelp—' "

Hawksworth stopped in the act of rubbing his left knee and stared up at Bullivant with a frozen face. " '—If you do not stop prosecuting and persecuting our people the whelp will suffer nine powers of six times what the bitch did.' "

"Hawksworth!"

"Oh my God." Hawksworth shook his head as if he had water in his ears. His eyes had gone bloodshot. "Why have I been saying all these stupid things? My head feels strange. . . . Sir? Could I have been hypnotized?"

"No, no!" Bullivant pushed away the idea with a wave of his arm. "We only came here last night, and you were with me on the *Zarandu* and then the *Clipper*, and there was no way for them to get at you. If you 'could have' they'd have bloody well not bothered breaking in."

A voice down the hall called, "Ah-kéké! Is anyone at home?"

Standing at the service door, which had opened with all

the others, were three Security Police. Two of them were Khagodi, looking like baby allosauruses, for whom the three-meter ceilings were not too tall, a brilliant-scaled man, and a woman of subdued color. Bullivant came nearly to the shoulders of the man, and only just above the Khagodi woman's waist. The third was a Solthree woman. Both Khagodi were wearing copper mesh impervious helmets to shield outworlders—the guilty as well as the innocent—from their powerful telepathy.

"Will you identify?" Bullivant asked.

"Yes, Ambassador," the Khagodi woman said. "I am Officer Tharma of the Burning Mountain Police." Tharma was an out-country woman who spoke *lingua* with a bright sharp West Ocean accent. She was carrying a serious-looking stunner in her harness and a huge old-fashioned key-ring in her hand. "This is Peaceman Heth, who serves this Complex—"

"Yes, I recognize him." Bullivant was grateful to see a familiar face; Heth was a trustworthy factotum who had served in other outworld Khagodi embassies.

"And this is Captain Smiryagin, Galactic Federation Security. What is wrong?"

Bullivant nodded to acknowledge the rest of the force. "My daughter has disappeared, and her bedroom door is sealed."

"You are sure she is gone?"

"Not absolutely. The machine valet told me she was not here before it went haywire." Bullivant told her of his adventures at breakfast while Heth and Smiryagin went scouring for hidden intruders.

"This is the door?"

"Yes."

"Will you permit me to open it?"

"Go ahead."

"You both have auxiliary oxygen?"

"Yes."

The woman took a stubby instrument from a sling bag and pointed its lens at the latch. The door slid open lazily.

The room was empty and without a sign of disturbance except that the glastex dome had a gaping hole with shrunk and crinkled edges as if something very hot had been put to it. Verona's bed was rumpled, but her fluffy slippers were paired with childish rigidity right where her feet would slip into them.

Bullivant said, "Vronni?" in a half-whisper, as if she were hiding somewhere asleep and he hesitated to wake her.

"She is not here," said the policewoman kindly, looking down at Bullivant like a mother. "When did you last see your daughter, Ambassador?"

"At midnight. We'd had a quarrel, I spoke to her for a while and we made up. She was peaceful by then, I know she was. She had no reason to run away and nowhere to go." He thought of her barefoot out . . . somewhere and shivered.

The Khagodi woman tilted her massive head to look through the hole in the roof. "I am sure she didn't run away." When she brought her head down again it was like a drawbridge descending. "Were you both asleep when this happened, gentlemen?" She directed her deliberate gaze at Hawksworth. "Secretary?"

Hawksworth swallowed, flicked a glance at Bullivant, and said, "I went to bed and fell asleep, and the next I knew I woke up kneeling in that doorway coming out of what seems to have been an unconscious hypnotic state. I have no idea what happened to put me in that state or whatever went on when I was out of it. I can't say more than that."

"Yes. You cannot. So you say." She turned to Bullivant, but he said nothing. "Tik! I understand the ways of diplomats, Ambassador, but they make it difficult for me to conduct my business. You need the advice of your Liaison Officer, and I suggest you get it immediately."

"I'll do that," said Bullivant, "and you can find me a medic to care for my friend here."

"Agreed." Bullivant's oxygen cap pinged its half-hour's warning and she moved around him to the bedroom entrance. "Now, if you permit I will reseal this room for Forensics." He moved back and she drew the door closed. Immediately the ventilators rose to an even higher whine, pumping oxygen to replace what had escaped.

"Mister Bullivant...."

He found Smiryagin at his elbow. She had been scouring the rest of the apartment. Smiryagin was a big hearty Miry—nickname for Russian—with a broad creased face, a head of coarse thick black hair and a mustache.

"Have you had any other message?"

Bullivant could not help twitching at the thought that the Secretary might fall to his knees and burst out in that hideous voice with some other fearful demand, and when that did not happen, wished that it had, so that he might know where he stood.

"No. My Liaison is Representative Evarny and it was too late to reach him when I came in last night."

"I presume you'll be staying here."

"I hope not! This place is a trap!"

"Just let me know where, Ambassador. Please."

"Ambassador," Heth said, "I am sorry we seem to be strained, it is only that our communications nets are overburdened with so many interworld lawyers and press people swarming about the city for the trials."

"I understand that well enough," Bullivant said. "Look, I can hardly think straight. My daughter's been taken and I want her back before she gets hurt or killed. I can be paged anywhere—whoever's trying to hurt me seems to be able to reach me easily enough!"

Smiryagin said quietly, "All we want is to make sure we can get in here when Forensics comes to collect evidence during the afternoon. The key to that front door weighs three kilos and we don't have entry to the back. None of Tharma's keys fits."

"Ring for the Housekeeper, I'll make sure she lets you in any time you get here."

Smiryagin nodded and turned to Hawksworth. "Will you come with us and permit yourself to be examined by our medic? We haven't authority to hold you, and certainly not to force you."

Hawksworth swallowed. "I'll come."

Bullivant said, "Hawks, I'm going to contact Evarny at the GalFed Office and I expect to be at his house."

They stood looking at each other for an awkward frozen moment. "Yes," Hawksworth said.

Bullivant pulled the big wheel that opened the front door latch. A Lyhhrt in a bronze workshell was waiting in the doorway. "I am the qualified medical officer who will accompany this person," he said in his beautifully modulated voice. Lyhhrt did not have personal names and only rarely acknowledged them in others. No one felt quite comfortable in the presence of Lyhhrt, though they made the best doctors and surgeons to be found anywhere. Hawksworth accompanied this one and Smiryagin very uneasily.

When they were all gone Bullivant did not touch any of the regular CommUnits, audio or tri-V, but used his personal key to hook into the redline in the wax-sealed wall safe.

"Galactic Federation Office. Who is calling, citizen?" The cautious whispering voice took him aback. The tone of it, hoarse and sexless, made Bullivant push the *record* and *scramble* buttons. He found himself sweating, and the recycled air became close and pressing.

"Representative Evarny gave me to expect that he would answer this line."

"We are sorry. Sta Memthe Evarny is communing with his Ancestors." The line went dead.

Communing with his ancestors . . . he knew that among Khagodi that meant dying or dead. But he had been using a direct line, not to be answered except by Evarny.

He was obscurely frightened, but there was no use in trying that code again and no one else to ask for advice. He was alone. He stood by the comm and tried to think.

There had simply been no more money for staff in this bare-bones embassy. In the midmorning of a day in which he meant to orient himself to this office on this world he had never felt more estranged in his life. He could think of nothing but his wife's horrible kidnapping, was stunned with terror at the thought of Verona suffering the same experience.

The redline chimed and he unlocked it quickly, desperately, wanting and dreading a whispered message.

"Bully!"

"Skerow? Is it you?" He knew it was; the way she pronounced his name, "Booey," had made him smile whenever he heard it, but not today.

"Evarny is dead, Bully. Can you come? I am at his house."

"Dead! What's happened?"

"I can't tell you now!"

"I'm so sorry, Skerow, I—"

"Please come quickly then, I daren't stay here long."

"But—" He had said he could be paged. "I'll come."

Evarny had been Khagodis's World Representative to Galactic Federation, the only one with such authority that Bullivant knew and trusted. Now with him dead and Hawksworth under the eyes of the police, there was no one in the world he could put faith in completely, except Skerow. *I daren't stay here long . . .* she was in danger then.

He slipped a handful of oxygen caps into his pocket and left by the service door down the big galumphing stone steps, three deep levels of them, to the Housekeeper's cubicle in the basement. He did not think that dozing woman had much to do with interworld plots; he might trust her to call an aircab for him.

Skerow

Skerow was waiting inside the crescent of dwarf ebbeb trees that gave some privacy to the doorway of Evarny's house. Not home, but residence; his home had been far northward in one of the provinces of the Northern Spine Confederacy. And Skerow was not his wife, really, had not been for forty-two years. He had divorced her on grounds of infertility back then after their only daughter died. Somehow after thirty-five years of separation, perhaps as short brisk Northerners trapped by their important positions in a languid equatorial country, the twenty years they had spent as a couple had accrued enough interest to bring them together once more in a shy and tentative way they were careful not to disturb.

"But he was murdered, Bully!" Skerow was swallowing air frantically to give herself voice. She was shorter than the dwarf trees and only a head taller than Bullivant: age had diminished her. "He died to save me." Her eyes were thickly red-rimmed with weeping. There were two tall guards flanking her, unhelmeted and holstered with lethal stunners and flamers.

He opened his mouth and could not say a word. But she and her naked-minded guards were ahead of him.

"Tik! My dear fellow, your daughter—I never knew, you should have told me! I would never have brought you here in such circumstances."

He caught his breath and forced out words. "You seemed to need me, Skerow."

"I do need you—you are my truest friend on this world now—but I must go into hiding, and so must you, Bully dear!"

"I called you on the redline and a strange voice answered. Was that one of your people?"

"No," she whispered. "No. Eka! I must surely move. And for you, I will find a safe place in another embassy where you will be comfortable."

"It's not likely I'll find comfort until she's found—but what of you, Skerow?"

"Come and let me tell you."

The small and seldom-used courtyard they had retired into was awash with the dead ebbeb leaves and blossoms of many seasons past.

Skerow had sent a staff member with a hand-held message to run the circuit of embassies whose officials she knew well, and now she crouched by the low retaining wall he had sat on and clasped his soft pink hands in her scaly pearl-taloned ones. "Evarny would have called you, but he was too late by one fall of the clock-weights. I am a witness, you see. Evarny . . ." Her hand went to her mouth for a moment. "Truly, such a harmless man." One huge tear ran from the corner of her eye and glistened like a falling crystal in its long track down her face.

He was not harmless to you, Skerow, all those long years of neglect. "How did it happen?"

She did not answer the unspoken thought. "You know how long the Zamos trials have been going on. . . ."

The long affair was centuries old, and so complicated that most of the witnesses, journalists and general audience needed to refresh their memories at least once every two days by some recorded means—audio, video or daily fax sheets published by the courts and media. This court was only one of scores trying connected cases on several worlds.

It had begun those centuries back with the rise of the Zamos Corporation, a chain of legal brothels which had established businesses in hundreds of locations on three worlds. It was certainly the largest brothel owner that had ever existed on any worlds in Galactic Federation. To appear more respectable Zamos had added circuses, gladiatorial and sports arenas, and gambling casinos filled with many thousands of well-paid employees, had kept this up for nearly two hundred years Standard, and certified its reputation by achieving membership in the Interworld Trade Consortium.

During that time it was also conducting secret research in creating ready-made prostitutes—slaves, really—by cloning.

This was the area in which Khagodis had become involved: Zamos persuaded the Interworld Consortium to buy a tract of land that was going cheap in the Isthmus States on Khagodis; here Zamos researchers conducted experiments and studies, particularly on an underwater species that had originally been developed on Earth. Their work over many years produced clones that were unusually healthy and vigorous. They felt that the installation on Khagodis would be well shielded among a people long considered to be overly high-minded. Khagodi themselves, of course, did not share this opinion, and the Khagodi renegades who guarded the clones did not worry much about high-mindedness.

When the clones accidentally discovered gold on Consortium property in the waters by the shore, Zamos set them to mining the vein and lent the gold back to the Consortium at high rates through a money-laundering company—basically, selling them what they already owned.

Zamos had aimed for hundreds of years to create fertile clones, and when one of the female swimmers was found to be pregnant—as well as dangerously independent-minded—she had been transported for safekeeping to Zamos's brothel on Fthel V in the Twelveworlds System, Galactic Federation Central Headquarters, in the city of Starry Nova. By chance she was put on display in the brothel window. By chance Skerow was presiding judge of the Quarterly Assizes in Starry Nova.

"And there I saw her, Bully!

"I was a circuit judge in those days and walking back from the Assizes session in the evening to one of those dreadful rooms they give you. . . . You know you can never see stars in Starry Nova, the sky is always filthy with clouds and smoke, the rain never cleans it, the water itself is filthy . . . the rain had just stopped falling with the heavy sky still pressing down and the old cobbled streets still wet, and the GalFed Residences you remember are old shabby buildings in the city center near where the casinos and brothels are clustered, all kinds of blaggers and huggards are scuffling about in the shadows and if one were more helpless than I am it might be dangerous. . . . I confess I almost loved that place because its life is so different from my own. It was dark coming along with only one burning bright place along the street, and that was Zamos's window like a bowl or bubble, with her swimming in it, sleeping and dreaming terrible dreams . . . my wonder at her, it was because she was so much like a Solthree, like you, in the shape of her face and limbs, though she lived in water, but her mind caught my shock and it startled her awake, she thought I was her enemy because I am a Khagodi."

What Skerow had been able to tell the Police gave Galactic Federation enough information to make them risk investigating Zamos's brothel, and Zamos's fall began.

"And I thought it had fallen for good, after all these long years, that my people had become a little less self-righteous, that the Federation had become a little less accommodating to the murderous and the greedy, I know by all my Saints that people will spend their passions somehow, no matter how strange the ways, but to enslave people that they may do this?"

She said wonderingly, "It was only yesterday that I

went into the courtroom after all those years to testify, and to listen, to watch that swimming woman tell her life's story . . . only yesterday."

The air-cooling system was new and like most contraptions on Khagodis, did not work very well. The city of Burning Mountain had always been extremely hot and damp, and it had been a series of outworld maneuvers that had installed the Interworld Court of Galactic Federation here; architects from the world Kylklar had ended up winning the contracts to design and construct the courthouse in a city that they themselves enjoyed for its heat. The Khagodi certainly did not like it. The streets threading the Court Complex were scabbed with vending machines dispensing allergy pills and lotions for scale-rot, psoriatic fungus, and other plagues that attacked reptile primates.

Yet the courthouse itself was pleasing, built by the feathered Kylkladi on their favorite architectural principle, the bower; the homely gazebo had been rendered on a great scale, a circle of reinforced ebbeb saplings of tremendous height, curved to join at the top, their slender trunks woven with boughs and preserved leaves layered to let in light and keep rain out. The banks of fans that hung beneath the dome kept the heat dispersed by their whickering leaf-shaped blades on all but the hottest days, when the new cooling system was intended to supplement their work. It had broken down on the hottest day of the year.

As a World Court judge, Skerow usually enjoyed attendance in this beautiful courtroom even on hot days; she was watching joyfully as the testimony came to an end. Toward evening the air had cooled under the ceiling fans and the bailiffs had wheeled away the tank holding the woman whose appearance in Skerow's life had changed so many thousands of other lives. One of the three presiding judges, all of whom had been students when Skerow took the dais in her first case, called out, "Citizens, the day's business is done, and is seen to have been done!" and the audience shuffled with relief.

The arches of the cold-light tubes that augmented the green light filtering through the leaves began to dim, and the green shaded into dusky blue, journalists and observers flicked off monitors and translation machines, a half-score of human species stirred out of chairs and slings and began the first exits. Skerow had a standing-place; Khagodi squat on their haunches and do not need to sit. She watched Evarny, a small Northern man with a lively step, climbing up the range of tiers toward her and moved out into the aisle to meet him.

As he came closer to her row . . . she felt strange, as if she were alone and wrapped in a sudden stillness, isolated in the glare of a spotlight. Then sensed a sparkling from above, heard an odd sound and tried to blink flickers from her eyes. Found herself forced to look up, though she did not want to, up to that source of black lightning and universe-cracking sparks, found herself becoming dizzy, fainting with the piercing ozone tang in her nostrils. Beyond the dizziness, faintness, nausea, she could just perceive a being, source of the disturbance, crouched high up in the curving branches of the ebbeb, aiming a weapon, a gun with a long barrel, plated with silver like a bolt of the whitest lightning, a weapon aimed at her. She saw nothing for an instant but the dark opening of the barrel leading to eternity, could not even swallow air to cry out.

But someone else was crying out: "No! No!" and she

was knocked over by the whole weight of a hurled body. She did not even hear the explosion. Evarny, the sharp-eyed quick-stepping Northern man, had taken its whole force and sprawled over her dead.

"I thought for one instant that I could see into that barrel, even its rifling spiraling down and drawing me in. That murderer was an Ix, and it is the Ix who are doing this, for the sake of Zamos. For nearly a century and a half they have done their dirtiest work for the slavemakers and now they are making terrorist raids on the people who dared hit back at Zamos. There have been more than a score of them these last seven years and I thought they were isolated incidents of revenge, but now I wonder if they are not part of a policy. It's one I find most frightening, I really don't want to believe that Zamos is still operating somewhere underground, because they have done their best to disgrace me but never until yesterday tried to kill me."

Bullivant had heard of the Ix. Everybody had heard of them but nobody knew them, and did not want to know either. What they knew was that Ix were egglayers who had polluted their world and themselves so horribly that they faced extinction. To survive they needed a new and richer medium in which to incubate their eggs; their scouting ships had found that the bodies of Lyhhrt were nearly perfect for them. Their world Iyax had attacked Lyhhr, a neutral world with close ties to Galactic Federation. The Lyhhrt had begged GalFed for help, but no one was willing to commit the huge sums necessary to rescue this strange people who were—at least seemed to be—only robots with amoebas inside them.

It was Zamos who came to the rescue of both parties by offering to help the Lyhhrt: they were prepared to create an artificial egg-hatching medium for the Ix if the Lyhhrt would serve them for one Cosmic Cycle—that is, one hundred and twenty-nine years in Lyhhrt terms. Zamos had plenty of uses for Lyhhrt because of their tremendous mastery of surgery and robotics as well as powerful telepathy. The Lyhhrt's cycle of slavery had ended as Zamos was about to fall, but by the end of that cycle the Lyhhrt, to their shame, had helped Zamos create the scores of clone varieties shipped as embryos by the millions to nineteen worlds.

So Zamos, swollen with greed, had stood with Ix terrorists and enslaved Lyhhrt as its right and left hands.

Bullivant knew of this deadly alliance which had kept the Lyhhrt subjugated. He knew that the attacks by Ix were made even more frightening because of the hallucinatory pheromones they emitted to disorient their victims. He was beginning to wonder what an ambassador could do here; whether the promotion he had worked so hard for was becoming an exile into danger.

Skerow was looking at him, and put her hands on his shoulders, a rare gesture. "Yesterday I believed that everything Zamos had created was almost completely shattered. Now that Evarny is dead and your daughter has been taken from you I see that I was mistaken. I don't know that Zamos or the Ix meant to kill you, Bully, but I believe the Ix have put their hands on you for the sake of Zamos." She clasped her own hands. "I must not put my burden on you. . . ."

Another huge tear ran down her face and glittered off the scales of her jaw. "He was a man of a hundred and twenty-nine years, and of course that is not youth but he might have had—we might have had twenty-five or thirty. At least he had his son from that other woman to beget his thousands. I must send you away, Bully, and keep you safe!"

The wind had quickened, eddying among the dead blossoms, and the sky was shading into the mid-afternoon rain-hour. "I'll go wherever you think is best for me, Skerow," Bullivant said. "God knows I'd give you comfort if I had any of my own to give."

He sensed the presence of Skerow's messenger at the gate, a five hundred kilo Southern woman swathed in the harnesses of stun- and stim-guns and bearing a packet with an official seal. Skerow knew what was in it even as she received and opened it. "It is from the Pinaxer Embassy," she said. "The Pinxin are happy enough to do a favor; they are here looking for a few for themselves." She looked up. "You won't mind staying awhile with five or six of those blue Pinxid women, will you, Bully? They can be quite pleasant when they want to be. They have the oxygen nearest your level and lately they seem to have hired quite a few guards."

"They probably pay much higher GalFed dues than my home world is willing to do." His mood was bitterly black. In better times he would have very much enjoyed the company of the Pinxin, who were always referred to in conversation as Pinxid women, as if the two sexes existed. Many other outworld peoples had enjoyed the company of Pinxin, some of them too well.

The messenger was waiting for his answer, and Bullivant said, "I'd be grateful to stay there until my quarters are repaired."

"No need to tell them anything they don't need to know."

He laughed shortly. "Not likely. I've been in the service over twenty years. Anyway not many people will look for me around the Pinxin and I'll be near enough if any messages come."

A harsh voice said, "That will not be necessary." The two Khagodi stared at Bullivant and he stared back at them in horror. The voice was his own. "You will make the Court reverse its rulings on Zamos," it said. "You will do this within ten days or what befell your wife will be sweetness compared to what befalls your daughter."

He sat horrified unable to move, with his mouth wrenched and stiff as if a serpent had forced its way out in writhing coils. When the words stopped he moved unthinkingly to find his handkerchief and spit in it, then clasped his hands over his mouth as if he were covering an indecent nakedness. There was one crack of thunder and the rain began with a few splattering drops.

Skerow's head tilted. "Now they have indeed proven how well they can reach everyone. We cannot go on this way, and the trials must be suspended, no matter how much comfort it gives to the enemy. But for yourself," her topaz eyes were the kindest in the world, "you need a doctor, Bully," she said gently. "And more than a friend to comfort you."

Verona and Acolytes

When Verona opened her eyes the first thing she saw was a woman with blue skin staring down at her. Woman? Eyes much like her own hazel ones but dark blue, some jade green shading to them, flat-saddled nose with nostrils and a mouth with green-tinged lips. Yes, green, and did not look wrong either. Her hair was yellow-white and close-curled. Maybe all of that was the color of a mind coming out of nightmare with bleary eyes. She blinked and the colors did not change. The strangeness made her shrink even before she dared think of where she was, but this person was a woman, a being with breasts under the coarse red shirt, and hands with four or five—yes?—fingers with yellow-orange nails.

The apparition said something. Verona's *lingua* was still very rough—the Galactic language was not often spoken on her native Earth—and she thought it was: *You are awake,* or *Are you awake?* She tried to nod, and found her neck very stiff. Her mouth was so dry she could not get her tongue free, and began to cough. The air was thick and warm.

The woman went away to find water or else someone who could speak to her, and Verona tried to move and look about but her hands and feet were numb. Her eyes were getting used to the light, what there was of it, and she found herself in a small square room lined with stucco that was flaked away in spots to show grayish-brown stone; one small round four-paned window of rough nubbled glass was set in a wall nearly half a meter thick. There were green leaves pressing against it from the outside and the light coming through was not twilight; but she was not sure what time it was nor where she was, except somewhere on this world in the daylight hours. An ugly terror was crackling at the edge of her mind, and she fought to keep it from coming in.

She worked a little saliva into her mouth and pulled up

her heavy head, supporting herself on her elbows. She was lying on a hard narrow cot, still in that fluffy nightsuit and bare feet. No place to pee.

The door opened and a dark glittering being came round its edge. The terror swamped her and she shrank back gasping.

"Silly little girl, did you think I was one of *them?*" the being said in English in a dismissive manner. "I am not yet worthy to be called one."

All she could think of, what filled her mind to bursting, was: *If I see one of THEM again I'll*—trying to put it in a package and shove it away from her mind—*(die-or-go-crazy)!*

She forced herself to look at this apparition and saw that it was in fact a person of her own kind, young enough to be more nearly a girl like herself than a woman. She had dark hair framing a narrow face that was so pale it seemed the sun had never shone on it. This stranger was dressed—swathed—in sheer black veils spangled with brilliant sequins of different sizes and colors, and her draped and gathered robes were harnessed by metallic bands studded with jewels too big and crudely colored to be genuine.

"Here is water, by the grace of our Lords," the woman said in English. There was a bright manic edge to her. She snapped her fingers; the blue woman brought a thick stoneware cup and pitcher, and a fresh oxycap.

Verona swallowed, licked her lips and said, "Thank you." She replaced the oxygen, took the cup and tasted the liquid gingerly, but it seemed only to be tepid, rather brackish water, and she was feverishly thirsty. The blue woman reached for the empty cup, her fingers slipped on it and it crashed to the floor.

"Lummox!" The veiled acolyte grabbed the pitcher

from her and slapped the side of her head so hard that it rapped against the wall as she stumbled. She did not cry out, did not even touch a darkening bruise but stood with her hands up as if in surprise and slowly began shrinking into herself as if she had been burned and were shriveling. The blue alien woman was small, smaller than Verona, who was a rangy girl almost as much like Bullivant in build as if she had been his daughter by blood, and who now felt herself shrinking as if she had been the one slapped.

"Bring a slop-pot," the acolyte snarled, "and see what happens if you drop that!" Then she caught herself up and repeated the words in *lingua*. She followed the servant out of the room.

The blue woman came back alone holding a big clay pot with ears, looking like the usual thunder-mug from Interworld Standard Plumbing, and Verona used it in gratitude while the servant looked away. When she turned back Verona said, "Thank you," from her small store of *lingua* and after a moment of hesitation, trying to remember the words, "Who are you, lady?"

The blue woman whispered, "I am a—" and used a word Verona did not know at all.

"A—?"

The woman hooked a finger into a thin chain around her neck, it was silver or silver colored and one of its links was in the shape of an asterisk. Verona could not tell whether the gesture meant what she thought it might, or even if she was anywhere near understanding this person, but it seemed to her that it suggested ownership or bondage. Not a piece of jewelry.

The chained woman licked her lips with a green tongue and whispered, "Tell them—"

But there was no time; the acolyte swept into the room

followed by two others like three unholy nuns, flashing with jewels and spangles. Before Verona could move two grasped her by the arms and the third by the ankles. When she felt the claws she realized that the third of these nuns was not wearing the flowing veils but had black feathers and talons, that her face, if it was a she, had a beak and fixed onyx eyes. Verona saw this in one blink, and in another the woman holding her right hand had taken a knife from her robe.

Verona shrieked and kicked out, her heel butted the hard beaked face, and the claws scratched and tightened. No one said a word; the hand clutched her fingers, the knife flashed across her palm: straight across: —, at one slant: / and then the other: \ until she felt the blossomed star: *

Then the narrow-faced white-skinned woman spread Verona's bloody hand palm-out against her forehead while the one at her left pulled out a tiny camera and took its picture. She said, "One of those every day until your father comes to his senses. Tomorrow, your face." She grinned with pointed teeth and wrapped a coarse cloth bandage around Verona's hand, and all three dropped their hands from her.

When they were gone, sweepingly as they had come, Verona lay curled up and shivering. *I used to go in and lie down beside her and rub her hands to warm them—they were so cold!*—and the palms were so rough and puckered. Scarred. She could not tell whether or not it was only her terrible imagination, but she thought she had glimpsed beyond the flash of the camera the horrible dark glitter of the being who had come to take her, and smelled its ozone crackling in her nostrils.

She did not try to keep track of the time after that, nor whether the light was brightening or darkening. The blue woman crept in to offer her some broth and biscuits but she could not stand the sight or smell of them, lay shivering with terror and anger; such anger that she hardly felt the pain of her slashed hand and such terror that she thought she would not live beyond the day. She thought she heard a shriek once, tensed and shivered. The time wore on gratingly into the darkness and no one came.

Half-consciously she heard a *tap-tap*, then scraping and grinding and again *tap-tap*. It came from the window and she had no strength to answer it. *Tap-tap,* her hand throbbed and seemed to keep time with it, then *tik-tik-tik,* stones fell to the floor, more stones and a rubble of grit, *TIK!* and a scrape, one more nerve-twinging *scrape!* and a muted clink. A drift of fresh air fluttered her nightsuit. She heard a stranger noise, *buzzt, buzzt, hummm . . .* something like "Awrk!" and a yelp.

She forgot herself long enough to turn over and rise up on one elbow. Dark shapes were plopping over the window-sill, landing on the floor and springing up, but before she could become swamped in horror the hums and buzzes resolved themselves into faint twanging voices: «*Come, miss, come along, come, hurry, come along, little miss, come!*»

"What?" she whispered. "What is it? Who's there?"

«*Us, miss, Aark, Tcha and Ki-Ki!*» said the hallucinatory voices, «*Come quickly!*»

She pulled herself up and the shapes gathered around her; they were hairy, animal heat and smell pulsed from them, and she saw three pairs of beady eyes staring at her. "Who?"

They were three shadow-dark rhesus macaques with bad-tempered faces and what looked like silver crowns on their heads. Monkeys? Here? «*Here is oxy for you, hop-hop and out the window now before they smell us, come-come!»* They jumped to her cot and she flinched away from their heat and the horridly tickling fur. The unearthliness of the metal structures capping them.

Her dull hurt mind would not let her move. They peered at her, rubbed her hair between their fingers, found her oxygen socket and replaced the capsule, plucked at her sleeve. *«Eh-eh, here is a hurt hand, we take care, touch-not.»* The biggest of the three was looking at her earnestly, speaking urgently in the electronic whisper: *«You understand all this, Miss? I am Aark, and we, are, here, to, bring, you, out! Please, say you understand?»*

She roused herself with the greatest effort. "I understand," she whispered, "I'll come," though she did not want to do anything but sink down.

«So now. Take this hand, come this way, up-up, watch the feet, here's stones to scrape them,» she saw the window, plucked from its frame, lying on the floor—*«watch out for that!»*—guiding her past the fallen bits of stone and stucco, *«out-you-go, miss—»* pulling her by the wrist, small hot hands at her elbows pushing her headfirst out of the tiny window, into the dusk, oh, oh, there was a deep well of darkness below the sill, far below and her head whirled, she cried out—

«Hush now!» Ki-Ki was lifting her legs while Aark and Tcha pulled her torso over the sill and passed her to many other small hands, Aark wound her around with a rope looped on a piton suckered onto the wall while Ki-Ki and Tcha set the window back into its frame. She dropped into space and for a lurching instant thought they had let go of the rope. In another moment she found herself clinging to the thick woody stem of a massive vine with cracking bark

that caught at her nightsuit and scraped her hands and feet, then the rope had been whipped off her and she was climbing down trembling among huge white flowers, like some princess or goose girl out of a fairy tale, favoring her hurt hand and grasping wildly for a branch, and being guided by thin wiry limbs to a handhold.

There was a heavy fragrance to the blossoms, each as broad as her shoulders, each leaf the size of an umbrella, the fragrance permeated the warmth and dusk, and beyond the dark leaf shapes through a thinner air than at home the stars seemed to be rushing toward her blazing. The dizziness twisted her head about and wrenched her neck, she had the thick stem hooked in her elbow with her knees gripping it like pliers, but the ground still seemed very far below, and the great vine spread endlessly over the broad wall. The macaques urged her, pushed and pulled at her, hummed in her ear. The sky grew darker and heat lightning flared on the horizon, she moved downward in a dream. . . .

A voice barked, "What's that! Who's there!" in *lingua* she found too easy to understand. A beam of light swept over the wall. She heard the leaves fluttering as five or six macaques dropped, and in a moment the light went out and there were no more shouts.

Further down she could see between the leaves that there were hedges surrounding the building, and beyond them a road illuminated by flickering lanterns. On it Khagodi were hurrying children and flocks of strange animals; a beast the size of a rhinoceros was dragging a lumbering wagon. They all looked very small and terribly far down.

«*Don't stop, miss, don't stop!*»

She wished for monkey feet, monkey hands and agility too. She went on putting one hand, one foot below the other. She did not look out again but only at her handholds; the sky beyond them was nearly midnight-colored in the quickly spinning night of the tropics.

It was when her feet touched the damp soil that she realized how sore they had become from the cracked bark of the vine-stems. Immediately her hand became thuddingly painful but that did not keep her from noticing the body she was stepping over, a Solthree man in dark clothes neatly parceled in the rope she had been descending on. She did not know whether he was alive or dead. She stumbled along blindly until the macaques slipped through the hedge before her; Aark would not let her pass for a moment and she froze, as if everything in her had stopped working, until he turned back and hummed, *«Come-with, miss, hurry-now!»* The hands kept pulling and pushing, and she was through the brambly hedge.

Shielding her from the open street now was the clumsy wagon with the lumbering behemoth. Another Solthree man dressed in a burnoose was holding the reins. This one grinned and raised his hand.

"Hullo, darling-o, I'm Ned Gattes and you're safe!"

The monkeys climbed onto the big dray and hoisted her up and under the coarse burlap that was covering its frame; before the cloth came down to hide her she glanced up, up at the stone tower and the horror rose in her throat. Then the monkeys crawled in with her and covered them all and the wagon rumbled on. She had some shuddering hysterics after that, but not much, before she fell asleep almost as if she were in her own bed and really home.

TWO *

Fthel IV: *Ned Gattes*

Ned Gattes had never wanted and never intended to visit Khagodis. The only Khagodi he knew by heart was Skerow, and even she intimidated him the way all the other Khagodi did. But he was an important witness for the Lyhhrt to some of the terrible conflicts that had taken place between them and Zamos. He had already made preliminary depositions and could have given his testimony on any of the five worlds where the long series of trials had been taking place, but he was always on the wrong one. He had sworn with his life that he would help destroy Zamos, but he and Zella had had to make a living for themselves and the children, and Galactic Federation never seemed to have funds available for the long and expensive interstellar voyages.

Eventually he and Zella had found themselves well-paying jobs running a school for gladiators on Fthel IV where the air smelled like perfume and the weather was beautifully warm in the tropics and sweetly cool in the temperate zone. When he and the family had settled themselves comfortably here, and on a fall day that was particularly mellow, his agent Manador sent him a message. She was still based on cold and desolate Fthel V in the grim port city of Starry Nova, where the Civil Service Divisions of Galactic Federation worked almost as hard as they played in their vacation colonies on Fthel IV.

The call came in on Ned's transcomm with a lot of other mail he was picking up. The trees were heavy with fruit on this warm day in Miramar on the Cinnabar Keys, also known as The Terrarium, like any other Solthree Community; it was Zella's turn to pick up the kids from the condo school and he was about to close the office early and go home because the next day was a Civic Holiday, one of many that Miramar celebrated. He would have stored the message without reading it for a couple of days except that it came from Manador. He hadn't heard from her in the two years Standard since he'd been on this world.

LOOK HERE NED GATTES, it said, THERE S A JOB FOR YOU ON KHAGODIS THEY NEED A TOUGH PUG DETAILS FOLLOW

His heart sank, yet the DETAILS FOLLOW made him punch in the decode number he hadn't used in those two years—and give up hope of leaving early. But the rest of the message turned up almost immediately:

GALFED WILL PAY YOUR EXPENSES AND MORE TO HELP CLEAN UP SOME BUSINESS LEFT OVER FROM THE BIG SCAN-DAL AND THE LYHHRT NEED YOU TO TESTIFY AT THE BIG TRIAL ASAP YOU CAN DO THEM BOTH TOGETHER LOVER

Ned shivered. He had once been Manador's lover and had escaped with his life, like a few who had loved Pinxid women. It was she who had recruited him as a GalFed agent, the career that had led to all the other near misses.

And there was nothing drawing him to Khagodis among those fearsomely alien beings. . . .

He left a line open for his answer but went out in the afternoon sunshine and walked along the avenues that were lightly scattered with newly fallen leaves from some of the few deciduous trees, and blossoms from some that flowered all year long. In the small plazas were stores with bow windows lined with lace curtains where the discriminating shopper could buy Balkan Sobranies and Meerschaum pipes with tins of Three Nuns tobacco, as well as lavender sachets, packs of tarot cards, religious icons and sexual aids.

Miramar was not known as The Refinery for nothing, although the people who shopped in malls and plazas were as likely to dress in yashmaks, anoraks and burnooses as they were to wear solar topees and wide-leg shorts. Even the big red cat padding down the street, wearing a huge blue Xirifor pearl on a platinum chain around her neck, was nothing to stare at. She grinned with sharp teeth and said, "Harroo, Ned Gattsss. . . ."

He paused at a bar that looked like a tea-room and advertised thirty-eight kinds of beer from seven worlds, but it kept British hours and was closed until evening. He went on down the road toward the area known as The Grottoes, where there were steps leading down to the sea. He felt a throbbing lump of resentment underneath his breastbone. He had nearly given his life—and more than once—for Galactic Federation.

He began descending the steps. There was a railing to one side to counter the sheer drop down the chalky cliff that beat back the warm wash of the sea, and to the other a series of natural caves had been fortified with concrene arches and they housed shops full of glittering brummagem, and the kind of glög-halls Ned had been very fond of in the years when he was a bolder and much younger pug, and ran whores on the side as a cover for his GalFed work. He didn't miss that much, missed it so little that he wanted only to stay home and risk only the few hard knocks he got showing raw street fighters how to move.

He was descending nearer and nearer the sea, and the steps began to gather windblown detritus in their lower levels either too quickly for the human cleaners to keep up with it or beyond the reach of machines. Dried leaves and petals, smashed glass needles, used condoms, and dopestick butts heaped themselves along with biodegrading beer containers in the dusty corners. There were shadows here and the bars advertised in flat cold-light letters across their fronts. He was about to turn back because in this kind of district it would be all too easy to find himself in a fight, but the letters caught his eye: DUSKY DELL—HAPPY HOUR!—3 FOR THE PRICE OF 2!

There was something nostalgic about that, and he went in. . . . The air was thick with smoke, and the men and women hunched over tables sucking beer out of bubble-thick glass mugs that did not last long between recyclings, and smoking dope or jhat, looked to him like old spacers who had served the freights from Kemalan to Qsaprinel. They had gotten spaceburned or dizzy, or lost bone mass, and come to an easy place to eke out their Worker's Compensation on the other end of a broom; they were cheaper than machines.

He found a stool at the end of the bar where the light was dimmest; hard eyes stared at him briefly and turned away. He kept his own eyes down toward the counter and drank the local beer, thinking of all the other places he'd worked, fighting in Zamos arenas in Starry Nova and in Zamos's Palace of Knossos on Shen IV, and in still other arenas that had once belonged to Zamos in Starry Nova and on Earth too. Places that were a little more honestly run now. Just didn't pay that much, because they didn't make most of their money shipping clone embryos to Demor V, Sem II and Kemalan. He drank harder to keep the guilt from settling in.

"Don't! Please!" It was the kind of voice and the tone of it that made him whirl about. The busser with her wrist gripped in the navvy's hand was . . . not quite a woman. Not with the khaki skin, the flat-featured, almost blanked-out face, thin body and sketchy breasts. A Zamos clone, of the kind that called themselves the O'e. He had seen too many of them on Shen IV. Her eyes were alive with fear.

"Give it back, you piece of shit!" The navvy was a stubby red-faced woman with frizzy yellow-white hair and a broken nose. She looked as much like an ex-pug as any woman Ned had seen, and with her free hand she whacked the O'e back and forehand across the face. "Give!" The clone shrieked. The drinkers looked up with mild interest.

"Hey!" Without thinking Ned hopped off the stool and pushed his arm and shoulder between the combatants. Not even turning her head the navvy swung her fist out sideways and Ned found the bar stool butting his kidneys and his mouth drizzling blood. Thinking this time he grabbed the old pug by the boot and flipped her so that she sat down hard and let go of the O'e woman, who jumped over the bar and hid behind it. He crouched to wait for the next onslaught.

"No, sweetheart!" A thick arm came round Ned's neck and a hard hand gripped his wrist and wrenched it up behind his back. "Wouldn't I recognize that funny jaw anywhere, that turns so white when you heat up? Ned Gattes?" Another voice he recognized.

"Lemme go, Dell!" He had found himself just short of breaking her arm.

"Just watch it, Ned! You're not welcome here." She freed him.

Ned mopped his mouth and rubbed the offending jaw, the product of a bad graft, and turned to look at the woman. "Dusky Dell. I thought it was familiar." Dell had been her fighting name, and her hair was still very black, perhaps artificially, though her skin had gone paper white from dark hours at the bar. Her real name—real as anything could be for an ex-Zamos pug—was Consuelo O'Brien, and she was still good-looking and muscular. Did her own bouncing, probably.

She was giving a hand up to the red-faced woman and soothing her down. Then she yelled, "Ama! Get out of there! I'm not going to fire you or hit you or anything!" and the O'e crept out from behind the bar, and Dell grabbed and shook her until her teeth chattered in fear.

"Dell!" Ned touched her shoulder.

Dell paid no attention, but tore back the O'e's sleeve until she had exposed the bracelet with the Worker's CreDisk. She grabbed it off and scratched the flat nose with it. "It's the last time you do this! Next time I kick your ass out the door and let Security have you, you get me?" Then gave the disk to the red-faced former pug, who seemed mollified and ordered more beer. Those who already had beer kept on drinking. "Now you come with me!" She grabbed Ned's arm.

Ned found himself being dragged into a corner even darker than the one he had occupied. "Hey, what—"

"Shut up and listen you damned fool," Dell said. "There's lots of pugs and whores got hung out and left to dry when Zamos closed down, some were smart like me and took care of themselves, that's why I own this joint, some fought themselves silly for not much pay, you can see them out there drinking beer, and they're lucky to push a broom, but they got the bit of pension and they're a lot better off than some I know—but those O'e folk, like Ama, that all got so much freedom after Zamos fell apart?—they don't get anything else because they're not even allowed to call themselves human beings! Most days you'll see them lying around on those stairs drunk or full of cheap dope, with their faces eaten out by skegworm or some other kind of filth that doesn't even come near us *human beings*. Most days you'll see seven or eight of them dead, and Security comes and kicks them into the sea! Some of them might even still be alive. I take them in, I give them food, I give them work and I even pay them for it. And I pay taxes on that money, too! You understand that, you dumb sonofabitch?"

After a moment Ned held his hands up. "I give in. You're right, Dell. Good-bye." He turned and marched over to the hefty woman with the frizzy hair and bowed, keeping a respectful distance. And waved to the O'e behind the bar. "Goodnight ladies, you'll see no more of me."

Outside, he breathed the fresh air gratefully and spat a mouthful of blood over the railing into the sea. He stood looking down into the sea a little dizzily for a moment, and went home to face Zella.

"Now where've you been? You promised you'd come home in good time to—" She saw his bruised face. "Good God, Ned! Are you all right? What happened?"

"Went fishing," Ned said. "Caught a flying fist. I'm

going to Khagodis—don't get the wind up, Zell, it's not for long!"

Bed was welcome that night, and good too. Zella was around him everywhere. "Don't even think of screwing around with any of those Khagodi women."

"You're winkin' me out, you are! You've never even seen a Khagodi woman, some of them are twice as big as the men, about five hundred kilos—and they know every thought in your head too!"

"You've always had a taste for dangerous women," Zella retorted, grasping him even more fiercely.

"Didn't I ever! Look who I married!"

During the night he dreamed of Khagodis with the deep skies and thick green equatorial growth he had seen on trivvy programs, and big scaly Khagodi thumping the heavy feet powered by those hugely muscled hips. Good gladiators they'd make, but very few of them wanted to be, and when they did had no proper trainers. Weight and powerful esp tended to keep them away from physical violence. Ned thought it unlikely that the call for a "tough pug" on Khagodis would have him handling the behemoths. Still, he was becoming a Khagodi in this dream, enjoying the brightly colored scale-suit along with the muscles and telepathy, working it all out as if he were a pug in the arena with another Khagodi, figuring whether his taloned fist was massive enough to jolt that huge head, remembering from the Khagodi he'd known how to move his hips and legs like a kick-boxer—that's where all the strength was, and the side-swipe with the tail—spinning out every move in turn . . . feeling a bit proud of himself for being able to imagine all of this, in the dream, until he realized that the floor and walls had become darker and he was working in a shadow wherever he turned. . . . All the light being taken up, absorbed, swallowed by this big scaly woman who was shining it out of her eyes, and beaming it all down again on him like God Herself, and that bright hot look becoming more than merely benevolent—he forced himself out of that one in a panic, and a sweat, and made sure he was well awake before he let himself fall asleep again.

Just a dream, Zell, nothing but a dream.

Khagodis: *Ned and Monkeys*

Khagodis was all Ned had anticipated and much more. He stared at the creatures in the cage. "Monkeys? Here?"

"Is that the name of these creatures? We never knew what they were called," said Etha. He was a very old man by his bent back and stiffness, though his colors were still bright. He walked with the help of a heavy stick of black wood that had a crook at one end.

"They're animals from Earth. Sol Three." *You could have dipped into my head to find out.* But Ned knew that— aside from their reputation for high-mindedness—among the Khagodi telepathy often weakened with age, and perhaps the old fellow's esp was as weak as his back. Just the same, he had kept up with Ned very well on the long day's hike.

It had begun in barren scrublands where the bay flowed to the south among the inlets and islands. Earlier had come the trip in the paddle-wheel barge up the Northern Branch of the Great Equatorial River, and before that the flight in one of the airfreight buses that carried Khagodi when they could be persuaded to travel by air. All after the long black voyage in no-space that mercifully could not be remembered. Now the mid-afternoon sky was a deep blue and two of the other worlds in the system were visible as small sparkles overhead. One of the moons hovered to the south-east and below it on the horizon there were three volcanoes distantly smoking.

"In those waters," Etha said, "was where Zamos kept the Swimmers—the ones that call themselves the Folk—fenced in by strong nets and made to gather the gold. Now they still do it, but the fences are gone and the gold belongs to them. There is not much of it, but it is enough to keep them in food, building materials, medicine. Sometimes when the moons are down and the night is very dark you may see their lights moving under the water."

Ned had never so much as glimpsed that swimming woman whose rescue had sent him into terrifying adventures seven years back. Looking out across the waters of the bay he thought there might have been a gleaming head rising above the surface among the ripples, or an arm lifted in an overhand stroke.

Now after the day's trudging, he was standing beside the monkey cage in a large clearing hacked out of a thicket; the area was centered with a group of three or four low buildings built of local wood and covered with vines. Their pointed leaves scrolled in deep green curls over two thirds of the roof surfaces. Six or seven Khagodi as well as three heavy matte-gray robots were going through the entrances pulling flatbed wagons and dragging them out loaded with wooden crates and cages. Ned did his best not to imagine what else the cages had held.

"This property is another part of the tract Zamos bought to use as their base on Khagodis. We discovered it very recently but it seems to have been built up years ago," Etha said, "and it stayed quite undisturbed because of that camouflage of vines in spite of all the trials and investigations. We make few air flights over here, it was a wilderness we had no use for." He shook his head. "Others did. The staff had kept on with whatever they were doing; I suppose breeding new varieties of slaves or whatever they needed, buying food supplies off the locals who knew nothing of what was going on. Likely they all believed Zamos would rise again."

"Were they all native people working here?"

"Some must have been Lyhhrt, since they are claiming these monkeys. Those structures on their heads had to be made by Lyhhrt. I'm not sure about the rest—from our world and several others, probably. They have all run off now."

Ned did his best to suppress the thought that from what he had tasted of Khagodi food, offworlders who had to live on it would not have gotten very far. He turned back to the monkeys. "You said they're some kind of fighter—"

"We assumed that from the records we found here."

"Are they dangerous?"

"Tik! no! Not to us at least. We have kept them in their cage for you because we are afraid they might run away, and they are needed for evidence."

"Those things on their heads are I guess radios to call and give them orders."

"Yes. Telemetry equipment. Whatever controls it was taken away by the staff."

"Can it be removed?"

"I'm afraid not. We found it was implanted in their skulls unit by unit from the time these monkey creatures were born until they became adult. If you look you can see that the bone has grown around it. It is part of them now."

Ned regarded the monkeys. "They're bigger than I

thought rhesus monkeys were. I suppose they'd have had to be engineered that way to stand the weight of the hardware." There were nine of them. Before they noticed him they had been occupied with grooming, coupling, feeding, or sleeping. As he came near the cage they put down their food, uncoupled, woke up, stopped what they were doing to look at him. The look was hard, even for those bad-tempered faces. One of the larger ones leaped to the bars and climbed up to stare him in the face. "I wonder if they've ever fought."

"Unfortunately, we cannot read their minds because of the instrumentation."

Ned sighed. He had never seen a real live monkey, though he had learned about them in his Primary School lessons about Old Earth. *They brought me all the way from Fthel IV for this?* He glanced up. "Sun's in the fourth quarter. Isn't the aircar due?"

Etha fished in his pouch for the CommUnit, fitted its plug into his gill-ear niche, listened, and shook it. Then punched in codes and listened again. "It is coming within the hour, citizen."

The sun was falling like a bomb, but the sky was still bright, and the darkness Ned felt was of uneasiness, not evening. Almost as soon as he felt it he heard the humming and after a moment the aircar appeared out of the west. "Is your pilot a local?"

"The craft is a drone. We could not afford a pilot. You have objections?" The tone was civil enough.

"I've ridden in them often enough," Ned said. *But I don't like them.* He watched the aircar descending noisily with the light of the late sun streaking its flank. It was a carrier designed for freight and had no grace. Cutting jets, it lowered and hovered over the landing pad, a small round platform of composition blotted by fuel and exhaust stains. Etha ticked a number sequence on his comm and the aircar settled gently to the pad. The monkeys had clustered at the bars on one side and were staring at it. After a few moments a door slid open raspingly and a steel ramp pushed out like a tongue. The car stood there, with the sun setting behind it, and a dim orange light beckoning within. Its inexpressive robot voice said: PLEASE LOAD YOUR CARGO AND PASSENGERS IMMEDIATELY.

The fearfully alien night was closing down around Ned, and ten thousand kinds of life he had never heard or dreamed of began to raise their voices around him, buzzing, chirring, flittering, trembling at his mouth on glassy wings to taste his lips, rising to the top of the sky in pterodactyl shapes on big web wings lit red by the sun's last rays. The chill of it hit him between the shoulder blades, and he found himself sweating. The monkeys were staring at him, and at the aircar, then turning back to him.

The aircar said, SECOND CALL. PLEASE LOAD YOUR CARGO AND PASSENGERS IMMEDIATELY.

Etha raised his little hands: "May I help you load the cage, citizen? We have the use of this car for just three stads."

"Yeh." Ned flung his arms out to shoo the bugs. "I guess so." He gave his back to the task of pushing the wheeled cage and waved Etha aside. Another Khagodi came with a robot to help him, but before they had made three or four meters' progress the monkeys clapped their hands to their heads and squawked, and in one more moment they were shaking the bars, thumping at the cage floor, and yipping *ek! ek! ek!* at the top of their lungs.

Shit, I've spiked them some way! Ned rubbed the sweat off his face. *I smell scared enough, I bet, but . . . is that all?*

"Something's got at them. Give it another shove." One step nearer the aircar and the macaques went shrieking crazy trying to push their heads through the bars.

"It's no good!" Ned snarled. "Pull back."

"Citizen—"

"I know it's damned silly, but do it."

Three pulls backward and the macaques were quiet. Ned faced them and snarled, "Christ, what's got into you bokos?"

The big male that had been staring at him so hard clapped his hands over his ears and with a grimace the mirror of Ned's said in *lingua: «The noise, mister,»* pointing to the aircar, *«that one makes big noise in the head!»*

Ned jumped. The voice was robotic, made by voders, but alive, not dead like the aircar's. He said to Etha, "You never told me this bunch could speak! What're they in a cage for?"

Etha bent down to peer between the bars in the dimming light. "They never spoke to me!" His tone was insulted.

Ned asked the male prime, "Why didn't you ever talk before?"

«We have no friends.»

"I'm not your enemy." It was the exact truth. Not quite the friend of nine rhesus macaques.

The aircar said: FINAL CALL FOR BOARDING. IF YOU ARE NOT BOARDED BY ONE QUARTER HOUR THIS VESSEL WILL LIFT.

"I guess it's static." Ned scratched his head. He touched the bars. "Maybe there's a current in here that interferes with them." He said to Etha, "Can you use your control to delay it for about another half a stad?"

"Only if I were to go inside to register myself on the sensors," Etha said.

"No, don't do that. Let the monkeys out and we'll see if we can walk them in."

"If they run off it will not go well for us!" said Etha dryly.

"I don't think they will—but I'll just let this fellow here come out, then."

«*I am Aark!*» said the male prime.

"Hullo, Aark. If they can name themselves and speak our *lingua*—whatever they may have been born as, they're people now—and they'll be going to start learning about human rights. Come on."

In a few moments Aark moved in free air for the first time. A smaller female clung to the bars staring at him. «*Not. Forget. Us.*»

"Nobody will forget you," Ned said. He took Aark's hand and led him toward the aircar, with the macaque scurrying on short legs and hanging back at the same time. But after five or six steps he balked, pulled his hand away from Ned's and slapped the ground, screaming, "Awrk! Awrk!" The other macaques yowled and screamed.

"We have promised to be in Burning Mountain by tomorrow!" Etha's low feathery voice was sharpening.

Ned sighed. Khagodis was no world to be stranded on with a barrel of monkeys. "Etha, you and I are not going to sit in that car for one whole clockfall listening to their screaming. That static might do them some harm."

"What then?"

"Yes, what are you fellows going to do?" one of the other Khagodi asked. It was the first time any of them had spoken, and Ned would learn that back-country Khagodi not only did not like to speak, but regarded with suspicion the effete city-dwellers who did.

He said, "We could put in a call on the radio here and then bunk down for the night. Tomorrow morning we'd leave by the same way we came, overland and by barge and airbus."

Etha said, "It would be far better if I were to take this car back to Burning Mountain and explain everything first. It will be easier than doing it later and better than making radio contact."

Ned had nothing to say against this except that he wanted to be on his home world and in bed with Zella, but he did not say it, and Etha did not behave as if he had esped this thought, but turned toward the aircar muttering, "Suppose these creatures cannot travel on the airbus because of those instruments?"

The aircar's voder made a sound like a throat-clearing cackle and said, NOW LIFTING and its door hissed shut. Etha croaked, "Wait!"

But the car gave a long, long sigh, then made a noise like sucking in breath, turned transparent and bright as if it were a bottle with a flame in it, and imploded. Slowly the flame deepened to the color of a rose and died with a whisper of ash. Leaving as it cooled a crumble of metal bits and a few lumps of plastic.

"Eh—eh!" cried Etha. "What—" The monkeys burst into yips of fear and packed themselves into one corner of the cage; Aark was wound around Ned's legs as if he were growing there.

After this moment of stunned shock one huge powerful wave of feeling—Ned could smell its reptile odor—swept, quick as the sudden starry darkness of the sky, over the seven Khagodi standing so quietly: *Damned aliens and their violence.*

Ned felt the blood drain from his head like beer from a mug thumped once too hard. All of this before the last cinders crumbled. He turned toward the other six, who were staring at him rather than the aircar's remains, but before he could say what he was thinking or anything else, Etha hissed, "No, no! I would also have died in that vessel and this fellow and his monkey what-'ems have saved me! All Saints bless you, citizen."

Ned realized, to do those six others justice, that none of them wished him harm, and he was simply in the same position as any other non-esp among telepaths. At his own risk.

"Who could have done this?" Etha extended his stick to poke at the clinkers and thought better of it, fearing that they might explode now. "I am as insignificant as one could want to be nowadays, and unless these creatures have secrets locked in their iron boxes. . . ." His eyes were resting on Ned.

Ned shook his head. Whoever had done it thought him important in a way that made him extremely uncomfortable.

Etha thumped his stick on the ground and stretched himself in thought. "Now what shall we do, Citizen Sol-three? One of our fellows is calling on radio for an aircraft *and* pilot, but I don't know when they will become available, or reach us here."

"I don't want to stay here overnight," Ned said. "Is there any other road back to where we came from?"

"The territory is foreign to me," Etha said. "I was given directions only this far."

"I know the way," said another, a fellow named Grussek. "It's long and hard around, but dodges the bay and comes out right on the Big River, where there's a barge station too."

"Good, then let's—"

"I would take you, but your friend Etha is tired and too old to run about in the bushes at midnight, mister. Better stay here by night and leave just before dawn."

Ned did not think it wise to disagree with any Khagodi just then. "Agreed."

"Good. And I will bring my mekko to clear the brush, because most of that path is hardly used these days."

"Just open that cage for me and let out this troop."

Etha did not object. Aark was still sticking to Ned's leg like a plaster, and, once freed, his mates did the same, crouching around Ned in the bunkhouse where he bedded on straw and shared with them the provisions he had brought for the trip: local bread and beer, cheese from Kemalan, and zimb-fruit from Nev.

Lyhhrt and No Spartakos on the Great Equatorial River

Khagodis turned slowly through its long night, and when Grussek woke Ned the darkness was still heavy and thick cold mists were settling on the brush like clouds. Ned felt the dew on his face when he came outside, droplets clustering on the new beard hairs because he had not brought depilatory; he could just make out the two faint white moons falling down the sky like lacrosse balls. The Khagodi had built a small fire not far from where the aircar had immolated itself and were roasting slabs of what smelled like rotten meat. The macaques were clustered around them catching the tidbits being thrown to them. Ned drank the local fruit juice—it tasted something like starfruit—and ate a few roasted wild glaur eggs.

He was almost sorry to leave the crackling fire. The Khagodi were grave and drowsy, but no more than himself, in reaction from the shock he'd had, and he felt—almost felt—as if he knew those fellows now.

Finally they roused themselves, threw a few waste bones and fat gobbets to sizzle on the fire, and warmed their hands for a last moment before they began the day. Then Grussek turned away and came forward with his big clumsy mekko lumbering behind him. The macaques jumped up on the mekko's loading tray; Etha hauled himself along on his stick, all still weary and thinking too much of what had happened the day before. Ned felt the thoughts rolling like the mists, as the three crossed the clearing without looking at the half-melted chunks of the wrecked aircar when they went by.

"That way," Grussek said, pointing westward where a narrow track disappeared into a stand of shrubby trees. The mekko traveled before them, whacking this way and that through the raveling mist at the spine-bushes and wild sour thorn that had plenty of eye-sticking twigs to dodge. Huge wide-winged humming flies with bodies like needles clustered around tiny berries, and every once in a while a wind would set seed pods clacking like xylophone keys. "Those are the silver trees," said Grussek, who had grown up in the Isthmuses and knew every leaf and branch; his mekko was picking nut-coins off the twigs for the monkeys. Ned looked where he pointed and saw the thin light of dawn glinting off the silvery pods. After some hours the sun rose and burned off the mist, the ground heated up and fragrant blue-green things that were too many for Grussek to name opened around him.

Ned felt the eyes everywhere. The feeling was not irrational; there were people who really wanted him—and probably the macaques—dead. But when he looked upward again and saw actual eyes on the thatched shelves of the cliffs that suddenly rose alongside the path, they were those of reptilian birds waking, and in a moment they began stretching their necks, squawking to their fellows and preparing to gather enough air under their wings to launch themselves and catch a thermal. When they lifted against the sunlit sky their skeletons stood clear black inside the glassy outlines of their thin membranous skin.

By the time the long twisting path brought the procession to a high-road the sun had nearly reached zenith. Ned had taken off his jacket and was using the hem of his jersey to wipe sweat off his face, and the finish had been gouged off his boots by ground-bristle. Etha was limping in his thick leather sandals.

Grussek pointed: "One quarter of your standard hours, citizens, you can almost see the station from here." His mekko unloaded the macaques and he turned away toward his long trek home.

The high-road that stretched southwest toward the Great Equatorial River was paved with ancient stone blocks and lined with the broken and listing stumps of thick carved columns. Rough as it was, it was clear and much easier to tread on. Etha trudged alongside Ned; he had become silent as a stone column in contemplation of his narrow escape, the first experience of the sort that he had had in his long life.

During the hours of hiking the macaques had been quiet

as well; they did not speak to each other with the voders. Now, somewhat freer, they scrambled along occasionally yipping, climbing the stumps of the columns, touching each other to reassure themselves. Aark grabbed and tugged at Ned's hand, matching his speed. «*What is coming,*» he said.

"Eh? What is coming?"

«*What is coming to Us.*»

"I don't know." He had a wincing thought and was glad the macaques were not telepathic. A thought of them being taken apart by scientists to see how their bodies had been modified and their telemetry equipment worked. "I was told you were fighters. What kind of fighting do you do?"

«*Wrestle.*»

"What?"

«*Like this.*» A moment later Ned found himself on his face under seventy-five kilos of monkeys, one sitting on his head, one on each foot, two on his thighs, the sixth and seventh holding his arms while the eighth knotted his jacket sleeves around his wrists and the ninth pointed his own stunner at his right eye.

Ned snarled and twisted, but before he could kick them away they had jumped off him, unloosed his hands and tossed him his stunner. He sat up with a red face, huffing. "Bandits you might be. Wrestlers I don't think!" He felt, rather than saw, that Etha was smiling, for the first time since they had met.

«*Now, Solthree. What is coming to us?*»

"Whatever it is, I guess you'll be able to handle it."

* * *

The barge was a very broad sturdy boat made of ancient timbers and powered by an efficient new gasoline engine of the sort that developed worlds running on solar and atomic power exported to low-tech worlds with plenty of fossil fuels. This was a dividend of Khagodis's recent status as a Headquarters for various Galactic Federation offices, and particularly the Interworld Court. Even the fold-down mast and neatly furled sails kept as insurance were manufactured offworld.

The barge, usually carrying tourists from Kylklar, Varvaryn, Dabirr, Szii and twenty-five Khagodi countries, putt-putted on the smooth green Great Equatorial River. On this pre-season day in late autumn there were only a few elderly Khagodi and a young teacher with a half-score brightly colored schoolchildren who were just as lively as the monkeys and wanted to play with them. Both parties were dissuaded with difficulty by Ned and the teacher.

The sun shone steadily in the deep clear sky; Ned socketed in a fresh oxycap and sat watchfully on one of a cluster of seats provided by a squatting people as a concession to aliens. The only disturbances of the afternoon were in the silent insults that the children were hurling at each other and the teacher was sharply snuffing while he tried to teach the day's lesson; the macaques were grooming each other, dozing or cracking nuts.

Into this silence came one sound like the skipping of a stone on the water.

The silence deepened. Ned looked over the deck railing and saw the round ripples mingling with the thousand currents of the water. Now the only other movement was that of the two moons lifting in the east and the thickening smoke pillar of a distant volcano. Then a smooth gold head rose out of the water like a new sun, and next two glittering hands. The head smiled as if its gold lips were flesh and said, "Give me a hand, Ned Gattes." In a dream, Ned reached out and his hand was gripped by a warm metal one.

He knew who this was: a Lyhhrt in a workshell; one who knew him, because every Lyhhrt knew everything any other Lyhhrt did.

Ned had never seen a Lyhhrt in what there was of its flesh and did not want to. He knew from school that inside their beautiful workshells Lyhhrt were ameboids who looked somewhat like brain-sized cowry shells with similar markings, were in fact all brain, all senses in one organ; that they did not truly want to do anything but lie in heaps twining pseudopods on their marshy world, in communion with the Cosmic Spirit. They never would have done anything else if some of them had not been discovered and carried off for investigation by GalFed, who found, not entirely to their liking, that Lyhhrt were as powerfully telepathic as Khagodi, were rabidly anti-individualistic, and tended to become mildly psychotic when separated from their fellows. These disadvantages were more than balanced by their genius for metalwork, surgery and philosophy.

This new-old Lyhhrt, long fissioned from whichever one Ned might have known in the past, and like all others having no personal name, climbed over the railing and stood brilliant and steaming in the sunlight. None of the other passengers saw him, or even looked in his direction. He said, in his perfectly modulated voice, "You did promise to testify for us, many years ago."

Ned said half-defiantly, "I know, but it's very hard to do." He had not forgotten that Lyhhrt had saved his life more than once.

"Yes, it is expensive and risky. I/we understand that. But now you will help us?"

"I will if I can. This is a strange place to call a meeting about it."

"No one knows of it. After the destruction of your aircar it would have been better if your guide had not made his call to Burning Mountain, but even so very few know where you are."

"Who was trying to kill us?"

"I cannot yet tell you that. I see that you found the monkey-creatures."

"Are they yours?"

"They are mine/ours and Galactic Federation's now. Better take good care of them."

Ned realized how very still it was, the monkeys curled up, the schoolchildren silent, Etha dozing. . . . "If someone's after me, how can I help—besides being a witness and collecting monkeys? There's got to be more to it than that."

"You must find Spartakos."

"What?"

"He has been missing for three demilunars."

"I don't understand."

Spartakos was a humanoid robot created by the Lyhhrt for a purpose Ned had never learned completely—partly as a mascot at the Zamos arenas, sometimes a novelty fighter, certainly a watching eye, a being who had become Ned's unlikely friend and pulled him out of danger as the Lyhhrt had done, a defender of Zamos's slaves, a work of art made because the Lyhhrt could not prevent themselves from creating beauty in metal—all of these, but perhaps these were not all.

I don't understand, Ned had said, because Spartakos was more than able to take care of himself, or he had believed so. But, remembering how carefully Spartakos had polished and cared for his gleaming gold-and-chrome body, Ned could not visualize him wandering too far from his creators, the Lyhhrt.

"How in hell could you lose contact with him—and why would he be on Khagodis at all?"

"Because he has switched off all signaling devices, and even we cannot esp a machine." A sore point with Lyhhrt. Ned had believed they could esp rocks if they chose. "And the Interworld Court is holding its most important trials here. Spartakos cannot testify because he has never been given the right in law, and we were planning to apply to make him a World Citizen for that reason. He has important information that we want to use in evidence. Ordinarily he would be the best guardian of it, but he has disappeared. It might be a mistake to make him a Citizen."

"He's a dangerous place to store evidence." He sensed the stiffening of the atmosphere around the Lyhhrt and dared go no further. "You think he's been kidnapped—stolen, whatever?"

"We are not sure. No one has asked for ransom."

"What could I possibly do that you can't? Except for being a low-rank GalFed agent, I was a good pug and a bad pimp. I've given both of those up."

"You served us well as an agent, and you can go among pugs and pimps better than we. We need an emissary among the vertebrates."

Ned shrugged. "I said I'd help."

"Take the monkeys back to Burning Mountain. Give them to the local Representative for Lyhhr at the embassy, and I/we will call on you."

The Lyhhrt raised his hand in salute, then slipped in one liquid gold movement over the barge railing and into the deep green water even more silently than he had risen.

The children were chuffing and poking at each other and the teacher hushed them. Etha, who had been crouching nearby watching the ripple of water along the flank of the barge, said, "He is teaching them the Great Mysterious Story of the World. How it was discovered that our people did not develop indigenously on this planet but were brought here by other beings in great ships. This was found out because of the New Sciences brought to us by other worlds of Galactic Federation, who proved what we had long believed, that one-quarter of our life-forms including ourselves did not in any way have a common ancestor with the rest and actually had chemistries completely inimical with theirs. Our religions developed out of these beliefs: the Diggers called the aliens theory a heresy and believed that we had not yet dug deep enough in the right place, and the Watchers and the Hatchlings that we had been delivered here by burning gods in huge eggs. It seems that both were in some way right, because only a few years ago there was an earthquake in the Northern Spine Confederacy, near where your friend Judge Skerow lives—"

"She's not quite my friend—"

"She remembers your meeting very well, just the same."

"I'd be glad to see her again. I need as many friends as I can find here."

"At any rate, the earthquake forced up a buried artifact believed to be an alien ship millions of years old. It is still being dug out after all these years, and we have not yet found its entrance. Nearly a hundred worlds are taking part in the huge dig. The area was cordoned off immediately the ship was discovered and Skerow was forced to leave her house. She is in Burning Mountain waiting to give evidence. You will probably see her soon."

Five hours later their landing in Burning Mountain was met with terrible news of murder and kidnapping, the trials had been set back for a tenday minimum, and Galactic Federation found other uses for Ned and the macaques; there was no question of spending an hour bantering with Skerow.

Verona

Things were blurry when she woke in the morning. Maybe she had been given something that—no, she remembered there'd been just the painkiller for her hand. It hurt in a dull way, swollen and throbbing under the bandage and sending occasional jets of pain through her wrist and fingers. She felt as if her brains weren't working right for a few minutes and then there was another slam of memory like a punch to the head: how she had been seized and slashed and dragged around like a sack, like one of the sacks on that jolting cart, pushed around, kicked around like any stone—no, her mind hurt too much in the same kind of dull throb as her hand to think about that any more now.

She was not in that bedroom where she had spent about half of the first night on Khagodis—of course, because that *thing* had burst through the dome. The small square room she awoke to startled her for a moment because it reminded her of the place where she had been kept by her captors, but there were stripes of hot morning sunlight coming in through the shades. She found herself lying in a big net hammock with something like a feather bed on it. She was wearing a plain shirt of rough nubbled cotton or linen that looked as if it had been softened by a lot of washing. Its sleeves and neck were edged by thin black embroidery patterns.

Beyond the door a low voice called, "Vronni!" Bullivant's voice, then a knock. "Are you all right? May I come in?"

"Yes, but—"

"Here are some clothes for you, Vronni." He opened the door slightly and tossed them into the hammock. "I'm sorry, dear, but you've got to dress as quickly as you can. There are people who want to talk to you and I've been holding them off—"

"Let the child eat something first, good man," said a voice behind him speaking English, and the speaker came around his elbow holding a tray.

Verona gave a gasp that held a little scream in it.

"What is it!" said the tray-bearer.

Verona stammered, "You're one like—your skin is blue. . . ."

"What of it, daughter? There's a whole world like us, yonder, and a whole house full right here," said the blue woman.

"But—there was one in that room—" She had babbled a few words last night about the woman with the blue skin, never knowing if anyone had paid attention.

"Yes?" The woman set the tray down on a small table and allowed herself one sharp breath. "Which room?"

Verona looked at her more closely. She was older than the other woman and her skin did not have the kind of bloom like a grape or plum that the prisoner—or slave—had had, but was purplish, with a light bronze sheen, like an eggplant; she wore a thin gold nostril ring with two big white diamonds in it.

"Where I was taken," Verona finished lamely, a bit frightened at the woman's intensity, almost afraid that she was going to burst into a fury like that terrible woman in veils and sequins. "I'd better get dressed."

"Wait—"

"No, Keremer," Bullivant said. "We'll tell you everything, but later."

When the woman had gone, Verona said, "What place is this? Who is she?"

"It's the Pinaxer Embassy, she's the Ambassador."

"Ambassador! Why did she serve me?"

"She wanted to see you—and find out if you'd seen that woman who was missing—but hurry, Vronni, they're waiting for you."

They were the same three who had interrogated Bullivant the day before: Smiryagin, the hairy Russian, Peaceman Heth, and Tharma, the big hearty woman from West Oceania. Most of the other Security forces who might have handled this case were attending to Evarny's murder, and all other embassy members and staffs had locked themselves into quarters.

Bullivant saw how achingly small and vulnerable Vronni looked beside the Khagodi, and even beside Smiryagin in the tiny Pinxid dayroom, and wished that he could tell these three to go easy; not only did he lack authority to say it, but he was almost suspect for having let himself be controlled by the Ix. No matter how willingly he and Hawksworth had allowed the local medical officer, whom even Tharma respected, to probe the recesses of their minds no obvious traces of tampering could be found.

Heth, ready to take notes, flicked on his daybook, and Tharma regarded Verona without blame or malice and said, "Just start from the beginning, dems'l." Verona was surprised to find that suddenly she knew *lingua* quite well.

. . . it was somehow melting through the dome and coming, lowering down over me like a spider, but, something like sparkling, and a smell, like a smell but more like a pain in my nose, and then a sting and I blacked out—

. . . and it was a little square room I woke in and the blue woman said, she said, "Tell them," but I'm not sure what she meant—maybe that she was a prisoner like me? Or a slave? She had a red shirt that didn't really fit and a chain around her neck with this design, like on my hand. . . .

—but no, they never touched me except to grab me and—and—they cut my hand—it hurts when I say that . . . what they were wearing, it was as if they were trying to be, pretending to be like that—

thing.

* * *

Tharma said, "That *thing*, as you call it, dems'l, is an Ix, from a world not belonging to Galactic Federation or its neutrals. We know all too little about them and their world, but they give off chemicals that drug you through your sense of smell, and make you feel strange and disoriented. The blue woman is a native of Pinaxer called a Pinxid, your father is staying at their embassy until the repairs can be made. The Ix or whoever they work with seem to have made her a slave, or tried to. The pattern on your hand, and on her chain, has something to do with them." She swallowed more air. "And those contemptible—but unfortunate—young women that tormented you so appear to be members of a cult that finds some damnable pleasure in the drug that the Ix secrete. We have been hearing rumors of them for some time."

"I thought I was catching a glimpse, maybe a smell, of the Ix in the shadows when they were. Cutting. I might have been off my head."

"Not necessarily."

"One of those women had feathers, if it was a woman."

"Yes, that was still another exoterrestrial, a Kylklad—probably a woman. I know how confusing it all is . . . but you will feel a little better to know that they have been seized—not without some damage. We did not find the Ix."

"Thank you for telling me all this."

"You have been through a great deal, child, and it is hard to look at it all directly, but staying in the darkness of ignorance would harm you more deeply. This is all we need ask of you at this time, and Officer Smiryagin will take you back to your quarters; it is just down the hall.

"Bullivant, your daughter believes we have treated her fairly, and I wish it were as easy to satisfy you, but you and your man Hawksworth are still conundrums to us."

"I have no one to speak for me now that Evarny is dead."

"Madame Skerow vouches for your trustworthiness, and we trust her. Now, Bullivant, I see no reason why you should not stay here for a day or so until we can make better arrangements. As long as you can eat the food and the Pinxin are willing to protect you. We are in the dark about your psychic condition and that of your secretary, though you both seem physically healthy, but if you should need any kind of treatment this is the one place on our world where you can possibly get it. I hope this seems fair."

"Fair enough. May I ask about those 'cult' members you said had been—'seized' was the word?"

"I believe it is safe enough to tell you that we took three of them. One we are still looking for. Of the three one died right away, quite spontaneously, as if she had had a cerebral hemorrhage. The others immediately went mad, or at least shouting and screaming. At any rate they could not be esped and were quieted only by drugging. We will keep watch over them, and possibly ask your daughter to identify them."

"Not right away," Bullivant said quickly.

"No. But at present they are useless both to us and themselves. So much for worshipping Ix."

"And the young Pinxid woman who had been missing so long?"

"It did not turn out well for her. I have put off telling Keremer for this hour, but I cannot do it longer."

"Can I help in any way?"

"No, Ambassador. She must have the word from an official mouth."

"Was I really speaking *lingua*?"

"Tharma was feeding it to you, but if you talk enough with Khagodi you'll learn it quickly."

"I like her better than that woman, Smiryagin."

"Tharma's at home here, and Smiryagin isn't, but she's all right."

"Will we have to stay here very long?"

Some of the staff had doubled up to accommodate Bullivant and Verona; the tiny suite was simply furnished, but every article was exquisite, like so many of the Pinxin. Bullivant found the surroundings almost precious: nothing was quite large enough for him. The sleeping areas were closed off by cloth-paneled screens embroidered with designs that hovered on the edge of familiarity and were so much the stranger for that.

"It's beautiful here, but . . ." Verona trailed off, almost picking up his thoughts. Bullivant felt as if he were smothering, as if he were, in relation to the Pinxin, what Skerow would be in relation to him. A Gulliver in Lilliput. It would be even more uncomfortable among the Pinxin now that the missing one had been found dead and identified.

"We'll move out as soon as we can find another place that's safe. In the meantime we don't have any choice. All your clothes and everything are stowed in that wall cupboard, most are still in the freight packing from the ship, and I gathered some loose things in a hurry when I moved here. I had to leave your furniture pieces. I must go look for Jack Hawksworth and find out who to ask to see what there is on this world for me to do."

"Wait—after I had to leave with Officer Smiryagin, did Tharma tell you whether they found that woman I met in—that room?"

"Nothing good . . . she'd gone missing a while ago and the police here had raided a place the Ix were supposed to be but had left. Everyone thought she had been taken off-planet. Pinxid women are in great demand."

Verona knew better than to ask for what, and shuddered. "I was found very quickly."

"The Security forces were on the watch after she'd disappeared. Someone reported seeing one of those acolytes—somewhere around that place—when everyone believed they'd gone, and Security kept the area under surveillance. I've got to find Jack now, and later I guess I'd better talk to Keremer. Your blue woman was her—I think 'spouse' is the nearest word for it."

Left to herself, Verona did not even try to put her thoughts in order. She sorted out her clothes and set up a mirror on one of the little tables. Looking into it, she found a stranger staring back at her skeptically. She combed her hair and plaited it into a braid running down the back of her head, put on a little light makeup. She had lost her taste for looking dramatic now that the shadows under her eyes were real ones. *What are you going to be when you grow up, Vronni?* Her eyes scoured the walls. She wondered how she could grow up to be anything here, trapped in an apartment again. This one at least had more windows.

There was a scratch at the door and it slid back a crack. "Yes," she whispered. It opened: Keremer was standing in the entrance. Her heart sank deeper.

"You were there with her," Keremer said, in rough En-

glish; her voice was harsh with grief. Her face looked much
more blue than before, because she was so pale, and her lips
were dull green. "You were the last to see my La'or before
she was murdered."

"Yes," Verona said again.

"I see you and not her." She pointed to the bandaged
hand. "They did terrible things to her, I know."

"They treated her badly." *Please God don't let her ask.*

"We are always the ones they steal, you see. And we
are not the ones they save, either. Why did they save you
and not her? Tell me!"

"It was luck, just luck," Verona said in a trembling
voice.

Keremer stepped closer, speaking now half in *lingua*,
half in the thickened blurry voice of grief. She smelled
faintly of a spice like mint or cloves. Tears burst from her
eyes, and the diamonds in her nostril ring lay on her cheek
like two greater tears. "What you say, luck, chance, means
nothing to me. I know that *you* are alive. She was sweet,
my lass was, and you are not more beautiful!" Her face
twisted into a terrible grimace and she howled, "Why?"

Her hands flew up and out. Verona would never know
whether they would have grasped her shoulders, clawed at
her, or closed around her neck. She saw her mother's fearful
suffering in that face and almost without thinking grabbed
and clasped the hands in her own.

"I know how terrible it was!"—speaking in her turn
some bastard mix of English and *lingua*—"I do know! My
mother was captured and tormented by the Ix, and she suffered all the rest of her life, she went mad from it, nobody
could save her, and she died from it—"

In the next moment the room was filled with people.
Verona, frozen, still grasping those strange-knuckled hands,

felt herself pulled gently and firmly away from them while Keremer receded among the bodies of others. She found herself facing Ned Gattes along with Bullivant and Hawksworth, and a hefty young Pinxid woman holding a stunner and draped with two knives, a flamer and a crossbow. They filled the room.

When the confusion cleared there were only Bullivant and Ned; the guard was at the door. She could still hear Keremer's wrenching cries, and her eyes filled with tears. "I don't believe she'd have hurt me; she's not very strong."

"Stronger than you'd think," Bullivant said, "but no, I don't think she'd have hurt you."

After an instant of silence, Ned Gattes cleared his throat and said awkwardly, "I came to find out how you were doing."

"Well enough, I guess." She was breathing hard.

"Maybe I'd better go. I'm staying down the hall for a couple of nights. . . ."

"No, I want to thank you for coming to save me—and those monkeys, are they really monkeys?"

"They were bred here, but they're monkeys, all right! I'm rooming with them, but I hope not for very long. I know the Pinxin will be glad to get rid of us!"

"I think they'll be glad to see me out of here, too," Verona said.

Bullivant put his hand on her shoulder. "All of us."

Why had he brought her to this world? Of course he knew, he did not need to wonder. Whatever prospects there might be for her, it had seemed to him that they opened up wider out among strange worlds than they did on Earth if she were to be stuffed into some school without family or friends anywhere on her world. And oh, how wrong he had been.

Verona, Bullivant and Hawksworth

One night and one day passed. Nothing happened in these hours and it was as if time had stopped. It was only in retrospect that Verona realized that there had been so long a calm; at every moment she half-expected some fearful outburst.

But she saw no more of Keremer, nor any Pinxid except the young woman, Adilon, who was standing guard, and who undertook to teach Verona a few useful phrases of *lingua* and a couple of words in a Pinxid language. After that she ran into Ned—he and his troop could hardly be avoided—and watched a demonstration of monkey wrestling. "We're getting an act together," he said. "I'll save you a ticket soon as I book the arena—hey, it's good to see you smile!"

And the day passed that way, with lame jokes, harmless activities, and meals of rehydrated "meat stew" served with boiled rupseed and sliced kappyx pickles.

After supper Officer Tharma sent for Bullivant, and he socketed an oxycap and went to meet her in the little temporary office she had established in what had been a broom closet. Its stone walls were pale green with mold and lichens and there was a drip in one corner of the ceiling, but she had found enough room for the compact work-unit with its fold-down desk and terminal, light standard and comm. And folding chair for interviewees who needed to sit.

She waved a sheet of onionskin that crackled with black

symbols and dove in without greeting: "Bullivant, I want to ask you a very personal question. As a member of Interpol I have authority to ask it. . . . Of course I cannot force you to answer, but the question is so important that your answer may save your life one day."

Bullivant, completely at a loss, said, "I don't know what you're getting at, but go ahead."

"Have you ever been subjected to psychic blocking? By whatever agency in your line of work. . . . I know it's quite common in your service, really no secret, but some people find it too personal to discuss."

"No, I never did. I was offered the option by the Security people, but since it wasn't obligatory, I didn't want anybody rearranging my mind for me. When I need security I wear an impervious helmet."

"That's interesting. It is not recorded in your curriculum vitae either."

"Are you implying that you found an esp block when I was examined?"

"First let me ask another question, Bullivant, a less personal one. How long has Hawksworth been your secretary?"

"I guess it must be a good ten years by my time. Why? What has he to do—"

"Even more interesting! My dear man, brace yourself. Before you came here he was not at all the secretary who was listed in the Staff Register in Headquarters on Fthel Five."

"You must be mistaken!"

"I believed so myself. So much so that I went to great trouble to have this printout made. I sent for you the moment it came. Look!"

Numbly he took the rustling sheet. "But Jack Hawksworth has traveled with me wherever I've gone for years. . . ." He pushed his mind back to those years. "My wife used to say he was so . . . trust . . . trust. Trustworthy."

He glanced at the printout and for a moment it was as if his ears had been plugged and he had swallowed to clear them. He licked his lips. "Why would she say . . . that? She hardly ever saw . . . didn't care to go . . ." He lifted his head enough to look Tharma in the eye. "She—she never met him. Because he wasn't there. My . . . secretary"—forcing the words out—"was a man named Hammadi. . . ." He had to stop and blink away the clouds in his mind. "He was dark like Hawksworth, much thicker in build. My wife had met him a couple of times, but she never went to embassy gatherings very often so she didn't really know him."

"Was this Hammadi intended to come here with you?"

"I—I suppose so . . . originally—I think—but I have a vague memory of some kind of trouble, illness, or family— if I could only get it clear in my head!"

"Your head will clear and you will be none the worse."

"Will it?" It was as if he had had a headache for years and only now realized it. "But somebody . . . did something . . . and I let myself be—"

"Manipulated, yes. It seems that your real secretary was moved out." At the least. "You were given a psychic block without your knowledge or consent. Then Hawksworth appeared in order to fill in for Hammadi, and somehow you were persuaded that he had been with you all along. Only that, Bullivant." Tharma was looking at him kindly.

He hated her kind looks. "Could Hawksworth have blocked me?"

"I doubt it was Hawksworth. He has a block of his

own—well installed and quite legal, and I am sure he sub-
verted the robots—but he certainly doesn't strike me as a
skilled Psychman."

"I could have looked at that registry anytime and seen
that he hadn't been my secretary."

"Only if you had seen the original Staff Register back
in Starry Nova on Fthel Five, and even then your mind
would have elided it. And somehow Hawksworth came to
be listed on the *Zarandu*'s passenger manifest—"

He realized how strongly he had been suspected for
Tharma to have investigated him as thoroughly as Hawksworth. "You said no worse was done to me, or I did, but
you can't be sure of that."

"You are *here*, Bullivant, with *me*, and if I feel you are
dangerous I will see to you."

He found this threat oddly reassuring. He did not want
to be dangerous. "But Hawksworth—"

"I have taken the precaution of sending for him as
well—but sending an officer."

His heart was thumping fearfully and he could not seem
to get control of his breath. "It's so—"

"Yes, Bullivant. It is a great shock."

"Finding out I've been a puppet. . . . What put you onto
Hawksworth?"

"The setup seemed strange to me. The Ix dropped in
through the skylight, plucked up your daughter, and was
pulled out the same way. Neatly, so much so that the emergency seal on her door was unbroken. That's reasonable
enough, because the Ix are so visually disturbing that none
of them could have come through these halls without being
noticed. Yet the robots were thoroughly tampered with—
and that the Ix could not have done without going out of
your daughter's room and breaking the seal. That had to be

done by someone else, and I can see Hawksworth as one who might know of a few devices to put robots out of order."

"You may be completely mistaken, though. He can't be convicted without a fair trial."

He could feel her suppressing one of her kind looks.

"That is so, Bullivant, and no one is convicting him or even judging him. We will ask questions and he will assist us with our inquiries."

"Even so, my daughter—"

"Your daughter is being well guarded."

Bullivant went cold. "You damned well better be sure of that, Tharma! None of the Pinxin know anything about Hawksworth!"

He found himself out of the office racing up the stairs before the last word was out of his mouth.

Looking at himself in the mirror, standing there in his sober suit, Master-of-the-Galaxy, bodyguard, secretary-with-a-sidearm suit, deep maroon with gold stuff over the left breast, that's where the heart is, looking good in the mirror, mirrors all over the place, sky-blue-Pinxids like to look at themselves, and so does sober, worthy, hawkish "Hawksworth." Bully's gone, gone to see Tharma, and they're talking about him, he saw it coming, they figured it all out, it had to happen sooner or later, and now he's got to get out and get her out. So he's working himself up to get on with it, looking across where it's free space, on the other side of the mirror, through the looking-glass, only you can't get there, it's all unreal, and this is even more unreal here, isn't it? NO, NO! WHAT ARE YOU MAKING ME DO! I NEVER

SIGNED ON TO DO *THIS!* THIS IS ALL WRONG! I WANT OUT OF HERE! *No, please, if you're esping, I don't mean all that, pay no attention! Really, all you have to do, Hawk's-eye, is press that little stud in the chronometer, the one that doesn't tell the time—the signal's going out now—then grab the girl, Miss Virgin—no no, the precious doll, don't hurt her, it's such a little gun, just lead her, let her lead you out on the roof where the buzzer's waiting, of course it's waiting, they said it would be there, they promised, they'll give you all the girls you want, blue ones, pink ones, boys if you want, do it, Hawks, do it. . . .*

Verona had been finishing up this peaceful day by continuing her lessons in *lingua* and playing skambi with Adilon. This young Pinxid did not have the air of lightness and delicacy that most of the others had; her skin was deeper colored and less reflective, and her muscles heavier—no, harder. Where others glided, she would bounce. Perhaps—most likely—she and the rest of the Pinxin had all come from different countries on that world.

Adilon smiled as if she had read the thought. "We play skambi all over the Galaxy," she said in that alien accent. "You don't need another language to do it. One more game?"

"*Please.*"

Verona had been about to say the word, but it was Hawksworth who spoke it. His step had been so silent that he simply appeared when the players looked up. Verona never knew what to say to him, or how to say it. "Yes?"

"May I speak with you?" He had tilted his head a little, and his hand was out in a tentative gesture.

Adilon had nodded and slipped away before Verona could say yes or no. But she was waiting there just outside the door. "What is it?"

"Miss Verona!" He was whispering. "I hate to tell you this now, but it's urgent. There's something you should know about your father."

Verona stared. "I know it already."

Something—artificial?—about his voice. "What? You do? Then why haven't you come to me for help?" He had got hold of her arm, but dropped his hand when she pulled away.

"Why should I? It's only—" *That he's not my father.* But that was none of Hawksworth's business. "I don't need your help, Mister Hawksworth."

"Ssh!" He held his hand up. "But you do, miss."

"I know he's not my father!" she said desperately, just to get rid of him. *Not her father?* He twitched. She saw this and saw him recover.

"That isn't it, it's—miss, it's—he's a dangerous man."

"I don't believe—I don't know what you're talking—"

"Keep your voice down!" He put his arm around her firmly. "It's my help you need to stay alive, now. I have a gun in my hand, if you look down you can see it," she saw it, a tiny blue-steel plug-ugly, "and I don't mean to harm you," his arm was very tight—

I know, I know you want her alive, I'm not going to hurt her, I swear, I'm just threatening, for God's sake, give me room to breathe!

But there's no one watching really. Is there? Are you there? Is the buzzer really there?

"—And I'm going to let go of you, but I've still got the gun, you see? They'll kill me if I hurt you, but I'll risk it just to get out of this—"

Out of breath, she whispered, "What do you want?"

"I want to take a walk, just us, you and me, because it's so suffocating here, can't you feel it? so hot and stuffy, you've got a headache, haven't you?"

"I—"

"Just go up the stairs to the roof, I've got fresh oxycaps, and the buzzer's there, yes it is." And then, "I'll kill them all, you know, to get us out of here. Your father and the big lizard and all the blueface ones."

"Where—" She had to say it. "Where are we going?"

"Back there. We've got to get back there."

A very powerful mind-voice said to Verona, GO WITH HIM, CHILD. DON'T BE AFRAID.

Hawksworth did not startle or falter, and she stood frozen for a moment in his terrible grip. Perhaps the message had not reached him, and she was safe, or . . .

He snarled, "Get on with it." She let him lead her out of that little fussy room, and through another one without seeing, or not being aware of Adilon or all the other Pinxin or Ned and his nine monkeys. The little chambers with their touches of brocade and delicacy seemed like the rooms of a dollhouse with Hawksworth and his gun ripping through its fabric. Then the hallway led to a foyer and one wall of it was nearly completely filled by a huge stone door whose brutal strength did not protect anything.

"Just lift the latch," he said. "Turn the wheel. You're a good strong girl."

Fuck you. But she did it. Three hard turns set the mechanism shrieking on metal wheels, and when the great slab gave way the damp heat of the landing and stairwell burst against them.

They stepped out onto the greenish stones.

She saw the gold statue before he did. No, not a statue, a robot, glimmering in the shadows from above and below. It said something she could not hear, but she was free, with Hawksworth's grasp on her arm a fading red mark, and Hawksworth was standing holding the gun muzzle in his mouth. Not quickly enough to do himself in.

"Stop that now and give it to me," the robot said, and when Hawksworth seemed compelled to obey, it spoke in that particular mind-voice Verona had heard before, I AM NOT A ROBOT, MISS, BUT A LYHHRT. She understood that there was a person inside that gleaming shell. One more different kind of person.

Tharma was coming down the stairs followed by Bullivant, and another robot—or Lyhhrt—in bronze, was coming up.

"Vronni! Are you—"

The Lyhhrt in gold said, "She is not perfectly all right, but unharmed. I am the temporary replacement for Evarny, and my landsman here is the house doctor. Hawksworth, there is no aircraft waiting to rescue you, and your chronometer did not send out any signals. If you are lucky, the doctor will find that it did not inject you with any poison either, or not much. You were no more use to your friends after the young woman was recovered, Hawksworth, and I am sure they hoped that you would destroy yourself, or that we would. Everything you believed was false. The doctor will examine you now. In one moment, Tharma, he will be yours."

"Thank you indeed!" Tharma said. "I'm not eager to admit this, but I would never have been able to penetrate his esp shield myself without his knowing it. At last we have a live one."

Verona was shuddering with strain.

"It's all right, Vronni." Bullivant's arms were around her.

She whispered, "I'm nobody. I could be dead."

"You're far from nobody, miss," the Lyhhrt said, as kindly as a gold-encrusted lump of protoplasm could. "You have no idea how valuable you are. We've been doing more than our best to keep you safe."

"I'm not staying here. You can't make me."

"Nobody will make you," Bullivant said.

"It is evidently not safe enough," the Lyhhrt said. "Doctor will come back and give you a medicine to ease you, miss, and make the world less black. Then we will find a haven for you. You will have more good quiet days. . . ."

Verona realized that the pain in her wounded hand, which had earlier ebbed enough to become bearable, had intensified, become an emblem of all the terrors she had suffered.

From hauling the wheel on that damned door.

Hawksworth Alone

Who are you, Hawksworth?
  I'm a bodyguard. Just a bodyguard.
  You were Bullivant's secretary.

I have a Business Certificate. I belong to the Interworld ProtectoGuild. Embassies hire people like me to stand in for staff and keep terrorists away. That's all I am! You got all my documents.

Yes, your credentials are in order.

What more do you want from me?

I want your real name, where you come from and who hired you.

I don't need to tell you anything. I need a lawyer.

You have not been charged with anything. You are helping us with our inquiries. What is your name, and—

You know all that, you got it out of my mind.

You see I'm wearing my imperhelm and so is Smiryagin. Esp testimony is not recognized in court. Go on.

I was born Herbert Ambrose, on Sol Three's Moonbase Fifty-eight. It's not against the law to change your name.

Herbert Ambrose.

It is my real name. Both my parents crewed the shuttle buses that run between bases. They might still be there. You can check it.

Who hired you to work for Bullivant? We know he didn't.

I don't know who it was. Really.

Someone did.

They didn't like me to remember things.

The people who hired you to commit crimes.

I've never hired on to commit crimes, and I don't have any record. Check it.

The sooner we get on with this the easier it will go with you. Whoever hired you, where did you meet them?

I think it was Moonbase, um, Twenty-five, in one of the big hire-halls. There wasn't much doing Earthside, people who want to work offworld and don't care where they go wait there to see who's hiring. There's help-wanted lists posted.

You answered an advertisement.

No. There were two fellows . . .

Describe them.

Solthrees. They were sides of beef, messengers I thought. They were carrying briefcases.

The briefcases held messages?

No, weapons and comm. A lot of the thugs carry them.

They approached you . . .

They weren't reading lists. Just looking around . . . fishing.

Looking for someone suitable, you mean. They hired you then?

Yeh. No, we talked and, and I don't remember.

Are you afraid of those men now, Hawksworth? They are very far away.

They're everywhere! Here and everywhere!

But you claim to forget that they hired you!

No! I was asked to meet them at the Port in one of the Civilian Offices next day.

You kept the appointment then. Was that place a Galactic Federation office?

A business franchise. It had a logo, Star Systems. They hire out servers who entertain while they dish out food. They need entertainment out there, in those places.

Not prostitutes?

I don't know what they do in their free time.

Was that business going on there? Where you went?

I didn't go very far in. Only through the Reception cubicle and then a small office. All the offices are small in Moonbases.

You saw those men, the Solthrees, again?

One of them. He led me into the office where there was someone else sitting at a desk. He hung around while the other one talked to me.

What were their names?

Smith and Jones.

Did they have identification?

No!

Describe the man at the desk.

He was a cyborg, not extreme. Just a hand, and an eye.

Nothing else?

White hair. Pale and old. Very old. You wouldn't notice him otherwise, only the hand and eye . . . what do I get for doing all this talking?

Extradition. May your gods forbid that you spend time in a Khagodi prison among violent criminals, Hawksworth. The crime rate is low here, because of the telepathy, but the ones we have are truly peculiar. Go on. Your man was a cyborg. He was not only a hand and an eye, he must have been something else.

I don't remember what else.

Get on with it, Hawksworth! He must have told you that you were to guard Bullivant and the girl, and do his secretarial work.

I remembered that was what I had to do when I came out of the office.

Do you believe your mind was interfered with in some way?

When he looked at me with that eye . . .

One of those hypno-eyes? an illegal one, with a flashing light?

It went on and off. Like in code. It said I wasn't to remember.

Remember what?

I don't remember.

Hawksworth . . .

CAREFUL. HE IS JUST NEATLY ON THE EDGE NOW.

Did he touch you, Hawksworth?

The hand was like needles. It was like a swarm of bees.

Bees.

With stingers. It was so fine.

Fine. You mean well-made.

It was gold and silver. Or platinum. Like jewelry. It had diamonds in the joints.

Like . . . Lyhhrt work.

He said it was Lyhhrt work. He said: The Lyhhrt have always worked for us. They do our clean work.

Smith or Jones said that.

Yeh.

His hand stung you.

Yes. A finger.

He told you what to do.

Stay with them and don't let her out of your sight until you get orders.

Verona Bullivant, that is.

Little Sister, he called her. Then he says, Cyborg says, no, that's not quite right. Think of her as Little Miss, Hawksworth, that's a good fellow. The other one kind of laughed and he laughed too, and said, Our little talk is one thing you needn't remember.

But you remembered that.

No! No, I didn't! I don't know anything about that at all! They said they'd find and delete me wherever I was if I tried.

Then what did they tell you to do?

There will be someone contacting you. Who? You don't need to know right now. Wait for orders.

What else?

You will go by the name Hawksworth. You will answer to it always.

And when you reach Khagodis they give orders. They say: Hawksworth, you are to . . .

Let the Ix into the embassy and take the girl. Then they will deliver her back to you and you will take her home.

But they never said what they wanted her for? Not as a prostitute for Zamos brothels?

Never, not for that! Why would they say they'd give her back to me then?

You have a point. You told Verona Bullivant, "Back there. We've got to get back there." That meant, back where the Ix are?

I don't remember. You wouldn't let me go back anywhere.

Were the Ix finished with her?

I never knew what they wanted her for, or how long.

Go back again to the time when you first came out here. Only a few days ago. You reached Khagodis and "they" gave orders. Who are "they"? Who are those ones on Khagodis who ordered you to give the girl to the Ix and then to wait for more orders?

It was the woman.

What woman? Where?

On the airbus, one of the *Clipper* line, coming to the port here.

A passenger?

No, she was serving drinks and food.

What else? Tell me about her.

She was a Solthree, there were some men too and some Kylkladi, all stewards. She had red hair, long red hair, they all wore black or dark blue suits, kind of velvet, with the Star Systems logo.

Go on.

When I was going to the can she calls out, Mister Bullivant! I guess she'd been reading the passenger list, and I said, No, did you want him? and she said, Then you're Hawksworth. Of course, I should have recognized you, then she followed me into the cubicle and said, I can talk to him later, but first—

And?

I thought she was going to fuck me, she nearly plastered herself onto me and—and I don't remember anything after that. And that's the truth! You know the rest. . . .

"Yes," said Tharma. "What did they promise you, Hawksworth?"

Hawksworth took a linen handkerchief from his pocket and wiped the sweat off his upper lip. "All the money I could spend, all the girls and boys I could fuck, all the jhat and ge'inn I could smoke."

"Did you get paid at all?"

"Only in some Interworld scrip so I could buy whatever I could find on shuttles and buses. I was supposed to get it all afterward."

"And when Smith-or-Jones paid you it was in the name of—"

"Star✳Systems, with that symbol in it, an asterisk. That's all."

"Yes," Tharma said. "Take him back to Holding, Smiryagin."

Tharma said to the Lyhhrt, who was waiting in Bullivant's apartment, :*If those people, who call themselves Star✴Systems, left him alive to say this much they may not care, his information may be useless. He has already failed them—or at least we thwarted whatever they wanted him to do.*:

:*Or they did not foresee that there would also be Lyhhrt listening to him so eagerly,*: the Lyhhrt said. He was watching Bullivant, who lay in exhausted sleep, tumbled still dressed on his bed.

:*Then I hope you got what you wanted.*:

:*It was helpful.*: The Lyhhrt broke contact.

Tharma was left with her own thoughts: *It was planned to bring Verona Bullivant here. An organization on Sol Three wanted the Ix to mark her, terrorize her for some reason. She remembers that her mother had the same kind of mark. And the Ix don't have—at least didn't have—the kind of ships that travel as far as Earth . . . and was not her mother kidnapped . . . ?*

Also, Tharma, it will no longer be your business once the man is charged with a good number of crimes, and it is well known that Lyhhrt and Khagodi do not sleep in the same water.

Tharma took off the helmet, which did not prevent the Lyhhrt from esping her. "Now, Smiryagin, bring out your bottle and a glass, I will find my bowl and jug, and perhaps we can wash the taste of Hawksworth from our mouths."

When all had quieted down in the embassies and their quarters, the two Lyhhrt stayed to keep watch on Bullivant.

:*I/we believe that went as well as one might hope:*

:*but she must be protected:*

:until this evil runs its course. . . . :
:Tharma would be a good choice as a guardian, but:
:she is too conspicuous so:
:let us give her to Skerow:
:a very old vertebrate who:
:still has some life in her.:
:Yes. And let one protect the other.:

They lingered for a few moments: two, drawn by the loneliness of the first night on a strange world, who did not care for each other but wished to be one.

After a moment one of them said, *:Shall we conjugate?:*

A wistful thought. *:You tempt me, Other. Would that we could.:*

:Not, one feels, on this world of strangers.:
:Too many of us at risk already.:
:And too few to defend ourselves.:

This was the nearest Lyhhrt ever came to romance. *:Now let us see what Ned Gattes has to say about taking care of monkeys.:*

THREE *

Skerow in Hiding

It was night when Skerow came to Smuggler's Gap. The gold smugglers were gone, but the black water rushed through the narrow channel as always, and the climb into the hillside strongholds was very steep. The doors into the hill fortress were reinforced with steel; clouds lay over the sky like armor plating too, and in the moisture of the sea Skerow could smell the bracts of the starweed that crawled among the mosses over the rocks.

She was forced to stop and catch her breath often on the rough steps, but Corpsman Ewskis did not hurry her. He could not help wishing himself back in the *Clipper* and heading back to civilization, but the *Clipper* had lifted, slanting its way toward the shadows of the Manganese Hills and its zigzag path toward a base whose location even Ewskis did not know.

Sergeant Dreytha came behind Skerow even more slowly; she was a large woman used to wielding authority among people, not hopping about on the stones of smugglers' country laden with pots and food supplies.

Finally Skerow could see, rising against the deep gray sky, the bulk of the half-buried fortress that was to be her shelter. As she twisted to pull aside a thorny creeper she glimpsed one brief flash of light on the horizon, and sensed that Ewskis twitched, and at the same moment shut his mind down tight.

"Have they followed us here already, Ewskis?"

Ewskis pulled up the heavy bronze impervious helmet slung on his back and set it on his head. "Madame, it doesn't matter that they know where we are, but that they cannot get at us."

After a few moments the party stopped before a stone arch and Ewskis tapped a key on his wristpack. Great wheels and pulleys swung behind the studded iron door, and Skerow raised her eyes once more to the dark sky and stepped through the white-noise esp-shield into yet another exile.

Inside was brightness, pots of green thuba trees and the smells of cooking. "Welcome, Judge Skerow!" A small quick-stepping Northern woman like herself came forward. She was wearing a chatelaine's chain slung around her shoulder, and the keys hanging from its ring ranged from old giants of rusty iron through merely large brass ones, down to little gold filigrees and beyond them three miniature keypads.

"Ksath!" Skerow cried. "How good to see you!" Ksath had been the trustworthy housekeeper to Skerow's friend Ossta, the Court Officer of Burning Mountain, not long dead of old age. Having Ksath here was almost as good as being with Ossta. She did not know the others; even Ksath had hardly known Evarny.

"I will do my best to make you comfortable. Ossta loved you dearly."

"I miss her." Skerow shivered and swallowed air. "And I'm sure you will take good care of me, Ksath. Tik! Those cannot be my own thuba trees!" Of course she knew that they were not; she had left them behind in her home seven years ago. Here in Smuggler's Gap she was closer to home than she had been all those years, only a day's journey in a wagon pulled by thumbokh, but still in exile.

Ksath touched one of the bulbous leaves. "Everyone knows you love thuba trees, Skerow."

Yes. Probably even the Ix know that.

"Thank you for bringing those, Ksath."

"You are welcome, Skerow. Here's dinner."

Fresh crock-bull joint, a favorite dish, with white-thorn essence to wash it down, and kappyx bulbs properly cooked and so marvelously different from the dreadful preserved form exported to distant worlds for unlucky travelers.

The gold smugglers had not stinted themselves in furnishing their hideout. The apartments were tiny but their lavatory basins luxuriously marbled, and several had gold faucets. Ksath had filled one of them and added lotion to the water, so that Skerow might sleep right away, as she wanted to from tiredness, but she forced herself to explore further among rooms for outworld tenants, several with taps for oxygen and other gases, and one for water-breathers lined with ceramyx.

Before she would sleep she arranged around her the few possessions she had managed to bring: her daybook with its spools: records of cases she hoped to write up before the next half-year session; some snatches of her own poetry; true accounts of travel to distant worlds she had only heard of, and fictional ones that were nowhere near as strange as the real; plus a hand-mirror, a jug of kerm oil and several loose robes, a few packets of herb tea.

She sank into her basin with relief and let the water flow over her head; her breathing siphon extended automatically from her right-hand gill to inflate the fold of membrane at its lip into the bubble anchoring its opening to the surface tension of the water. The lights dimmed around her and she wondered when she would next see the sun, or whether; half-fearfully she extended mental feelers for the stranger and the alien. But in this stone fortress wrapped in a white-noise esp field there was no one else even awake except Ewskis, monitoring satellite transmissions, and the sleepers were as apprehensive as she was.

Waking was much harder, in a place with artificial light where she had nothing to do but keep herself alive. Evarny was dead, her sisters Tikrow and Nesskow had been told only that she was in hiding. Sergeant Dreytha was not a friend, but a bodyguard rather resentful at being cooped up here, and Ksath was a housekeeper who had more to do than entertain an old woman.

She pored over her dreary cases: a dispute over protective tariffs between Eastern Oceania and her own Northern Spine Confederacy; an appeal of a judgment in a suit brought by three Equatorial countries against the Sluices Corporation regarding freshwater levels of the Great Equatorial River. . . . She pushed them aside. She could not bear to learn more about imported fomb shingles and sluice-gate controls. She pushed another key to call up her poems.

o
this desert
I drown in moonlight

The seh is written by Khagodi of the Northern Spine
Confederacy in three lines of one, three and five syllables
in any order. It is not the only form of poetry produced in
the Spines, but certainly the one considered by critics in
Equatorial lands to be the most dry and frigid. Of course
the poems, the epics of the Great Equatorial River poets,
tend to be long winded and melodramatic. Skerow had continued to specialize in seh and gone on writing her reticent
desert poems.

where
ice ages
folded the seas under

and
wave-crests are
combs of ancient salt . . .

But those are from the old days when I was free. And
today they really did seem dry and crumbled.

there are stone poems
and I am
one

Her mind would not budge further. Perhaps she had
fallen into a reverie then, because she was startled when
Ksath appeared with her late-morning bowl of yagha-root
tea and a slice of toasted glauber.

"No need to serve me, Ksath. I can get those things for myself, and I'll help with the cooking too."

"Skerow, I am paid for cooking; you are paid for the work you do. I came mainly to tell you that Ewskis has had a message—eh, we are to have another, eh, guest, I suppose, with us." She stood looking at Skerow almost doubtfully; she was wearing her helmet, a copper net, and had anyway always kept her thoughts to herself.

"Don't make me guess, Ksath! Could I possibly object that someone else might be kept here safely? I have outlived everyone I have ever disliked as well as almost all I loved."

"It is the Solthree Ambassador Bullivant's daughter."

"Eka! That child who has had such a difficult time. . . . It will not be easier for her here either."

"We have plumbing and pumped oxygen for that species."

"Will there be others of that kind coming with her?"

"None that I was told of . . . yes, I understand what you mean. But we will do our best for her."

Yes. She will be made "comfortable."

Skerow watched her go. Ksath did not have far to go: one step.

Skerow looked about her at the walls of her apartment, the sleeping basin she fit exactly with no stretching room, the ceiling that rose above her standing height by one fingerlength, the drinking bowl that set exactly into its niche and was just wide enough to fit her jaw and deep enough for her tongue to lick at, thinking that Bullivant's child should be forced into just such a deadening environment to fit her much smaller frame—and found herself looking into a vertiginous depth echoing with the realization that Evarny, whom she had scarcely found again, seven years worth out of her hundred and twenty, *was* dead, did not exist, was denied the death rituals that recognized his life, because someone wanted her, Skerow, dead because of what she had fought for, and fought against . . . and that same entity, that same monster of greed made up of men and women, only men and women, from twenty or forty or a hundred worlds, was reaching out for that one child who had been left as unprotected and alone as that one Swimmer, Kobai, had been seven years ago.

And here I am, where I can touch the walls without moving, with my tail in a cramp, and cannot get out to do anything!

She was dizzy and breathless, her thoughts were buzzing and confused, she had no space, not enough air.

It is the shock, Skerow, she told herself, reaching up out of her darkness, *only the shock.* But she could not get out into the light.

I can't bear this, I must have some room. . . .

She pulled on her impervious helmet, shuddering at the way it rubbed her scales the wrong way, and pushed her head into the corridor before the door had slid completely open. The corridor ceiling was still no more than one fingerlength above her head. To the left the lightstrip lit the way to a dayroom where Dreytha might be enjoying her own afternoon cordial with Ksath or Ewskis, and to the right ran for a few steps to what seemed a dead end where a door or wall blocked the way.

Momentarily distracted from her unease, Skerow took the few steps. It was a door that stopped her, with a metallic surface very cold to her hesitant touch. No, the very cold part was the electronic panel with touchspots that changed from silver to bright red after contact with her hand. The door slid into its socket, grinding with the rust of unused tracks.

She smelled dead stale air and darkness faced her. She wondered if she had inadvertently opened a strongbox, but there did not seem to be anything stored in it. There was another, hinged, door before her. As if in a dream, she pushed it. Its hinges shrieked like demons.

A whirl of cold dank air blew around her. Wrenched between fear and curiosity, she stepped forward onto a square stone piling set with three mooring rings, below it the water flowing down toward the Gap through a man-made arch hewn out of the bedrock. The stone, stained green with mold and lichens, chilled her feet through the thin soles of her sandals. Not quite above her head a faint greenish light winkled its way through an airshaft in the vault and did no more than dirty the seeping walls.

Skerow heard a buzzing that rose above the skirl of the water and found her mouth and nostrils beginning to tingle. The feeling was horribly familiar, and she backed away, but the door had shut and locked behind her. The sensation deepened and she clapped her hands to the sides of her jaw over the gill-slits, trying at the same time to hold her breath and reach up out of her fear and confusion.

The light coming down through the airshaft dimmed, and Skerow saw the first flicker of the Ix. Her mind became more clear than she would have wished. She stopped breathing, bit down on her tongue with twenty or so of her forty-six teeth to blunt the terrible memory flashes of that day in the Court, and quickly pulled off the loose zaxwul robe she was wearing. She looked sidelong with half-closed eyes, and when three of the Ix's clawed and flashing limbs were only too visible she wrenched off her helmet, swallowed air and shrieked with all the fury stored up in her.

"MONSTER! DEMON!"

The Ix, who had been coming down on a line, seemed

to cringe and curl up like an insect flipped on its back, and then Skerow was reaching out, shrieking again at her loudest and with all the force of her mind, flinging herself forward, clasping it with her great billowing robe.

:I HAVE YOU! MURDERER!:

For a moment it buzzed dreadfully in her arms and its chitinous joints gritted as it clawed through the fabric.

She had to let go. Her foot had slipped and struck one of the mooring rings and she squealed in pain, with greater terror of falling over the edge and into the water than of being hurt by the Ix.

:SKEROW!:

The door had been wrenched open, Ewskis was pulling at her and she fell back into his arms. Her head was whirling and the flashes in front of her eyes did not come only from the Ix.

In a moment she was back inside. The Ix had fought its way out of the robe and gone up the airshaft as if it had wings. The robe was torn and stained with two kinds of blood.

"Not much harm to either of us," Skerow croaked. "It had no weapon."

"Neither did you!" cried Ewskis. "What in the name of the Seventy-Seven Saints made you do that, Madame Skerow!" He was using all his strength trying to hold her upright. With her burst of energy over she had become a dead weight and felt like one. Dreytha came along to support her properly.

Limping on her bruised foot, Skerow trembled and felt foolish. *What can I say? I had an attack of grief.*

She forced herself upright. "Not my room! Let me rest in the dayroom." Dreytha bandaged her ankle and she let Ksath stroke her head and bring her another cup of yagha.

Ewskis said, "We believe the Ix came in a Bri'ak dinghy. It's a kind of airboat the Kylkladi make, a tiny thing with signal-silencers. It was just scouting, but you made an easy target, Madame Skerow."

"Except that she had no weapon," Skerow said.

"She?"

"Yes," Skerow said, and trembled again. She had had a sharp plunge into the Ix's—the Ix woman's—mind: a mother feeding her newly-hatched young the kind of jelly that Ix had once found in Lyhhrt, clutching the infant bodies against her belly to soothe the hot brooding-spots on its plates. The vision of a world where a thousand million Ix slaved and enslaved others; nights of huddling in dim rooms brooding over their children, days of yearning for freedom while they turned the huge unceasing wheels of steel machines in endless rows.

The great Vastness was blind and silent until God and the Saints gave it the eyes and ears of awareness, and they included the Ix. I know it, I have always known it, but— have mercy, Saints!—I don't want to know it now!

Ewskis said from his command post: *:The young woman is on her way.:*

Ned and Robot Serpent

The monkeys had been taken away by a Khagodi Ned had never met, under the close supervision of the Lyhhrt in gold. Verona had been spirited away with Bullivant's deep misgivings, and he himself had ignored the best advice and moved back into the Ambassador's apartment under guard.

Ned was left alone in a small room that still smelled of nine monkeys.

Lonely and at a loss, he resented more than ever having come to Khagodis where he knew no one and did not know what he was to do.

He was staring through the small square window at Khagodis's misty green-blue morning when the door opened, and Gold Lyhhrt came in.

Ned felt his face reddening. "I thought I came here to find Spartakos, not herd a pack of monkeys!"

The Lyhhrt came up very close, as if he were examining Ned pore by pore, and had never noticed that some beings would change color with their moods. "What you did also needed to be done."

Ned stared at him. "What's so valuable about them? All those telemetrics . . ." He forced himself to face the crystal lenses without backing away; the Lyhhrt was not behind them, but somewhere in the torso. "And if Spartakos is so valuable how could you let him take a step without making sure you could trace him?"

The Lyhhrt raised his hand palm outward and spread the fingers. Ned felt the mind-touch as the light caught the Lyhhrt's gold palm, and cried hotly, "Don't put your mindblocks on me! I'm not Hawksworth! I did better at this work when I knew what I was doing and what for—you/yours were willing enough to trust me then!"

The Lyhhrt took a step back and said mildly, "We trusted Spartakos to be always loyal to us. We were, you would say, anthropomorphizing."

Ned doubted he would ever say that, but thought he understood. "You didn't think of him as having a mind of his own." Because, of course, the Lyhhrt did not have minds of their own, and did a machine have a mind? Evidently, Spartakos did.

"Yes, and we were mistaken. We did not think far enough ahead."

Ned nodded, almost awed that the Lyhhrt could admit to having faults. "I've also got a mind of my own, but it doesn't mean you can't trust me."

"We know that Spartakos will not give away our secrets," the Lyhhrt said quietly in the electronically warm voice that no one found appealing. "But I will give you one of them to show that we trust you: the monkeys are our strongbox and Spartakos is the key. You are the only non-Lyhhrt who knows this, and the only Solthree we trust because you swore that oath to help us. . . . no one else here knows this, not Etha nor any Khagodi or offworlder. Will you let me block you enough to ensure that you do not tell about it in your sleep?"

Nobody liked Lyhhrt. It was that combination of coldly beautiful metal and slimy center. All Lyhhrt knew that. "I suppose that's fair enough," Ned said. He was tired of being reminded of that oath. "I didn't know how much you needed the monkeys." He remembered Etha's words: *Unless these creatures have secrets locked in their iron boxes.*

"They are safe for the moment, but they must always be a secret, and keep their secrets—even more so as long as Spartakos is missing. Now you will be unable to tell. . . ."

"I didn't feel anything," Ned said dully. He was beginning to wish he didn't know anything. He was chained to Lyhhrt now.

"You are, in a manner of speaking," said the Lyhhrt. "We cannot help that. We must have Spartakos. We ourselves cannot understand how he went missing. He boarded the airbus with us and was gone when we disembarked."

"He's conspicuous!"

"He knows how to change shape to disguise himself. He might look like a carpet sweeper for all we know. With access to energy he can maintain himself perfectly. He cannot be esped. He is completely beautiful and beautifully complete, a model of robotics in every sense, so wonderfully made that—" The Lyhhrt broke off his self-congratulatory flight. "However, whatever else he can do, he has broken off contact and disappeared."

"Why would he leave?" Ned wondered, and before he could stop himself, thought: *Maybe he doesn't like being named after a slave.*

But the Lyhhrt did not answer this and only said, "It is barely possible that he has been stolen, barely."

"If he can disguise himself how can I find him?"

"You must go where he is and let him find you."

Ned shook his head like a wet dog, trying to make sense of this.

The Lyhhrt went on, "Spartakos will not go far by himself. We have given him freedom and would give him citizenship, but he is not yet used to them, and he is very cautious in unknown places. He has always been associated with arenas, and the only arenas on this world are in Burning Mountain. We feel that the best place to look for him is in the Old City. Where the amusements are. No one there likes Lyhhrt either."

"That's where I'll start then," Ned said, and sighed.

:Can this crude being possibly find our Spartakos?: said bronze Lyhhrt to gold, from the little office where he was mixing ointment for a Pinxid's tropical rash.

:Spartakos has made Ned Gattes his friend. He does not know one Lyhhrt from the next, but he will remember Ned Gattes,: said Gold. "Listen, Ned Gattes, if you believe it is

impossible for you to find Spartakos you may go back to your world and live your happy life. We know you will keep our secrets. No one will take them from you because you will die first, but we will remain here for twenty times twenty Life Cycles if necessary until we have repaired the harm we have done and that is done every hour in our name. Spartakos and the monkeys are not pets or toys but our treasures. Say that you will do or leave us to do."

:If it were my choice alone I would eradicate that one,: Bronze said.

:But it is not "your" choice, nor does "I" exist. It is I/ we that makes our choices. Are we not sufficiently steeped in evil and falling faster?:

"Just because I'm made of flesh and not gold doesn't mean I'm any goddam animal!" Ned said. "My oath is as good as yours or anybody else you want to call on."

Ned packed a low-grade stunner and a clip of ceramyx knucks he had bought from an old stunned pug begging in the spaceport. He did not believe they would help him find Spartakos, but he was not quite young enough now to be rash.

The Old City had been built higher up on the volcano's flank than the modern Burning Mountain, as an ancient walled fortification that had grown in peaceful times into a haven for bored tourists. It was a place where Khagodi did not worry about morality or its hypocrisies. Khagodis had allowed GalFed to designate the area as an Interworld Zone, and the local Peacemen patrolled only to stop violence.

Ned came in through the great wooden doors bound with iron hinges and armed with bosses and spikes. He was

sweating in the fierce heat, and had not dared to come before the sun was low in the west. Half a score of revelers
came in with him, three gray-dyed Kylkladi in red embassy
sashes, a red-haired Solthree woman in a crimson wrap, another Earther woman, the bodyguard of a man who looked
too powerful to need one, an ancient crinkled Khagodi man
whose faded colors had been brightened with sprays of
pearl and gold, and a Tignit in a filter-suit and bubble helmet. Ned wondered what a Tignit could find to enjoy here,
and how.

The streets were just awakening in the evening shadow.
Gas lamps popped their flames, merchants called out into
the streets hawking three for the price of two. The thick
stone fortification walls were lined inside with souvenir
stands selling pennants for tour groups, knucklebone toys,
feather necklaces from Kylklar, cheap handmade cigarettes
of coarse jhat grown in the Southwest Marshes, imitation
Xirifri pearls and miniature sundials. Pinch-faced children
of five species offered necklaces of cheap silver coins.

There were clusters of tiny shops that sold food, oxygen
capsules and filters, allergy sprays and headache patches, to
all of the outworlders—lawyers and their staffs, journalists
and their crews—who had been flocking throughout the
years to the sensational trials. There was a historic stone
mill powered by twenty thick-shouldered tzammer that
pulled a huge stone wheel round and round unceasingly.
And then there was the Arcade of Delight, which in pre-
historic times had been a lateral cone along the fissure line
of the volcano, much later an underground shelter for the
besieged, and now had become a place where aliens, and
sometimes even Khagodi, took their pleasures.

Ned went into its depths down a coil of grimy stone
steps and limestone walls, accompanied in a straggling line

by the customers who had come along with him through the gates. A brawling clamor welled up along with thick vapors of jhat and beer, and the dark walls became tinted dull mauve and green by the cold-light ceiling strips.

Further down the heavy smoke of ge'inn arose with the other smells. Ned stepped down into the well of it, saw stars and blinked away dizziness. Beyond the ge'inn he could smell fried tidbits and ancient urinals. There was a bubbling croak from behind him, and the Tignit swarmed past in a snarl of tentacles, hurrying to some mysterious pleasure. One or two other shadowy characters slipped down into the depths of the pit; none came up, so early in the evening.

The tunnel was paved with ancient cobbles and walled in moldy tiles. The naked rock ceiling had been jerry-rigged in a Laocoön's tangle of obsolete electric lamps: globes with naked filaments, tiny glaring halogen tubes, mauve fluorescents, and stuttering neons that said JOE'S PLACE in eighty-seven languages. Loudspeaker voices were screaming songs of love or hate accented by gubu drums and Asturian pinh bells.

The first thing Ned saw in this glare was a thick cluster of nervous journalists clutching cams and keybos, looking for human interest stories; they had gotten entangled with the Tignit, who was thrashing to get free. Ned made his way carefully around them. What could Spartakos possibly want here?

The curving walls beyond him were lined to the left with sideshows, some with a spieler on the bally, and to the right with cubicles where gamblers spent their old silver pistabat on game machines or squatted in circles to play skambi with plastic disks and brass rods. He passed the old man sprayed in pearl and gold, who was staring as he tottered by at three tired-looking women who were swishing their tails in time with the finger-cymbals they were playing and thinking mildly salacious thoughts.

Ned picked up a jug of weak local beer from a passing vendor while he watched two Sziis dancing through hoops of fire, and an acrobat juggling thin glass bubbles. And beyond that, where the man and woman were writhing with the serpent, he stopped and stared.

The man was a Varvani and the woman an O'e, and except for the faint gleam of their copper filigree helmets, they were naked as far as he could see in the quivering light that cast such strange shadows; the Varvani's slaty skin was warmed in it, and the O'e's dun color softened. They were standing on a turntable with their arms reaching upward, turning, twisting as the table rotated so that their bodies touched belly-to-breast, side-to-back, buttock-to-thigh, and did not pause anywhere while the serpent swarmed into the spaces between their bodies, arms, legs, in a sinuous endless embrace. There was no accompaniment; they did not need it. Ned had always thought of Varvani as awkward and clumsy, and this one, no better looking than any other, was not. The O'e woman looked so healthy as to seem another species entirely. As for the serpent with its coils always in motion, he could not tell at all what kind of being it might be, only that it was as huge as a python or the devil's wife of Thanamar II, huge enough to weigh the dancers to the floor, but it did not seem to burden them at all.

For a moment Ned found himself once again a schoolboy in Religious Studies watching Adam and Eve, Garden tree and snake displayed alive in one completed being. It seemed to him as if no one else was watching. He stood without moving as the turntable slowed, the serpent's coils loosened and spiraled away, the woman brought down her arms and lifted her head, which had been resting on the Varvani's shoulder.

Ned was startled to see she was wearing around her neck the thin gold chain with the little heart-shaped lock that had been the whore's badge of subjugation in Zamos's brothels. He was even more startled when the Varvani took a tiny key from his mouth, unlocked the heart and fastened it around his own neck. Varvani had always been the bouncers in Zamos brothels, just as Lyhhrt had always been the doctors. He hardly noticed that someone was pulling on his arm and whining, "You wanna have fun, baby? You wanna have fun?"

"Not tonight, lady!" He half turned to push her aside, and she yelped. "What—"

Her eyes were on the platform. He turned back.

The serpent in unwinding its great swath from the two performers had completed a circle around them and now lifted its head arching and turned it toward Ned as if he had charmed it. It came forward with diamond eyes glowing and a small leaf-shaped tongue flickering. The O'e woman was standing turned to stone with her mouth open, and the Varvani, too astonished to stop the turntable, was running along its rim to stay where he was and gasping, "Ho! A-ho!" as if he were out of words.

Ned thought he wanted to be away from all three of them in a hurry. The people around him were crying out and shrinking back, and Ned backed with them, but the serpent swiftly caught up with him and flicked its tongue at his mouth—it was cool and dry—then wound a great thick coil around his body. It did not weigh him down but supported itself on him like a living caduceus. And it was of metal, a robot serpent.

All the while the diamond eyes remained fixed on his

human gray ones and Ned stood very, very still. Everyone within five meters' radius of him was still. He was sure of being crushed, it would be like being up-country with the monkeys; as the drone had been waiting to incinerate him, this had been waiting to make sure he did not escape for long. The scales, gold, silver or chrome, smelling of warm metal, reflected the lights like flickering water, flowed around him like water, or perhaps mercury, tarnished in spots, the way mercury will pick up a greasy fingerprint. Ned could not help observing this through his terror. It was what made him a GalFed agent.

Gradually he lost his fear because the metal body did not press on him, barely touched him. This was no attempt to destroy him but something else: the robot was investigating him as an animal would do and sometimes other robots did. The thick coils flowed, around, under, in between, and then fell away and retreated, freeing him.

Ned shuddered and stepped back quickly; a yelp told him he had trodden on the foot of a Khagodi Peaceman. "Ik-ik! What's going on here!" He was a big Southern man with a helmet and livid blue sash fighting with his brilliant colors; he was trying to rub his foot and had to bend anyway to keep his head out of the electric lights.

"Sorry!" Ned gasped. "Nothing's wrong!"

Seven or eight voices around him cried out, "The thing grabbed 'im! The Thing! It was gonna eat 'im!"

The metal python was slithering away—Ned could hear the faint hiss of its scales on the stage—and the O'e and the Varvani were cowering behind it. "It's all part of the act, mister!" Ned said, pulling himself together with an involuntary shiver. "First time on this or any other world, warming up for the Grand Pandemonium on Skaparan Four next stop!"

"Is that the truth!" The Peaceman bent his neck to peer into Ned's face as the serpent had done, obviously wishing he was allowed to take off the helmet and find out. "Let us have some ID for safety's sake."

Ned produced a medallion with his real name and profession on it. He was a legitimate traveler and registered with the police here. The peace officer held it to the light "Ik! You are a long way from Fthel Four! Business bad for pugs with no more Zamos, eki?" The Varvani crept forward tremblingly and offered an Exhibitor's and Operator's license. "One of the few here that is not expired, I see. Go you in peace, man, and keep a good hold on that creature of yours!" He moved off. A few of the curious hung about for a short while and Ned ducked out of the way of a camera eye.

Then the O'e woman came forward to put her arms around the Varvani, and he and Ned looked at each other over her shoulder. The robot had slipped away behind a curtain. Ned dug into his money pouch and found a handful of the worn pistabat he had exchanged credit for at the gate. None of them spoke. The music flared up again in the background and someone lit a fire and swallowed it. Ned put the money into the Varvani's hands and said, "Take really good care of our friend."

The Varvani grunted. "You come back. You good with that one."

"Maybe I will."

Let him find you, the Lyhhrt had said. Ned was thinking furiously. He had set out to find a robot and he had found one. If that sidewinder was Spartakos the Lyhhrt's property seemed to be in good shape, and in good hands. If. Did he dare leave it at that and report back now? He didn't know whether it was Spartakos, and he wasn't going to try taking possession of it. And he didn't dare linger near it after he had caught the attention of the Peace force.

All right. Damned if I know what this monster is, I'll work my way round and come back when the Peace are gone.

When he turned to sidle among the pleasure seekers in the lane, Ned saw the Tignit standing across the way in front of the skambi machines. He could not tell through that dark featureless bubble whether the fellow—of whatever sex—was staring at him. That was the only Tignit he had seen since he came through the Old City gates; he maneuvered swiftly to put himself among groups of people, and far away from the serpent.

He was wondering whether the Tignit was an ESP. Ned did not wear an impervious helmet, though he owned one and sometimes used it in the arena. He had studied esp-shielding and -blocking techniques for both the arena and GalFed, and as an agent he had always worked as an observer, not a keeper or transmitter of secrets. Terrans were not a powerfully telepathic people, and there were probably fewer than a hundred esps among the billions and no more than four or five of them esp-one. The Lyhhrt had tied his tongue to protect the only secret they had given him, and there was nothing about him to stir suspicion except his interest in that strange display.

Why the hell did he leave the Lyhhrt anyway? And if I do find him how am I supposed to bring him back? He might kill me . . . no, I don't think he would. He saved my life.

He went on with the feeling that the eyes of the Peaceman were boring into his back, and that the diamond eyes of the serpent were on him. And someone else. That though the destruction of the drone flier had been meant for the

122 * *Phyllis Gotlieb*

monkeys, whoever was willing to see him die in it was here
stalking him in the open, under the eyes of Khagodi authority.

He passed a platform where two Kylkladi, a man and a
woman, in plumage of yellow-orange and orange-red, were
kick-boxing, using their ankle spurs to rip at each other
with cruel grace. They could not have been watching him,
they were so busy dodging each other's horn-shafted legs.
He went on, drifting further into the reaches of the Arcade.

The floor sloped downward around to the left and the
whir of the ventilators deepened. The game machines on
the concave wall to the right gave way to booths where
players used gold crediscs to play genuine games, Kylkladi
ekka squares, blueblack jack, and skambi at a proper table
with a dealer and plasmix disks with gold rims and numbers
on amber rods. A half-score of others.

Ned bought another beer and hung around near the
star-shaped skambi table while he sipped at it, turned very
slowly and looked about carefully; no sign of the Tignit.
But as he turned his head back he saw that the tall Peaceman
whose foot he'd trodden on had been joined by a shorter
one; both of them were watching him with a curiosity that
was mild but persistent. He swung away and shoved his
face into his beer. His mind swarmed with its usual fantasies
in these situations: that the Lyhhrt, whom he would never
wholly trust, did not really trust him either and had put
him under surveillance, or that the Peace officers were in
the pay of whoever owned Zamos's collapsed empire now,
or that . . . As fast as he could drink the beer he was sweating it off. He licked his foamy lip and went down toward
whatever delight waited in the depth of this Arcade.

The cavern widened into greater space, the game rooms
became larger and more brilliant, some with crystal doors

and blazing chandeliers reminiscent of the more expensive brothels run by Zamos. The tables there had smoke-cones hovering over them to draw up the fumes of more powerful and costly hallucinogens than the jhat and ge'inn that had already dizzied him, and the figures beneath the cones were veiled in their own smoke. There were tall doors set in the marble-lined walls and beyond them perhaps women, men, children or machines waiting to give the players deeper pleasures.

The flocks of media, civils, legals and other soberly dressed gents and ladies that peered at such places were just daring to venture to this section, but Ned was thinking, *Maybe I've come too far.* Too far away from that serpent, the only robot, the only hint of anything like Spartakos. He began to move across toward the other wall where, as the evening lengthened and more pleasure-seekers swarmed down the stairs to fill the space, the fire-swallowers and jugglers of crystal balls were gesticulating ever more passionately to the rhythms of steel drums and palpitating bucciphones.

As he began the move upstream he was swamped by the force of a group of well-roused workers who looked like the crew of a ship or construction site. They were a mixed lot: Kylkladi and Varvani, a few Bengtvadi; some of the Varvani, women among them, giving piggyback rides to frail-looking but wiry Bengtvadi. Ned could not fight this lot, especially the Varvani; short of letting them flatten him he had no choice but to run with them.

He was driven along under the jittering lights toward a line of small arenas that curved to follow the cavern's shape. In the first one two young Khagodi wearing massive impervious helmets were thrashing at each other with their tails; they had cut off the tips, stimulated the stumps to split into three or four, and armed them with steel spikes. Both were bleeding a little from scratches but neither had the skill or grace to make an interesting show. Ned pushed back toward the wall.

But the crew behind him were scuffling and looked about to dissolve into a free-for-all, and there was no way back. Ned rode the wave past two fighting Khagodi reptile primates wearing gold collars enameled with cloisonné work, who were being prodded with zapsticks by Kylkladi handlers and squeaking pathetically. They would vanish if the Peacemen came within sight of them. Looking back, Ned could not see either of the officers, nor the Tignit. He began to feel like a fool for all his idiotic fears.

When he turned about to find his way beyond the third ring he found someone purposively looking at him. The broad and powerful man who had come through the gate with the young woman bodyguard was standing at the edge of the ring staring at Ned Gattes. The way the lights worked their flares and shadows above his head they seemed to lay a cruel and flickering smile across his face. Seemed... When he moved his head his look was only thoughtful. But looking at Ned.

Then Ned saw that the woman who had come with him was in the ring taunting a young Varvani she had evidently challenged. More than taunting, she was lunging at him with thrusts of her double-edged knife, laughing, purring endearments and tender promises to carve him into chops. The Varvani, who was grasping a wrench and a heat-sealer and might have been part of a local maintenance crew— certainly no fighter though he was twice-and-a-half her weight—was taken aback at her vehemence, and wondering how he had been caught in this trap.

"Sweetheart," she cooed, "come on, sweetheart!" She

was dancing in the heavy ash that littered the ring, her boots were gray with it, and everything else she wore was gray, as suited a shadow-stalker serving her master. Ned thought she was younger than he, but fresh-faced and unscarred except for missing an earlobe. Her hair was dark brown in a long braid, and caught the lights. He thought of Zella, in the first light of his meeting her, and her braided cornsilk hair.

Something else caught the lights and distracted him, one bright flash and then another. It was glittering from the face of a dark figure standing two paces behind the broad man watching his woman in the ring. Ned could not make it out for a moment, until he recognized the bluish tinge of the face: the Pinxid woman, Keremer, was back there wrapped in black lace and leaning on a thick wooden staff. The glitters had come from the brilliant diamonds on her nose ring, and Ned wondered that no one had stolen them from her. She was staring at the broad man.

She had not yet seen him, but Ned shook his head, thinking for a moment that he had drifted into a paranoid fantasy in which everyone had come to this place for some purpose connected with him. He wiped his forehead with his sleeve. He had sweated in rough denims all the days since he had landed on Khagodis, and no washboard could scrub them clean. The heat was somewhat less oppressive this far underground, but not much. When he looked up again he saw that the Varvani was marching off shaking his wrench at the jeering crowd, and the challenger was smiling, with that joyful icy smile, at him, Ned Gattes. She swiveled her head to glance at her master, he nodded with a tic of his eyelid and she turned back. The crowd fell silent. "Here's a one," she murmured.

At that moment Ned could see the future as if he had

already lived it, but there was no way he knew to dodge past it. "I don't take dares from alley-flickers," he said levelly.

"I thought you were a real fighter," she half-whispered, as if for his ears alone. "I thought you were a pug called Ned Gattes who'd fought in arenas on seven worlds."

"Five," he said, "and what are you called, lady?"

"You don't need to call me anything, pommster. But I fight for Councilman Brandsma, and my name's Palma. Something you won't need to remember."

"I'm nobody's hire-on and I fight for cash," Ned said. Then he wished he had not, because he saw the next move.

"Here is money," the man who radiated power said. Councilman Brandsma. He dug into his money belt and tossed a handful of silver coins across the ring at Ned's feet. He ran his hand over his darkly grizzled head and smiled.

"I came here for pleasure, not the wallops," Ned said mildly, carefully turning away from him. Certainly he could not fight a duel with ceramyx knuckles, no matter how hard, and his stunner was not a weapon for a crowd.

"And maybe you're just shitting-scared," his challenger whispered, as if she were inviting him into her bed.

Ned shook his head again to push away the nightmare of noise, heat, lights. He could see Brandsma edging away now, swiftly, into the dimness. Headed somewhere, like the Tignit. Keremer turned and stood with her eyes following the man, mouth open and one hand raised as if she would call him back. All this in an instant.

Ned's mind would not stop running while he faced the knife: *He thinks I'm following him, I dunno why, his babby's here to hold me, kill me if she thinks she's got to. Yeh, that's a one would kill me all right.* Ned was not afraid of fighting in arenas, though fear sometimes spiced the pleasure he took in it. What he feared was dying for nothing, worlds away from everything he cared about, in a street fight fired up by a chophead. This dems'l was none of that sort, but even more dangerous. He made himself grin and said, "Call me scared if you like that kind, I see your mister the Councilman's run off with his whole skin."

"Too much dicker, Ned Gattes." She was sweating and the loose hairs around her hairline had burst into little curls. Her ice-cold eyes had begun brown, but white and blue lights were glazing them. He thought the eyes said that one of them must die before he could take one step away from this nightmare. Zella and his sons and daughter swarmed up before his eyes in flickering visions.

A Kylklad standing just behind his shoulder cackled, "Kill the whore!" and thrust a dagger into his hand.

A half-score voices cried, "Yeho, man, get on with it!"

Ned had not fought with a knife since his young days as an alley scrapper, but he grasped it in a dream. Palma leaped out of the ring, and he ducked in time to avoid having his throat sliced open but got a flick of the knife-point from jaw to cheekbone, felt the blood blooming like a rose on his skin.

Palma grinned, and the crowd fell silent, because no fair fight stepped beyond an arena. Ned dodged around her into the ring, reached out and catching her knife hand aimed a blow at her right shoulder. She went down on one hip but her foot came up kicking and caught his right knee hard. He gasped as it gave way and lost his knife when he landed on his hand to keep his whole body from slamming down into the crumbled ash. And she jumped up with her knife driving at his ribs.

A high thin voice screamed, "No!" and again "No! That's enough!"

The voice came from Keremer, standing now where the power broker had begun by watching Ned, and Palma startled and looked up with her knife poised one centimeter away from Ned's flesh and blood. Twice Keremer pounded the floor with her thick staff of black wood, the second time with an explosive noise as the tile beneath it cracked. Then she swung it to one side and holding it horizontal with her two hands bulldozed her way to the edge of the ring with her black lace fluttering after her and the sheen of her purple-bronzed face picking up lights in their turn, cracking heads and screaming as she came, "Enough of this stupid business, no more, enough!" Ned saw that her arms were less like thin bones and more like steel rods. And that her diamonds might be hard to steal.

An uproar had started around the ring but by then Keremer had reached its edge. She swung her heavy staff upright and brought it down on Palma's knife arm. Ned heard the sick sound of crunched bone.

Palma fell to her knees in turn, remained so for a moment in shock with her mouth open, then gave a scream that turned to a whimper, until she swallowed on the pain and howled, "You old turd! I'll kill you, I'll kill you and him both! You'll pay! You'll pay!"

Keremer jeered, "You sniveling blatteroon! Go lick your master's arse, you've got the right reward from me!" She swung her head around snarling at her surly audience. "Not satisfied, you sewerskates? Want more blood?"

But they were muttering, "Move off, the Peaceman's coming," and shrinking away from the ring.

Keremer grasped Ned's arm with her wire-sharp fingers and hissed, "Come with me, Ned Gattes, and quickly! That thug Councilman that stole my La'or has got together with a clutch of felons like himself, and we must stop them!"

Ned pulled away frantically. He was breathing hard and dared not touch his stinging face. "What are you talking about? I have nothing to do with them!" God knew where the serpent had slithered by now, into some bolt-hole where he could never follow.

"What have I saved your life for then, you dolt? Those demons killed my darling, my children's mother, and they have worse things in mind! Hurry!"

"For God's sake—" Ned stumbled, limping on his bruised leg. Who were the "demons" and how did she know of them?

"Yes, for any deity you choose, I want them dead if not alive!"

Ned, having escaped one killing, was desperate not to face another. But Keremer was desperate too, dragging him along by her passionate strength past the last two arenas, now emptied by the excitement, further down into the pit where there were no more entertainments and nothing to catch the eye but tangles of lights and pipes, and blankfaced doors leading to rumbling generators and ventilators. Finally he dug in his heels and pulled her back.

"Stop it, Keremer, stop!"

She glared at him. "You are a coward, like everyone else on this world!"

He socketed in a new oxycap—they became exhausted quickly in this foul air—and took a breath. "I'm damned if I'm going farther into this hole without knowing what's down there! Where did you hear about this meeting?"

Keremer said sharply, "I have employees and some of you hemisexuals seem to find them attractive. You will even whisper secrets to them in the dark. Some of you belong in the dark!"

Keremer knew nothing of his past, and Ned was grateful, remembering the darkness in which he had slept with Manador, and the danger, too. "I'll see what I can find—but you have to go back. If anyone twigs what you've done already I'll be kicked off the world for letting it happen!"

"I will never—"

"You've got to carry a message for me, find the Lyhhrt Ambassador and tell him that you saw me, and where I am, nothing else, do you have that?" The message would not say much but its existence would be a hint of something.

"I—"

"I swear I'll try to help!"

Keremer said grudgingly, "I will do that much for you."

"Keremer!" A Pinxid was running toward them, one of the young embassy guards, draped with an armory of holstered weapons. "Keremer—" She gave Ned one startled look at his bloody face, grasped Keremer about the shoulders and drew her away back toward the lights. Keremer went quietly, not even cracking another tile with her staff.

"Remember!" Ned called, and left them quickly, pausing only an instant to rub his knee and damned glad to be rid of the old woman, savior or no. Here was another unwanted errand growing out of the first one like a wart.

But so far there was no one to dodge but two or three stooping Khagodi slung with tool kits and lumbering under the close ceiling, a couple of twittering Kylkladi, and then no one at all, and the music and cries were fainter than his footfalls . . . or the echo of some strange noise that might be footsteps and might not. . . .

Why can't I get rid of this feeling? Nobody's come after me. The robot thing was only curious—the Peacemen I guess knew of me because I've been around the embassy for a

*while, but they didn't bother me, the Tignit and that stud
councillor wanted to get away from me. . . .*

For a moment he thought he had come to the very end
of the labyrinth, a blind pocket of stone. The lights had
thinned out and grown dim. But there was one more faint
sign in cold light, a symbol that pointed to an exit in what
had seemed a solid wall; when he came up close he found
another wrought-iron railing around a spiral stairway going
downward, this one much darker and narrower than the
entranceway. He backed off at first as if it had been the
opening to Hell's pit, but when he smelled not sulfur but a
waft of fresh air blowing up he reoriented himself and realized that the stairs must lead only to an exit further down
the hillside, perhaps outside of Old City altogether. Not
many people seemed eager to use it.

He went down gingerly, hoping against hope not to
meet anybody worse than himself. There were only about
fifteen steps and each one that he touched safely left him
very slightly more relaxed; he could hear the chirring of
insects and the squawks of bat-winged fliers, and was beginning to think—a thought he never completed, because
among those sounds in the lower noise level here, was the
ticking of something like an antique clock, something behind him that he could not see when he turned his head,
and just below him a mutter of voices.

As he took a turn onto the last-step-but-three the voices
grew loud and angry, and he found to the left a huge
wooden door set flush with the wall, a dusty cone of light
coming from its keyhole, and to the right the heavy metal
grille which had been pulled back to leave the exit open.
Behind the door, just slightly muffled by its thickness, there
was a rumble of overturned furniture and a crash of glass.

The voices gathered in a tremendous cry that was too blurred for him to make out the words.

Ned's heart thumped sickeningly; he backed away and slipped the knucks over his fist. While he was trying to decide whether to scramble back up the stairs or jump for the dark opening to the outside where he could not see anything at all, and might fall down a hillside or another flight of stairs, the door burst open.

After that there was a great confusion he could only sort out roughly: Brandsma—that bulky shape, the cropped frizzy hair—flung himself through the doorway, saw Ned in its burst of light, yelled, "You!" and lunged at him. He ran into Ned's fistful of knucks and his rush knocked Ned's head against the grille.

Ned saw stars and clung to the metal rungs while Brandsma yelled and staggered, then hurled himself howling out into the night. The ancient gold-sprayed Khagodi, quivering hands clasped to his gill-slits, hopped out and away with surprising vigor, followed by a gray-dyed Kylklad with a red sash striding on long horn legs, and last a tall woman swept out with her face shrouded in a deep red velvet cloak. They did not even notice Ned, clinging dizzily to the gate.

He smelled something horrible, a smell that went up his nose into his eyes and ears, and deep into his brain and its dizziness, and in the depth of all this confusion he heard a buzzing that he had thought was the noise of insects coming from outdoors, and now just dimly realized was coming from the nakedly lit room beyond the door, where lying half across a table was the Tignit with its limbs twitching and helmet smashed, and inside the helmet the head of the Tignit or something else that was black and hairy, oozing into a pool on the table with a liquid that was black, and yellowish too and slowly congealing around the slowly dying buzz that stopped and gasped, went on most faintly for a moment, and with a last twitch died.

Ned felt himself fainting and sinking with the poison in his nose and eyes, and heard the too familiar sound of ticking, clicking that had been following him down through the cavern all along, his nemesis, thought *I'm done for* and saw through fading sight a half-score of metal things on invisible wheels swarming from their hiding place among the ceiling pipes and wires down the walls, humming as they came. He gaped dully while these mechanical mice skittered around him into lines and circles, clicked as if they were communicating in signal dots and dashes, no, were joining themselves together, one-two *click* and *click-click* two-three, no, four-five meters of sinuous length, the beautiful length of the metal serpent, in coils on the floor before him.

It raised its cobra head and brilliant eyes to Ned's face for one instant, then reached across the hallway, dimmed the room's light and pulled the heavy door closed. All this movement from its first appearance through the process of metamorphosis took no more than a few blinks of Ned's heavy eyes. In another dim confused moment the serpent wound its length that felt like warm satin around Ned's torso and carried him outside into the hot but fresh air, down six Khagodi-sized stone steps, and laid him down in a clump of greenery.

Ned lay still and could not even see the stars while his head slowly cleared, though it did not stop aching, along with his kicked knee and the bloody slash on his face, the skin now pulling tightly as it dried. The serpent's head hovered over him as if it were anxious; he saw, finally, the stars beyond the head, and a lamp on a pole set into the rock wall around the back doorway. He was lying on the hillside in a thicket of weeds with narrow green leaves, and a path ran alongside him to one side and crookedly downward. He heard noises and twitched, but there was only a Varvani, drunk on smoke or drink, tumbling out and down the stairs, staggering off singing what sounded like a space chantey in a very deep bass rumble.

Ned found that he could move his arms and changed his oxycap. He was stunned as the old pug he'd bought the knucks from in the port. *Never got to use them, either.* Though somehow they had whacked Brandsma good and proper.

His first rational thought was, *I remember Brandsma from somewhere.* He could not think where, and for the moment did not care. Also, though he had never before seen or smelled an Ix he realized that the dead thing with the horrible smell had been an Ix disguised as a Tignit. *He knows how to disguise himself, says Lyhhrt. Yeh, somebody did.*

The two moons hurled themselves up the eastern sky and the serpent stirred. In the moonlight it was changing shape, not separating into pieces but shifting, twisting, writhing as it re-formed itself with the scales swimming over its surface, blunting its head, absorbing its tail, pushing out a gleaming limb, two, four limbs, stretching out fingers, separating toes, flickered its eyelids and nostrils, licked or pretended to lick its lips with a leaf-shaped tongue, smoothed down its sleek belly and seemed to grow genitals under the sweep of a hand, and last, arched its back and rose slowly, to maintain balance, opened its eyes, and became Spartakos with his gold head, hands and feet, and chrome-washed body.

He hummed for a moment, as if clearing his throat, flung wide his hands and said in his warm baritone, "My friend Ned Gattes, it is your old acquaintance Spartakos! Do you not know me? I am Spartakos! Say that you know me, Ned Gattes!"

Ned and Spartakos

"I know you," Ned said.

"Are you in good order, Ned? Tell me that you are in good order!"

"I'm not in any kind of order." Ned sat up slowly and waited for a few moments while the throbbing blood eased its way down from the top of his head. "What were you doing in that Arcade?" He looked at the dim opening where he had brushed death, and saw how Spartakos must have hidden himself in his strange shape and slipped inside.

Spartakos folded himself neatly into a sitting position and opened a minuscule drawer in his side, where his twelfth rib would have been if he were fleshly, brought out a piece of chamois leather, switched on a tiny light in his forehead, and began to polish himself with innocent sensuality, revolving his head a hundred and eighty degrees so as not to miss a dull spot on his back. "So many chrons we have been apart and you have no more to say to me than 'What were you doing in that Arcade?' "

"You saved my life again, Spartakos, but I took the risks to find you. What do you know about all the crazy things that happened back there? Why in God's name did you run away?"

"God's name is Lyhhrt," Spartakos said.

A few revelers tottered down the steps from the back entrance, two or three misstepped and fell into the greenery with thumps. In their state they paid Spartakos no more attention than they would have paid Ned if he had taken off all his clothes and painted himself purple. "I don't understand."

"That One God has no great sum to do with me, does That One?" Spartakos's voice, a baritone instrument like every Lyhhrt's, muted itself so that no one but Ned could hear it. "No, it is He or She or Tree or Stone. Not what made me, which is Lyhhrt. I was made—by Lyhhrt, by flesh like yourself under that gold and bronze—to believe that I was a guide and a lighthouse until Zamos was destroyed, when the Lyhhrt would be safe and the O'e were free. Now the Lyhhrt are safe enough because they are protected from the Ix by Galactic Federation, but the O'e are swept into corners and left to rot. And my *self* that worked so hard to bring all of that to pass is as nothing, and I find that I am no more than an adding machine for Zamos's sins against the Lyhhrt. I did not know where else to hide myself from that."

Ned stared at this glinting figure, the robot with a social conscience, and wondered what would happen when Spartakos learned of the monkeys.

"Not only that," Spartakos said, "but the other part of my filing system is fitted into hideous creatures from your world!"

What will happen to Us! the monkey Aark had cried.

"And what will become of me?" Spartakos went on. "Me! this self! when they are done with addition and multiplication? How can I help the O'e then? And how can I leave my friends?"

Ned was about to ask who they were, when the Varvani appeared in the doorway with his arm around the O'e woman's shoulders; they came down the steps and made their way toward the shimmering android. They were familiar with his form.

"I have shown myself to them," Spartakos said. "They know nothing about Lyhhrt."

"Maybe not. It looks as if everyone knows where you are except the Lyhhrt," Ned said.

"I can go into narrow places, but they are the prisoners of their machines and cannot go anywhere."

"What have you told your friends then?" The couple, weary of performing and looking for their serpent, huddled clasping each other with their eyes closed, disregarding a conversation they barely understood.

"Nothing they need not know. I cannot tell them Lyhhrt secrets any more than you can, Ned Gattes. If we could we would not be here. Alive."

"The police soon will be."

"They are not looking for us."

"The Lyhhrt are."

Spartakos began the tricky balancing act of pulling up his massive body. "They will not find me no matter what you may tell them, my-friend-Ned-Gattes."

"I am your friend. If you want to keep going in good order you can't do without them."

"It is *these* friends! I cannot leave my friends! If I cannot help even one of the O'e how can I save the lot of them? Before they found me they were performing an animal act."

"Animal?" Ned tried to imagine the kind of Khagodi beast that would have taken the part of the serpent.

"A nonprocreative act of copulation."

Ned untangled that one and said, "I see."

"They have no other skill."

"Um." Ned scratched his head. "The Lyhhrt really need you, Spartakos. I don't see why you shouldn't do a bit of bargaining with them. Everybody knows nobody loves Lyhhrt. If they do a favor to a couple of other human beings they might have somebody who's at least grateful. Think about it."

"They have sent out a buzzer for us," Spartakos said, and was silent. The moons swept over his head like lacrosse balls and began the long descent into dawn, while his brilliant surface reflected their fall.

Ned could not hear the machine, but he knew that he would. The Varvani stirred himself and fished in a drawstring pouch for dopesticks.

Ned accepted one, and they sat smoking while Spartakos settled himself back into his fakir's position, humming faintly with thought, ticking every once in a while as if he might shift and slither away into the leaves.

Three or four of the musicians who had been performing for the bally shows came out of the doorway and settled on the steps to tighten a string or run up and down a scale. They were a mixed lot, gathered in some fellowship of sound: an old thin Khagodi who played a xylobou, a Bengtvadi woman with a mandolet, a squat Varvani with a little harp and a Kylklad with an electronic soundboard. They strummed a bit and the young Bengtvadi began to sing, in a thin high voice like silver wire, flavored with strange harmonics, a song in Ned's own English, though he would never find out whether they knew what the words meant. . . .

> *Give us this day, Lord, our daily monotony*
> *Yea Lord, give us this day*
> *our daily monotony*
> *gather the flocks, shepherd the sheepy clouds*
> *down to the western sea . . .*

"Lyhhrt must swear an oath to pay some price for my return. I will find some way to do what I must for these friends."

Ned remembered the devil's oath the Lyhhrt had sworn to Zamos, to serve one Cosmic Cycle—one hundred and twenty-nine of their years—of labor in Zamos's laboratories and whorehouses, in exchange for power and glory within Galactic Federation. "You might get a promise, Spartakos. I doubt if you could make them swear any more oaths. You know the Lyhhrt. As long as you have something that's so important to them you don't have much choice."

Spartakos hummed for a moment, a long moment, and said, "Yes. You are right, Ned Gattes. I am not sorry I saved your life all of those times." He turned, swiveling his torso by ninety degrees, to the O'e woman and the Varvani. "I must leave you, but I will come back. I can make this oath, that the Lyhhrt will lose me again if they do not let me help my friends."

Now Ned could hear the breathy hum of the aircar that Spartakos had been waiting for.

They were well airborne before the lights of the police helicopter swept the sky. Finally a passerby had realized that the stuff seeping out under the door of the plotters' meeting room was somebody's blood. The morning was laying its first deep blue streak along the limb of the world as if no blood had been spilled ever.

FOUR *

Verona and Hasso

The Pinaxer embassy had lent its shuttle pilot to crew the aircar taking Verona Bullivant to Skerow's fortress. Nearly a quarter of a world away Skerow had leaped into battle with the Ix, and Ned was taking the first breath of relief at being free of nine monkeys.

The pilot waved from her glass-walled cockpit as Verona climbed aboard; she was a small weathered woman with skin colored mainly by a shower of purplish freckles. After Ned's experience, nobody was taking risks with drones, and this pilot looked capable of crewing a battleship.

Verona found one cabin space occupied, where a seat had been removed to accommodate him, by a Khagodi who was like no other she had seen, a small man with dulled colors and a thin wasted leg. His massive head was lowered to his chest and he seemed asleep, but perhaps was only in a dream. As she sat down and fastened the safety clamp he raised his head slowly and whispered, "Hasso, I am Hasso. I know your name."

She felt the press of his mind against hers and flinched, though it was not intrusive. Hasso's was a heavier, deeper, more powerful mind than Tharma's, seemed to need all the space around it, and somehow, intrusive or not, had let her know it. It could not help but be fearsome.

At the same time there was something almost timid about it, about Hasso. He pulled his consciousness away from her, and for a moment she imagined that he had lifted the huge universe of his thought and was balancing it above his head like Atlas. Then her own mind drifted away from him and she was free to look out of the window while the jets hissed and the world dropped away, taking with it the afternoon storm that was whipping the trees into green froth.

When she looked down at this storm and its chaos of mists and bluish greenery it seemed to take on the shape of her experiences here and all through her life too. The parts of that life seemed to have no pattern or shape at all, from the years when she thought she had a mother and father, through the years when they became a crazed mother and an estranged father, then her mother's awful death, the hurried voyage halfway across the Galaxy to an alien world, the quarrel when she found she did not have a father anyone knew, with the Bullivant she never knew deeply and might not see again for how long? then the horrible thing that seized and drugged her, the nine monkeys with metal crowns, the man with sacks of cats and wives, *no, no, Vronni, you're off your head!*—the man was Hawksworth with his blue steel gun, nothing held together and everything was chaos and—

Hasso's mind rose up once more alongside her own

from whatever depth it brooded in and he said in his dif-
fident whisper, "I did not welcome myself to you properly,
dems'l, not knowing quite how, because, forgive, I have
never before met an alien and I have only a few words the
lingua. I am the son of that Evarny who was murdered and
I am journeying to be with Skerow, my goodmother."

The clouds whipped away, the sun shone its slanting
light in the sky over there, the world was here just below,
and the raindrops were diamonds on the curve of the aircar's transparent chassis. . . . She pulled herself together. "I
have only a few words the *lingua* myself," she said, mim-
icking him unconsciously, and then flushed, because she
might have insulted him.

If he noticed, he did not take offense, but closed his
eyes and settled his head on his chest once more. She re-
clined the seat, the nervous fatigue that had gripped her
since her mother shrieked and died loosened its hold on
her, she drowsed. With Hasso resting his mind next to hers
she imagined herself swimming alongside a whale, leaning
her weariness against its massive heartbeating body.

She thought in a dream that she was seeing everything
far and wide, that all the outlines of hills, trees, even leaves
were glitteringly clear and brilliantly green and blue-green;
marveling how clearly she realized that she was dreaming,
then the sky thickened and darkened, clouds swarmed up
around the aircar, water drops or flecks of ice were crackling against its surface and jags of lightning darted at her,
the clouds pressed against the glassy surface, an Ix cracked
out of each one as if it were coming from an egg, a lightning
shot from each claw of each Ix, blazing asterisk, she raised
her hands to ward them off, spread the fingers so that she
would not see, felt the scars break and bleed on her palm,
turned it inward, a bloody asterisk.

She fought her way out of the nightmare through a mist of stars and saw Hasso's kind ugly face turned toward her but looking beyond her through the aircar's transparent surface. It had been polarized darker, but outside the sun was in the last quarter of Khagodis's long afternoon, and there were none of the clouds she had dreamed of, not the vaporous kind. The pilot was calling to base, "We're being ordered to land now, they've threatened to force—"

Verona turned her head to follow Hasso's line of sight and saw the craft shouldering abreast of the aircar. It was black above and silver beneath, a twist of tubes and coughing jets that looked as if it were meant to scuttle over the ground like a beetle, but it easily maintained a course just a little ahead of the aircar, and threatened to cut it off.

"They are Ix, dems'l," Hasso half murmured, half thought, *"it is a space shuttle, no weakness to it."* Verona shivered.

Hasso closed his eyes and devoted his mind to the Ix.

Verona saw through his mind's eye the chitinous Ix body lying inside the shuttle with its limbs splayed out on a polymer grid set with dials and gears mounted with mill-edged knobs; it turned this way and that like a wheel, a wheeling asterisk, to reach the controls with four of its six limbs.

She tried to pull away from Hasso's consciousness, that massive universe crowded with pain and terror, but she could not get free of it, as the pilot could not, and she was forced to find herself in three, no four minds, minds of people of four worlds, her own and Hasso's concentrating inside the Ix's. The pilot, her awareness drawn in willy-nilly, struggled to keep her attention on maintaining altitude and direction; the back of her neck became suffused and greenish as she flushed with effort.

The weight of Hasso's universe pressed crushingly on the Ix, and it could not suppress its thoughts: *death home-hearth-fire brood mate death . . .*

And then: *dying for my people—*

But even the purity of its feeling could not keep it from pulling away from death, and the unconscious movement of its body shifted the grid it rested on so that the shuttle-craft rose into the bluer depth of the sky and the world fell away below it, far from the fierce mind that pursued it.

For a horrified moment Verona, pinned in this force, thought that Hasso, in his terrible anger, would pursue it to its death, dragging her and himself with it, but the Ixi ship kept its new course away from them and did not swerve to attack again. In the next instant she found herself in her seat as if she had fallen there, free and unharmed, the edge of her mind still with the Ix while he stayed there on the grid, paralyzed with terror, and his crew squawked from their stations. Then her mind freed itself.

The pilot called through the intercom, "Are you all right, miss?" Her skin had paled again under its purplish spatter.

"Yes," Verona found the word. She turned her head to look at Hasso.

He was watching her with the point-lipped Khagodi smile, swallowing air not altogether calmly. "You are well, eki? I think?" Then added, without vanity, "I am only a young fellow. When I am older I shall learn to do such things more swiftly and neatly." He lowered his weary head to his breast and dozed again.

"I hope you never have to," Verona whispered. "Not soon."

The westering sun shone benignly again, but as they flew, the green land, which had been refreshed by rain, lost its lushness and the vegetation became gradually sparse and stunted, the grasses thinned and outcroppings of rock broke the level plain. The thought of the fearful Ix still pulsed in her mind like a waning headache.

Dying for my people . . . Just as they always said on the trivvy news and all of the adventure shows: Earthers, outworlders, Colonials, a thousand kinds of them, and some hardly imaginable. Think of it going on all over the Galaxy, the universe . . . The terrorist anthem. *Nation, Hearth fire, Brood.* She wished that she had not been made to think of the Ix as "human."

Hasso roused himself and lifted his head. "So do I myself wish, dems'l."

There was that steep climb among the stones under the deeply starry sky with the sea in the distance and two long lanes of moonglade rippling in it. The air very sharp and clear, fragrant with small blossoms.

"That is starweed," Hasso said.

Verona did not know what it was about Hasso that kept her feeling easy and alert even though he'd dragged her along with him on that mean ride in the Ix's mind. It was hard to imagine being angry with Hasso. She had offered him her shoulder as he climbed out of the aircar, and he had given her a very small part of his weight; he walked quite bent and stunted and was not half-a-head taller than she.

A very strong hefty Khagodi woman, not Skerow, had come down to take charge of him and the baggage, too. "Quickly, quickly! The Ix are too near all of us." Verona scrambled up ahead of them on the broad stone steps that seemed made for giants and perhaps had been long ages ago.

When they reached the big steel door it opened immediately and an old woman half-a-head taller than Hasso reached out to take Verona's hands in her own knobbed and twisted ones. "Good child! I am Skerow, and you are Bully's lovely girl!" Verona was never sure what language she had spoken in, but she understood her quickly enough. "You shall have some supper, I have saved my own, and we can eat it together with . . . with Hasso." She turned to him and touched his shoulder. "I know. You are Hasso. I always hoped that we would meet, but at a—a better time."

"Nevertheless, Goodmother," Hasso said, "I am deeply satisfied to be with you." The speech was shy, but not as stilted in manner as in its words.

There was a depth of feeling in the exchange; neither hid it from Verona; both understood that Evarny had divorced Skerow in order to beget his one son. Hasso gave a painful little shrug in the direction of his wasted leg; he did not expect ever to find a woman who would risk her fertility with him in his underpopulated world. Verona, watching this swift interplay between two newly met people with a deep and painful bond, felt herself drawn at the same time into a fortress and a family.

"And you, dems'l," Skerow said, returning the intense beam of her regard to Verona, "I hope you are well after that dangerous journey."

"I think so, ma'am." She felt stupid and at a loss before this formidable person.

"You call me Skerow, my girl, and I will call you Verona, even if I don't pronounce it very well. We have no time for formality. I hope the food is no worse than you expect." And Skerow added doubtfully, "Ksath has followed all of the directions in preparing it."

"I'm not very hungry."

"I cannot blame you, but you have many good reasons to keep up your strength. Perhaps you would like to look at your quarters and wash up now. The cabin is just down that little hallway, everything is little here."

Skerow would hardly have been able to squeeze through the doorway, and the Pinaxer embassy was vast in comparison. The tiny unit seemed to have been grown out of a plastic vat into a vaguely organic shape that was just off the natural, like a tomato grown in a box. The wall was pale and restful green, with embedded porthole-shaped holograms of Earth trees and blue sky, neither of which Verona had seen much of from the smog-shrouded towers where she had lived.

But it was hers alone, for a while, too much alone when the door was locked and the impervious wall activated, no one to speak with in her own language, not the most basic human family, *Mother! Father!* They were shadows drawing always further away from her.

No Khagodi-human family either, but an old woman and her stepson eyeing each other. Three or four Khagodi altogether keeping her from the Ix.

Why do those things want me? Yes, things! Why? Remembering how before the Ix had attacked the aircar she dreamed that the scars on her palm had burst and bled. They twinged now, but remained faint under the translucent skintex.

For this moment she was safe enough in an apartment of her own, *air waiting in tanks here until I came to breathe it,* air at the right temperature and pressure; Skerow, hating equatorial heat, would have liked it a little cooler. It felt odd for a moment, and then good—not having to use the oxycaps—but still odd, especially with the lighter gravity, just a little lighter, but. Felt less weighted down, a bit childish, when she thought of it, hippety-hop goes little Earthie, great thumping Khagodi had to have a little less pull from the ground, on her own Earth would be dragged down hauling themselves, Godzillas. Great big pleated-brow and just as ancient God Zillas. She put down the duffel crammed with her few rough clothes, unpacked the hideous music box she loved so much, one touch of home, and explored this one more apartment.

At the touch of a button a bunk opened out of an almost seamless wall, and recessed beside it a shelf provided a bookassette with spools in English, French, Spanish, German, Russian, Mandarin, kanji, Hindi. Another cassette: *Readings from a Thousand Worlds . . . God, I don't want to be here long enough to read all of them.* A lucite cube with a picture of a landscape—

No. She picked it up. *No, it's a terrarium.* She held it to the light and inside she could see a lichen-covered stone and a tiny tree, like a twisted bonsai—its leaves trembled to her heartbeat—surrounded by grass, or a kind of moss that grew just visible blue and yellow flowers. She didn't know if it had come from home; it could have represented any world that was good to live on. It did not look quite Earthly; the tree's leaves were dot-sized globes that pulsed with luminescence, and when she put it down the slight jar made the whole tree spray like a miniature firework. No, she thought, not from Earth.

*   *   *

"I brought it with me when I came home from Kemalan where I was holding assizes," Skerow said. "I thought it would not harm the ecosphere, and it was the only pretty thing I had time to buy on that world."

The dayroom walls unfolded into tables that could be raised to various heights, and Verona sat at one, with a stool and footrest arrangement, nearly at the height of the others, who were standing supported by tails, and hardly needed furniture. She felt somewhat like Gulliver among the Brobdingnags, or more nearly Goldilocks among the bears. Baby Bear, though, would not be wanting her bed; Khagodi slept floating in basins. . . .

They spoke *lingua* in muted voices, and did not let their thoughts run deep, a sign of courtesy not only to Verona but to each other, beginning with what they had in common, their connection to Evarny. Verona wondered about this person who had deserted the woman he loved for the sake of begetting the son who had been maimed before his life began.

:*Weak, twisted and with only the one heart,*: said Hasso, presenting the sober facts.

:*And a mind worthy of strengthening it,*: said Skerow. "Come, children, eat your suppers, and let us not dwell on grim thoughts."

Verona, among alien telepaths, managed to fork it in, with some wisp of appetite left after all the terrors, grainy wafers that were crisp enough, an unidentified vegetable, rehydrated tomato slices, and a protein something that was far from chicken. Hasso, for all his self-deprecation, made her feel comfortable, and Skerow cared only that she was safe.

"Evarny has—had told me that you were working in Interworld Law, Hasso," Skerow said.

"I have been doing researches for these trials, which I believe have just been suspended. Perhaps I will decide to make the Law my life-work, as you and my father did, Goodmother. But I don't care for the courtroom. Even if I could present a good public figure, it would be tiring and I hate impervious helmets. But I am making my living at this, and of course I want to see the famous court in Burning Mountain . . . for years I had been saving money for this visit to you, and—" He shivered. "And even then I missed him. He did not come back when my mother died, you see."

"If I had known of that I would have made sure he did."

Hasso rubbed his arms down the sides of his body where the scales had tensed up when he shivered. "Now there is no way of smoothing down those roughnesses that were between us."

"It is the case more often than not, Hasso. But years ago he risked his life to save me, and in the end gave it, and perhaps it will lift the weight of the wrongs he has done you to know that I owe him my life twice over, and now I am alive to have you here with me! I am more than pleased to know you at last, Hasso, and so happy that you came in spite of the danger!"

Hasso said shyly, "The danger was to this young lady. I only came along."

"Eki! Tharma and the Lyhhrt were more than quick to trust you, good young fellow!" There was a shrewdness in her eyes that even Verona could not miss, and she did not miss another of Hasso's little shrinking movements either.

"It is because I am so candid, Goodmother," Hasso said.

*   *   *

Really sleepy now. Tired, too . . . leave the door open a little, a crack, don't even need an oxycap, good to get real air, at least.

Not listening in on them, can't understand most of it, they won't mind, don't give a shit what I think, anyway, shut up, boxed in here in one more apartment, too much . . .

Mother? Can't have been that good for you in Singapore, that I thought was home, if you couldn't stand it—

—*damn it, woman, that's no life for a child, crammed in together with no place to move or see anything, nobody but guards around you*—

IT'S THE WAY I WANT IT!

—and she did it.

Please stay with me, Darya, I love you, please don't do this!

—and she did it anyway. Two of us alone. No sisters or brothers, either of us, as if she'd been born in some laboratory out of nothing but a tank with an egg in it. And all his family was in military outposts or governing colonies, nobody to help him either.

And all we had for company was those guards, in that second apartment, that sneered at both of us and drank most of the whiskey; but they wouldn't touch whatever she shot up her arm, keep her from thinking. I have to say that, and they kept us safe—that one time, dropping down from the roof, I don't know what it was that tried to get at us; it wasn't a lesser thouk. They wouldn't tell us, but it didn't. Not that time.

Where's the cupboard to put clothes in here? . . . this one, and that's where you put the dirty ones to be fumed, glad to give it every sweaty thing I've got on, awful nights with her in that place begging me not to leave her in the dark, how I learned not to be afraid of the dark, knew everything that could be in it . . .

. . . she would have screwed them, just to have somebody hold her in bed, just the way I wanted, thought I wanted those bokos on the mopeds in the street, that she called rotten thugs. So we wouldn't let each other, did that much together. Rubbed her hands to warm them, those scars, yes, like mine, didn't know what they were. Slash across and aslant and aslant. Somebody got to her, that one time. Why? Why? Took her away somewhere, didn't care if she screamed, slash across and aslant . . . O Mother! You were only dead eight days when we lifted, how many months or years from Earth?

There you are Vronni in that tiny mirror, knob knees and little tits, even up somehow sooner or later—if the Ix let me, oh shut up, find the sleepsuit, not that fuzzy one I was wearing then, when It came, when Ix It came, so tired, bunk soft, no pillow, um? bunk shapes itself, cushions what bone and blubber sleeps here, ha,

: . . . *sad child* . . . :

Skerow talking, thinking, thinks: *alien child, pink, pale, scaleless, pink-nailed alien . . . daughter . . . child:*

Not your daughter . . . get up, close the damn door, no, let them talk, don't bother getting up, *no, Mother, they're not talking about you, those studs don't give a damn except to keep us safe, let me go back to bed, Mama!*

Stay! Please, oh please stay! A real daughter would stay with me, protect me, hold my hands, so cold . . .

: . . . *strange scars on her hand . . . heard the Ix did it*—: says Skerow.

Don't think about that.

My eyes are full of sand and sleep, I sleep.

Beginnings

"She is sleeping at last," Skerow said. "I have a jug of white-thorn, Hasso. Will you share it with me?"

Hasso said, "No, Goodmother, I must not allow myself to become dizzy. Listen, I must tell you: the kind of scar-ring on that youngling's hand is like what has sometimes been done by our own monsters with hot irons."

"At least she was spared that."

"Not always as torture, but for identification and bra-vado."

"I have known of such cases."

"In my legal researches I have found records of trials going back hundreds of years, and on many worlds—only Sainted Skathe the Just knows how many years it took merely to transcribe them into electro*lingua*—and this symbol has been found in criminal families on more than one world and in more than one human species—"

:Hasso, is this a matter of public knowledge?:

:These records are open to anyone who can read them, Goodmother, I am not giving away any secrets.: "This is the first time I myself have ever seen such a mark on a person."

"You are not telling me that the child is some sort of crim—no, I understand. Somewhere there is a family . . ."

"Yes. Even a branch named Zamos."

"Truly? I always believed it was only a made-up name."

"So did everyone else. The problem is that no one knows where this Family can be, even if it still exists. It began on Sol Three, and I have traced the Zamos branch, but there are private colonies I of course have not heard of, particularly on Fthel IV where there are so many Galactic Federation officials living, and so many of those who are Solthrees."

:Does Galactic Federation know all of this?:

:Of course, Goodmother.:

Skerow regarded him for a long moment.

Hasso bowed his head. *:I have not come only to visit, only to bring you the child to keep. . . . I have got permission from GalFed to ask you to join me, help us work to clear our communities of the scourge Zamos has inflicted on us— of course not to hang around watching people or dash about all over the place, but—since Coordinator Threyha died you are one of the greatest living archives we have and likely the very greatest—:*

"Hush!" Skerow cried, though he had not spoken aloud. "I am much too old for such doings."

"I said, no dashing about, Goodmother."

"And I am here, my good son, where we are both no better than prisoners."

"You have traveled to many worlds, and everything one could want is in your memory. Of course you may refuse."

"Tik! I may refuse! But can I?" She moved away from him a little. "I am not sure that I love you for this situation you have put me in, Hasso."

"I truly have been saving to come here," Hasso said. "That money brought me from Northern Oceania, and I have earned my way from Burning Mountain by guarding Verona Bullivant. Police Officer Tharma gave me that commission. I regret that I missed seeing my father, but nothing else. I feel blessed to have met with you—and—and that child. She is full of courage, and—she likes me, Skerow. . . ." He gave his little shrug. "Of course I cannot force you to do anything. I will visit with you for a while and when conditions are safer I will leave satisfied and look for other sources." After a moment he added, "I am not sorry if I have made it hard for you to refuse."

Skerow snickered, a light *keh-keh-keh* sound. "There is little here to laugh about, Hasso, so let me laugh at you a little. You are a clever manipulator."

Hasso bowed his head again. "Thank you, Goodmother, but I am still not sorry."

"Yes. Of course you knew that I would not refuse. And of course you are an agent of Galactic Federation—otherwise you would not be able to tell me all of this."

"My clearance is not greater than your own as an interworld judge."

"My clearance is at too high a rank for my own taste. Are these investigations for the sake of Galactic Federation and the trials, or do you have a personal interest in all of these Solthree matters?"

"These go far beyond Solthrees, far beyond the Fthel System where they are so populous, beyond the Ix who are so fearfully dangerous now, out to—yes, the Lyhhrt, who have wound themselves too tightly into the structure, and—"

"—back inward, where too many of our self-righteous Khagodi have shown themselves to be as rascally a pack of knaves as you may find anywhere else in the Galaxy."

"Yes, and eventually all of their records will be in my hands! They are so complicated, and I love them so because they are so complicated! Goodmother, I am going to compose my Scholar's Dissertation on the Structure and Assembly of Legal Archives, and one day I will be known as Hasso the Learned for this work."

"Take care you are not first known as The Man Who

Knew Too Much, Hasso." She could not resist another snicker at Hasso's innocent self-puffery.

"It will be a long dangerous while before that happens," Hasso said more soberly, and for a few moments he and Skerow contemplated the vast structure of deceptions and torments, murder and slavery, greed and agony which had begun so long ago.

He saw Skerow through her mind's eye, walking the wet streets under the dark skies of Starry Nova, the grubby port city of clerks and brothels, drawn to the bright window where the swimming woman dreamed terrible dreams. And then saw himself, as Skerow saw him through his own mind's eye, being fitted for the costly spectacles with heavy lenses and painful clamps, that barely improved his sight as he peered through the endless records in tapes, spools, photographs, fibers, crystals, in twenty-three dialects of *lingua* from five worlds. Seven years of them. It had not been ignorance of *lingua* that made him shy when he met Verona, but shyness that twisted his tongue.

"I have drawn it together," Hasso said. "I have synthesized it. On Sol Three there was a Family . . ."

Trying to envision such a grouping, a mingling of men with women and children under one roof with its quarrels and accommodations, placing himself there, leading Skerow with him into a world of small people with strange shapes and drawing on her experiences of life on the worlds where she had stood on the judge's dais, he went on, frightened at last by his own boldness—

"Go ahead with it, Hasso," Skerow said. "You have come too far now."

"I can only barely imagine those people in their species and the spaces they live in, and not at all in their behavior.

No. I needn't understand them. I think you have believed until now that they were faceless men and women who sat on committees and didn't touch evil with their hands, but they were not all of them like that. The man named Sandomir Zamos . . .''

Our criminal minds on this world run to bad eggs who come by ones, rather like the Lyhhrt when they turn bad; we do not breed them by clutches the way other peoples do, thank the Seventy-Seven, and these people from Sol Three that they call Earth were clustered into families, including that of Zamos. They gathered money by thuggery and extortion, then bought and formed legal businesses to hide it in—I know that you presided at trials concerning their trading in gold, and also their dealings in laboratories that conducted genetic experiments and produced some of the earliest clones, the ones who later became a basis of the huge slave trade we are still trying to dismantle.

(I am curious to trace the careers of our own home-grown knaves who colluded with them in selling and lending gold, and I hope you will help me with that, Goodmother.)

Then when the world Earth was discovered by Galactic Federation—eki! we are so lucky that it was our GalFed and not one of those New Worlds Assemblies that the Ix have lately joined—when Sol Three became a member no one worried about those kinds of dealings, and that stream of evil drained into those of the Interworld Trade Consortium like the tributary of a mighty underground river, or more like the conduit of a great sewer rushing ever more quickly and freely . . . but I am running ahead too fast and free myself, and I don't want to think of my Dissertation as the flowchart of a sewer . . . as for Zamos—his group of families had the habit of marking victims, sometimes after they had killed them and some they didn't trouble to kill, but the symbol they marked them with has not come down to us. It would be only too neat to say it was that star. Barbarous.

But Sandomir Zamos . . . that was a barbarous alien. What I have to say of him may be only a legend; it is the garbled testimony of a man who worked for Zamos—he ran one of the Zamos genetics laboratories, and he told this before he died after a long and dreadful lifetime bearing the horrible wounds he swore that Zamos gave him—those people have terrible passions—and it is this:

He claimed that he was the lover of Zamos's wife, that Zamos found him out and came to believe that the son his wife had born was her lover's, that Zamos had the boy killed and then forced this man to remove his wife's ovaries. . . . I don't know what became of her, I don't want to think of it. But Zamos ripened the proto-eggs and fertilized them with female sperms from his own seed-sacs until he had the embryos of a hundred daughters . . . and the end of it is that he had one of them brought to bear in the body of a hired woman—*ek!* I am glad to be the son of egg-bearers—in order that when this daughter became an adult she should bear one other of her sisters, kept in frozen storage all these many years, and onward in that way, each sister the next one, so it would always be known that they were the inheritors of Zamos, even if only through the female line that he despised. That is the legend.

*　　*　　*

"It gives much to think about," Skerow said.

"It has filtered through the generations," Hasso said. "Who knows if it is the truth?"

An explosion, a white-lightning one, broke through their thoughts. Skerow and Hasso turned to see Verona standing in her open doorway, eyes like blue flames in her white pinched face.

"But it explains everything," she whispered.

Ned, Palma and Lyhhrt

When Galactic Federation Representative Evarny of Khagodis, Northern Spine Confederacy, had lived at the embassy in Burning Mountain, his apartment had included a dayroom-office, a lavatory and a nightchamber with two sleeping basins large enough to hold Evarny along with an assistant or guest. But Evarny was dead and the Lyrhht who were taking his position had removed half the interior of their ship: cabinets, walls, shelves, power generators and other storage cupboards, and fitted them into the apartment. The only spaces left were one or two small rooms that might have passed for doctors' offices, and their only spaciousness was in the cathedral height of their ceilings.

The woman gladiator called Palma had been brought into Lyhhrt quarters, jeering and cursing, by Arcade staffers in the pre-dawn hour. She did not look at her surroundings, or say what she thought of them. Her impervious helmet was tattooed on her scalp; it would have been transparent to the gold-shelled Lyhhrt if he had had any interest in penetrating it, but like other Lyhhrt he was afraid of individuals and their isms. Her hand was resting unwillingly in one of his, he had extruded two extra ones from the torso of his shell, and was bent over a wrist splint that looked much like a wide bracelet of silver filigree, carefully locking its pins into the segments of cracked bone beneath the skin.

The Lyhhrt did not want to talk about the bruises on her mouth and cheekbone either. After all the fights that had broken out in the Arcade during the night, he and the other Lyhhrt were the only doctors left in Burning Mountain who were capable of treating her species, but they were still only the Temporary World Representatives on Khagodis and not the police, and whatever had happened to her in the Arcade or by the hand of her employer was not under the control of either. Gold avoided her sullen face.

:We are not here to do this work. It is no better than being slaves of Zamos,: Bronze Lyhhrt said.

:You think not? Truly? She is in pain. I ease it.: Half-stifled by their shells of metal, the Lyhhrt had gotten into the habit of thinking separate thoughts, and both were uneasy. Now that the trials were postponed they were unsure of what to do with their evidence, whether to deliver it to the courts or store it somewhere else.

Bronze was taking breakfast, his day's only meal, in one of the small rooms; he was keeping mindwatch while Bullivant and Hawksworth ate their breakfasts, the one in his half-repaired apartment, the other in a basement cell. They were eating reconstituted bacon-and-egg omelets. Bronze, who needed to do more than add water and stir, had pressed a stud in his neck to open the abdomen of his workshell. The workshell's hands then reached in and removed a glastex globe, twenty centimeters in diameter, containing the Lyhhrt's actual body, which the bronze shell, acting as a robot, placed on a tabletop in a gold basket. Holding a tiny remote in one pseudopod, the Lyhhrt had directed the shell

to unplug the globe and siphon off the liquid he was im-
mersed in and replace it with a fresh mixture of food and
oxygen from a jar stored in the wall refrigerator.

He was splashing around in this, activating his light receptors in order to look around himself, and carefully keeping his mind free of Hawksworth's ugly thoughts and
Bullivant's frustrated ones.

He had only just returned from escorting Ned and
Spartakos back from the Arcade and was examining his experiences of that quarter hour. He could not escape a strong
feeling that during the short hop the buzzer they were traveling in had been shadowed by an Ix aircar, hovering just
over the foliage on the mountainside. Ix craft were hypnoformed and radar-blind, and heavily esp-shielded as well,
but not from Lyhhrt or Khagodi who were alert for signs
of danger.

At the moment that his bronze shell lifted the englobed
Lyhhrt in its hands to replace him, his colleague Gold
clasped the splint bracelet one millimeter too hard and
Palma yelped.

Her impervious barrier split under the press of pain and
anger, and Bronze barely missed dumping himself on the
floor like an egg.

Gold in his turn found himself actually stammering, "I
don't—I mean—I cannot—" He rectified himself and murmured, "I beg your pardon."

Palma said through gritted teeth, "Go fuck yourself."

But his mind had joined into one unit with that of
Bronze, and that unit was tracing the threads of thought
both had drawn from her outburst, and weaving them together with all the images of the Old City and the Arcade
roiling in the stoned-drunk memories of Ned Gattes while

he slept. All of these had been too confused and disorganized to make sense of earlier. Now the Lyhhrt began to set them in order.

Palma Ruiz, the fighting-woman, bodyguard of Councillor Brandsma, the officious factfinder, travels with him on his way to meet—whom?

Ned Gattes believes that Brandsma, fearing that he was being pursued, has placed Palma in his path to scare him away, to kill him if necessary. She has been stopped short by Keremer, the angry old being with the blue skin and diamonds. In the noise that followed, Brandsma has run off to meet that group of beings whose connections are not clear. . . .

Now all of that excitement is over and it is the long predawn of Khagodis's long day. One of the two sharp-white moons is rising like a whacked ball as the other is falling into the still-deep sky; the spy-eye lens on the topmost tower of the building can see them.

Brandsma is where? sleeping in his residence. Drunk and with a bruised face, he writhes in a sweaty bed . . . but his implanted helmet is an expensive one with a warning trigger, so let us not disturb him.

Ned Gattes, who has just dropped off to sleep with his hammock still swinging and his dirty clothes flung on the floor, is dreaming of all the noise and confusion, and all of those who had hurried to the fateful meeting: Brandsma, with the pearl-sprayed Khagodi, the cloaked woman, the Kylklad with the red sash, and that Ix! in the disguise of a Tignit—and all of those had set to arguing first, then screaming—and finally murder. Dead Ix. There had been two parties at that meeting, the Ix on one side and on the other a committee: Star✳Systems? Zamos?

Gold and Bronze gather all of them into the fibers of the net, Bronze and Gold thinking of the Ix pilot that Bronze had sensed when he was returning in the buzzer with Ned and Spartakos.

:Why did he not attack us?: Bronze asks.

Gold answers, *:He might have been hovering in that district waiting only for the end of the meeting to pick up his landsman, not planning to attack at all, and did not know of the killing.:*

:That particular Ix surely knows of it now, and has told all the other Ix on the world.:

Bronze and Gold are very sure of that.

All of these thoughts flash out in very little more than an instant. Gold presses home the last lock ever so gently. "When the bones are whole they will reject the splint and it will fall away by itself."

Palma pulls back with a sharp gesture of her shoulders as if to say the words with her body, "Thank you for nothing."

"If you want to stay alive, dems'l, you will keep yourself at a good distance from Kees Brandsma. But you need not thank me for telling you so."

"Just stay out of my mind!" *You lump of slime!* her mind says. Gold, very delicately, opens four hands to release her.

:She still has it in mind to go back to Brandsma,: Gold said to Bronze. *:Of course, the Ix may make sure that the coun-*

cillor does not stay alive long enough to abuse her again.:

:It is going too far,: Bronze said. *:There are more and more Ix landing here and we are the ones who'll die if we stay.:*

:We cannot let him die on that account, nor this woman either, no matter how sinful a piece of work she is.:

:We should fission, or conjugate first and then fission— we would at least have some reinforcements, and there is no need of special license for doing it in emergencies.:

:That would take too much time and food now. Let us see what can be done first. We must guard the woman until I can warn Brandsma.:

:I won't take charge of her!: Bronze was near to bursting his arterial valves. *:I can barely keep track of the ones I am watching now.:*

Gold said resignedly, *:I will find someone.:*

Gold did not call Officer Tharma on the comm but went to her broom-closet office. She was waiting for him.

"There was an Ix attacked and killed in the Old City arcade yesterday at 26.37.49 hours standard," he said.

"It has been reported." Tharma lifted one shoulder. Teach your grandmother to suck eggs.

"I am not accusing you of ignorance. I would like to request the help of your forces in guarding—but also watching—some of the persons I believe are involved."

"Eh, we have the murders of Evarny and Keremer's woman La'or to handle and we have officers running about for them. We've sent everyone else I have available—that's two officers and an army officer—to say nothing of recruiting Skerow's stepson—and they are guarding Skerow and Bullivant's daughter, and the Main Office has put extra Peacemen on patrol in the Arcade for the next few hours because of all the media people with nothing to do except look for entertainment—and trouble. If you can think of anyone who might be left you are welcome to that person."

"What of Smiryagin?"

"I have had to lend her to the Arcade force along with an officer on leave from West Oceania, an amateur archaeologist who has been saving for seven years to visit the Great Ship Excavation, and was just stopping over. All I have left is Heth and I must keep him."

The Lyhhrt stood in thought, arm rattling a little against his side.

Tharma said, "You have that little fellow, the Solthree. Ned Gattes."

"I want someone to guard the fighting woman, Palma, and she did her best to kill him."

"In that case he'll be so much more on his guard with her."

Ned Gattes dreamed of being pursued by Ix, with a sense that it was no dream, and woke with a fiercely throbbing hangover he could not blame on Ix. He had taken enough beer, dopesticks and ge'inn fumes to account for it, as well as dodging knives, getting knocked on the head, and finding his way through the hideous noise and flickering lights in the Arcade of Delight. He pulled himself up and sat rubbing his sore head.

After a few groaning moments he rose out of bed and ripped the film off a wetcloth, swabbed himself and made a face in the tiny mirror at the thought of wearing his dirty clothes. Yesterday's had been his last change of clean ones, and he'd left the rest in the Common Laundry.

He found them folded on a chest of drawers, and as he picked them up he saw that they were clean and smelled faintly of disinfectant. Someone had put them in a fume cupboard overnight. Adilon, perhaps. Pinxin made their own laundry arrangements; they did not like local servants coming into their quarters, least of all big thumping Khagodi. He held the clothes gingerly. Adilon was attractive, but he did not want any more attention from Pinxid women, not Adilon and least of all Keremer, even though she had saved his life. No, when he thought about it, he was safe from Adilon if she was the protégé of Keremer, whose feelings for hemisexuals were strong and bad.

While he was pulling his jeans on, there was a knock on his door and Adilon's voice called, "Mister Ned Gattes, your Mister Gold Lyhhrt wants you now-now!"

Ned finished dressing quickly, wondering if Spartakos had had an attack of rust, and skip-dashed down the big stairs.

The Ambassador's door slid open before he could touch it and the gold Lyhhrt said, "No, we know what to do for rust."

"Then why—" He saw Palma and said, "Now what?"

"You," said Palma as if it was the worst insult in the world.

"I want you to stay with this woman until I come back," the Lyhhrt said. He paused for an instant. "Stay with her. She has been disabled sufficiently, I believe, and she will have no painkiller until I come back and find you both alive." He had no more time for them but left, and Ned wondered what new Hell he had fallen into now.

Lyhhrt and Sin

The Lyhhrt slipped into something more comfortable, a darkened brass workshell that did not reflect light so blatantly as gold, and its matte texture blended with the sandstone and rough adobe of the walls and buildings. As he went down the staircases and into the hot streets his mind was locked on the faint electric pulses of Brandsma's expensive helmet, and he kept it so rigorously to himself that he was only barely noticed; if noticed, soon forgotten. He need not have bothered. The streets that had been crowded with media crews from seventeen worlds while the trials were going on were now almost deserted. Some of the flocks had gone north to the Excavations to look for stories, disappointed but freed from the heat, and the rest into the Arcade for a few hours while they waited for transport.

The higher the sun rose the harder it beat down, and the Lyhhrt opened his cooling vents. Two or three old Khagodi women clustered on stone verandas. They had cooler places to go, but they were so very old they could not get warm enough. Down one alleyway there were three children playing, a noisy Varvani tossing a ball with two silent Khagodi, the Khagodi not too obviously getting the best of it because they were telepathic. This one voice made the only sounds in the streets. The city was so quiet it might have been a trap waiting for its prey, but the Lyhhrt knew nothing of hunting and cared less; he did not think that way.

As he came nearer to where he believed Brandsma was, the trace became fainter, and the Lyhhrt walked very quickly through the lacy shade of a beq-tree grove toward the Guest House Wing that was attached to the Courts and

Administrations complex, a group of noble old edifices of adobe built with bases of limestone blocks, and untouched by Galactic Federation technology. New annexes were being added to these buildings, as well as the embassy complex—slowly and still in the old manner—to accommodate the outworld visitors who were finding Burning Mountain increasingly popular.

Gold had lengthened his legs slightly to increase his speed, and they served him on the deep steps built for massive Khagodi thighs. His movement now was like molten brass.

Up the one flight of steps he found himself in a rotunda paved with flagstones and lined with the doors of guest apartments; the occupants were away or else very well shielded, and he did not try to penetrate shields or helmets but swiftly extended the sensor attached to his mass spectrometer through the keyhole of one door after another until he smelled his quarry. The door was locked and he configured his fingers to reach in and lift the tumblers, then pushed the door open screaming on its hinges.

Brandsma was on the bed, bound with thin black cord that twisted around his throat. His face was purple and he stirred only feebly, though the coverings were tossed about as if he had been writhing. In two strides the Lyhhrt reached him and sliced clear the ropes, all the while aware that the Ix he had smelled so strongly was hovering under the domed skylight. Its shadow and that of the window frames rested on the floor in a circle of sunlight like a spider in its web, an image the Lyhhrt took from Brandsma's mind. He had no breath with which to give Brandsma air, but he noted that the oxycap was still full, and without pausing to think of anything else he had reached his sensors down the man's throat and pushed down on his belly.

As Brandsma took his first breath the Lyhhrt stood up in time to back up two quick steps and dodge the Ix, who had dropped to the floor on a length of the same kind of rope it had used to bind Brandsma.

For this complicated suit of brass, the Lyhhrt had a hand like a Swiss knife, and he flashed a blade to cut the hanging rope so that the pieces fell—Brandsma would say, like licorice sticks. Then he retracted his knives and sensors; they were delicate, not for defending himself.

The Ix rose up on its feet, buzzing like a hive in no language the Lyhhrt knew. The Lyhhrt did not understand the Ix's pheromone-language either, and access to its mind was partly blocked because now, as a warrior on a mission, it was wearing an armor of jewel-studded platinum mesh with openings for its six limbs, and its hump of a neckless head was armored naturally by its skull of hard bubbly gristle to protect the brain and sense organs.

The Lyhhrt also realized that he did not really want access to the mind of the Ix, his ancient enemy along with the slavers of Zamos, and the first he had seen in seven of this world's years. At the same time he was so filled with hate for this enemy that the nutrient liquid he swam in seemed to be boiling, deep in the belly of his metal body.

Behind him Brandsma was gasping and retching on the bed, on his way up to consciousness, but though he had slid beneath Brandsma's helmet the Lyhhrt paid no attention. He was trying to find a way, beyond his passion, to scotch the Ix without killing it. Another dead Ix might mean twenty more reprisals. Its pheromones did not affect him, and he was not aware of the blinks and flashes that bothered others with direct senses. His camera eyes saw only the creature with its black chitinous body and the six limbs that quivered with antenna hairs, and he did not need to read its mind to know that it would draw a weapon, one of the flamers or heavy stunners the world Iyax bought on the open market.

It appeared very quickly—almost invisible in the leathery black hand—a long-barreled Quadzull that shot exploding bullets, and dangerous enough to make the Lyhhrt back away a step.

The Ix's three black bulb eyes moved independently, and the light from above flickered on them in their whiteless rims. There were no escapes for either Lyhhrt or Ix.

The Lyhhrt raised a hand. "I will not harm you."

"You are lying," the Ix said in thought and tongue, and shot off the Lyhhrt's hand. The Lyhhrt extruded two other hands he had been keeping ready and moved forward under the gun to grasp the armored body and pin down the Ix's arms with the three of his own. But the sudden movement made the Ix pull its gun-arm inward against its breast, and as the Lyhhrt and the Ix clasped each other, the gun exploded between their bodies. The sound of the first shot was still ricocheting in the narrow walls. Whether the Ix had meant to kill itself no one would know; the thought dispersed before it left the Ix's brain. Ix and Lyhhrt were flung on their backs.

The Lyhhrt rolled over and pushed himself up on his legs and his three remaining arms, suspended in the circle of sunlight (through the eyes of Brandsma) like a dull gold version of the Ix. The Ix's bullet had burst into an area of his torso taken up by small storage compartments, and beyond them had charred some of the padding that protected his globe. Inside he was horribly shaken, but unharmed. He did not bother to pick up the detached hand but withdrew the rest of the arm into his side.

The Ix was still twitching, but its belly was a cavernous

ruin and there was no sign of life in its mind. The exploded gun was embedded in its body, and the flesh smoked around it.

The Lyhhrt quivered within his workshell. Lyhhrt had killed Ix before, but not this Lyhhrt, nor had he come so close to violent death. He stared down at the Ix, wondering if it was truly dead, but did not want to touch it, even with the instruments of his shell. All that black chitin . . . Perhaps it was wearing a shell. . . .

"Who the hell are you?" Brandsma was gagging and coughing behind him. "I know who you are, you're a Lyhhrt. Yeah. Nearly too late, but you came. Is the fucker dead?"

In horror the Lyhhrt watched the other activity going on in the Ix's body. Between its legs, a grayish fleshy bulb began to push outward, and in a moment the Lyhhrt realized that it was an ovipositor; translucent white globes were slowly emerging from it in the body's final spasms.

The eggs were very small, and the forms of the tiny fetuses, just discernible shadows inside the membranes, did not move. Though none of the eggs had been torn open the Lyhhrt could esp no life in them: the fetuses were mindless. He thought they must have been stunned to death by the shock of the explosion.

"Hey?" Brandsma pulled himself to his feet, coughing and shuddering. "You! You listen to me!"

The Lyhhrt swung about and grasped a handful of Brandsma's hair. His mind burned into Brandsma's mind, shredding his helmet as if it were also the membrane of an egg. "You piece of filth. You trafficked with those monsters and took their gold for Zamos. Whose bodies do they buy now that Lyhhrt are no longer slaves?" He found control

of himself and stood back a pace, while Brandsma gaped at
him and rubbed his throat with bruised and trembling
hands. The Lyhhrt knew that the Ix no longer used organic
materials to hatch their eggs in, but that long Life Cycle in
the grasp of Zamos, one hundred and twenty-nine years of
slavery, had changed the Lyhhrt world-view forever.

"That son of a bitch was killing me! It was me he was
killing, not the other way around!"

The Lyhhrt turned aside both from him and the dead
Ix while he activated his personal radio and called Tharma
to report another death.

"I'm supposed to be protected by the law in this place!
What kind of law are you?"

"For this moment I am the Galactic Federation Ambassador in place of Evarny, nothing else. I will find protection for you in the embassy. Dress yourself and bring
along your baggage. You are not safe here."

"I don't have to go any goddam where with you!"

"The next Ix that comes for you will kill you before I
can reach you." :And I will not hurry either.:

While Brandsma dressed and packed the Lyhhrt covered the hole in his workshell with a fine wire grid so that
none of his contents would spill, and looked at the dead Ix.
He deeply wanted rest/in/prayer in touch with him/them/
self/selves around him on his home world to help him forgive himself for not finding some way to keep the Ix alive.
He cursed it again and doubly for being gravid. His sin had
been multiplied by its eggs. Worse, he could not even use
the long history of crimes he had collected from Brandsma's
mind in that one angry instant, because evidence gathered
only by esp is nowhere admissible, not on Khagodis or
Lyhhr or any other world whose peoples are telepathic.

Ned Remembers

By chance the Lyhhrt met Peaceman Heth at the gate of the embassy complex; he put Brandsma in Heth's keeping to be escorted to Tharma's office and did not listen to protests. In his own compartment he not only did not attend to Bronze's frightened outburst but did not even open his mind to it. He changed back into his gold shell, sent the brass one into a closet with keyed-in directions for self-repair, and returned to Tharma's office.

She was resting with a bowl of herb tea; in the last hour she had coordinated the gathering and shipping of most of the media visitors from the Old City and the Arcade to the Heliport for the trip north to the Excavations. In the quarter hour since the Lyhhrt had called to tell her of the Ix and its death, she had notified both her superiors at the Main Office and the WorldPeace Forces stationed in West Vineland.

The Lyhhrt, still wrangling with sin and self-forgiveness, and weary from all of that, plunged in, "I regret adding Brandsma to your troubles. Have you found some place for him?"

Tharma twitched her shoulder. "I thought to have him stay in Bullivant's apartment, but he was curiously unwilling to face Bullivant. The Pinaxer Embassy has no room, and besides, Ned Gattes is there—"

"I had forgotten Ned Gattes." Not really. He had wanted to forget Ned, and Spartakos, and the nine monkeys.

"So I lodged him temporarily with the Bengtvadi, who have sent some of their members home because of expense account fraud. They breathe nearly the same air."

"Certainly as far as fraud is concerned," the Lyhhrt said. "I/we regret that you feel we have not been forthcoming about what has been happening."

"Yes. Lyhhrt and Khagodi do not sleep in the same water." Her smile and her metaphor were lost on the Lyhhrt.

"We are filled with shame, you understand, for letting ourselves become slaves to save our lives. We swore that oath knowing we would be made to do evil."

"Moral people have sometimes even done more for less." She poured another bowl of tea. She knew better than to interfere with a Lyhhrt's self-castigation.

"We are determined to root out all of the evil of Zamos."

"I hope you have not sworn another oath," Tharma muttered. "Do you think it is all centered on this world?"

"No, but there is enough to keep us busy."

"The courts are closed, Ambassador. The principals, the witnesses, the media are all scattered, or will be. Two of our people and two of the Ix are dead, but the losses have not evened up. There will be more terrorist attacks, I am sure of it."

They regarded each other, carefully shielding thought. The Lyhhrt had immunity, but Tharma had authority.

"What do you want?" The Lyhhrt's question was a formality.

She did not say that Khagodis would be safer without Lyhhrt. "You may not have been forthcoming about what was happening, because of your shame, but now you are one more target that will draw fire here, along with Skerow and the little Solthree child. To say nothing of Brandsma. It's time to put shame aside and share information."

The Lyhhrt took his time, and said, "Yes. I have been remiss."

"No more shame, Ambassador! Just let us begin. I've found out a lot in the past day because Evarny's son Hasso came looking for him, but there's a deal more that I need to learn."

"Whatever I may have learned by telepathy is not admissible in court."

"The trials have been put off and I don't need evidence for the court. I need it to be able to keep hold of dangerous felons. At the least we can detain both the councillor and his guard for their activities in the Arcade, particularly about his connection with that murdered Ix. Let us first see how we can turn the inadmissible zinc into gold."

Twenty-five steps away in the Lyhhrt's embassy apartment, Ned found a bit of wall to lean on and stared at Palma. The sight of her made the cut on his face sting as if he had been slashed that instant. He watched her warily, with his hands loose, but Palma had angled into a corner—there were no chairs—and all her violence was in her icy face. There was no room to swing a kick, and her mouth was tightened by the pain of her wrist.

Ned did not know what to say to her and except for the hums and tickings of the instruments in their glassy cabinets there was silence.

Finally he burst out, "Why in hell did you come after me like that? What were you trying to kill me for? I never saw you in my life, or him either!"

"He knew you from somewhere, that's all he said. He

told me to get rid of you and I don't ask why, I do what he wants."

"Yeh." Ned looked at her blackened cheekbone and swollen lip, and wondered if that was part of the service.

She kept her face turned to him. "Say what you like, I do what's wanted. If you want to fuck me, the price is letting me go."

"You have nowhere to go," Ned said. Neither did he. The locks the Lyhhrt had fitted in their apartment doors were so complicated he had no idea how to get out. He turned his head away, left her in the corner of his eye, caught up in a train of thought: "Knew me from somewhere." He had wakened up lying in the weeds outside the Arcade exit, thinking: *I remember that Brandsma from somewhere.* "Where did he know me from? You must have known me! Down there in the Arcade you said I'd fought on all those worlds."

"He didn't tell me! If you're not going to screw me, leave me alone!"

"I've got to know! If he wants to get rid of me I should know why!"

She gestured with her injured arm and gave an involuntary shiver. "He said, I want that one off my tail!" She spoke through stiff jaws. "Then he said, I can tell you something—that's a pug has fought on six worlds and thinks he's big, but he has no jaw to speak of and the rest of him cracks the same way!" She sneered. "That's all he said."

"No jaw to speak of," Ned whispered, and tried to think beyond his anger. "He must have been in the fights, somewhere. An old pug, no, probably did something that made him more money, if he's a councillor now, or calls himself one. He never was a name I ever heard of, not a fighter, knives, swords, blindfolds, Kemalan tsukka bugs, blitz, nets, Akido—what was it?"

She closed her eyes and nursed her pain.

"Slocked his name, shaved his b—" He stopped and thought. "Yeh, shaved his beard . . . lots of knuckers grew beards to hide the brands they got in the prisons on Deng Shen One," he grinned at her, "—you ever meet him there?" She opened her eyes and closed them again. "Or just even dyed his hair, found a corner taking inside bets, made himself a promoter . . . I knew that bunch of touts too, when I was a greenass yobbo from the alleys, no Manador booking for me back then," he felt his mouth hardening, "one more lump of meat thrown in to suck up some old dog who used to be a lion or think he was. Ends up other end of a fistful of lead knucks, gets carted off in a net with half his face missing." He rubbed his jaw to feel the rough skin that covered a polymer jawbone, the skin that got so white or red when he was hurt or angry. "Wakes up in a fleshpot clinic where the whores sell their bellyfuls to the genequacks for Nuflesh . . . Yeh, I did, couldn't get my mind clear for half a year Earthtime."

"I cry for you," Palma said.

"Promoter, wasn't he? hey? Your promoter too, that Brandsma? Took care of his bozos all right, insurance on everybody? Had an in with the skinners so he could skim the money and buy cheap phoneybones and cheaper skin to cover them with, no matter what kind of itch it'd give'm . . . called himself Jakes? Harry Jakes? Jesus, no wonder he thought I was after him! If I'd sussed him then I damned well would have been! And you—you want to keep—doing what he wants, and get beat up some more!"

"Oh shut up! Just shut up!" She bared her teeth and

made a fist of her good hand, looked about to spring on him.

Ned lifted his open hands. His anger had run out. "I only wanted to get it clear." He shook his head. "Now it's too goddamn clear." She was broken and beaten, and he, after remembering what he should have left forgotten, was still far from home.

They went on watching each other from their corners like two cats who had run out of spit, until Bronze opened the door and let in something like daylight.

Bullivant Learns

That morning Bullivant had awakened in a blaze of anger at his own helplessness. Knowing he had been manipulated, was being watched, might even yet be forced into some dangerous action against his will. He ate and drank the concoctions that had been left in his kitchen by some unseen force. Breakfast was a mess of something like eggs mixed with something like bacon and a brownish drink that did not taste like anything. At least there were no glaur eggs served by a crazy robot.

I said those awful things, made threats, didn't even know Hawksworth was a plant when the records were staring me in the face. . . . Why did they want her? why?

There was a knock at his door. "Oh, come on in!" Bullivant yelled.

Tharma, wearing her dull female Khagodi scales and decorated with a blue official sash and a black stun-gun harness, was followed by Gold Lyhhrt, glittering as he came.

Ah, the robot, Bullivant did not say; he got up and sat on his table in an attempt to be near eye level with his visitors.

"What kind of bloody thing now?" He was feeling quite wild, and turned his face to the green-filled window wishing he could plunge through it into the leaves. Into another world.

Tharma looked at him soberly while she took what looked like a child's wire toy out of her sash pocket, unfolded and pulled it onto her great head. It was her helmet, evidently. "Mister Bullivant, I understand how angry you are."

"You're damned right I am! You've taken my daughter away from me and isolated both of us! God knows what's happening to her, and everyone on this world knows more than I do about us and what's going on here!"

"I have felt the same way myself at times," Tharma said dryly. "But except for yourself, Bullivant, at present there is no one else on this world or any other who can take care of your daughter better than Skerow and Evarny's son Hasso. Now we are here to tell you all we can. You will not like all of it—perhaps not much of it."

Bullivant felt himself turning pale. He said stiffly, "Everything I said, terrible things, let myself be hypnotized . . . I might incriminate myself without knowing it, without even knowing what I did, if anything. I believe I need a lawyer."

"I don't know what a lawyer might tell you but you are not under suspicion for any reason, Bullivant. We have examined you carefully and satisfied ourselves about that. I am not recording anything. I am here to ask you questions as a witness, certainly not to hypnotize you, I don't know how—but to try to discover what really has been happening, and clarify it for you."

"I suppose I must risk it, then," Bullivant said quietly, but the fear beat against his rib cage. "The awful things done to Vronni, it's all made me so terribly angry."

"I cannot help that."

"And the worst of it all was when she, when my wife died, you know . . ."

"I understand. Now I want to ask you about what happened when you met your wife and married her. It has a lot to do with what happened later."

"Really? Must I do that?"

"It will help."

Bullivant looked into space as he pushed the words out. "I met her nearly sixteen years ago in Singapore, my time, at one of those embassy parties, very correct, and she was with one of the families, I don't think it was her own. I'm sure it wasn't. I'd been trying to make an important call that hadn't gone through, and when I went to the comm room to try again, she was there . . . she was crying. I didn't want to look, of course, and was just turning away, and she lifted her head. . . . she had such dark eyes, black hair, her skin so gold against the red dress—and she said, 'Please, please, get me out of this, take me anywhere!' Just a cliché, but she was very young—no more than eighteen, and I was much younger myself." He looked up. "Do you think I was being hypnotized when that happened?"

"I don't believe so, Bullivant," Tharma said firmly.

"Well, then I fell in love. Just like that. I'd always been lonely, even with all the people I kept around me, and I fell. I took her to a little apartment where I used to bring women sometimes, and tried to find out what was troubling her.

She'd insisted on creeping out of a back exit and we took three different helicabs. She wouldn't eat or drink, and when I got her talking after she'd cried everything out—it was just a whisper, as if everyone would hear us in that huge city—she'd only say that she was pregnant, hated the family, never wanted the child, wouldn't say anything about the father of it, was afraid to have an abortion because 'somebody' might find out. She said all that before she told me her name. Darya Merriam."

He stopped to take breath, and Tharma and the Lyhhrt watched him as he forced himself to speak, sitting on the table with his hanging legs crossed at the ankle.

"I did ask, but she told me it wasn't rape, and I couldn't push it. I didn't know whether that 'somebody' she was afraid of meant the family; I never did meet any of them, those Merriams. They were religious NewHavenites who lived in a colony on New Southsea. I only found out years afterward from an old news report that she'd been kidnapped not long before I met her, and her family never called the police—took care of it privately, they said. Now, when I remember that I can see a pattern in what happened to Verona, I never quite realized that the scars on her palm were so much like . . . but then she must have been raped. Verona—"

"Your daughter was not sexually assaulted, Bullivant. If she had not been found—" She saw that he was shivering and said quickly, "Go on with your story."

"The way it was then, we two were alone in the world, and I was in love, that's all that mattered. I married her, I adopted Verona and loved her too, I was glad to have a baby ready-made, and thought we'd have more of our own, but we never did. She was always frightened, no matter what I did to reassure her, was always afraid of a mysterious *them*, afraid to go out in the street even with the guards we always had, when we went to parties she always stayed close, and was afraid to be alone in case *they* came to take her away. I never could find out who." He shook his head. "She was never happy, that's all. And she left me, finally, because of her fear. . . .

"When she died—I was afraid she'd been murdered, and that I should have watched her so much more carefully—" He wiped his eyes. Then he flushed and lifted his head angrily. "Can you leave me alone, do you think? Are you satisfied now that I've been babbling like an idiot!"

"An innocent one, Bullivant," Tharma said, gently for her. "Would you tell us now what happened after your wife died?"

Bullivant said dully, dutifully, "I came from Singapore—I'd never seen her since we . . . separated, and the police wouldn't let anyone near her at the funeral—they might still think she was murdered—"

"We do not think she was," the Lyhhrt said.

"Oh. I guess I'm glad of that, I'm not quite sure why. She was only thirty-three. I went back to the apartment with Verona and saw how they'd been living up there north of Toronto in those big slab buildings with their underground markets. She'd never let Verona go to school, she had to get her education off the TrivvySchool run for shut-ins. The guards were thick-headed brutes who were sniggering among themselves during the funeral. One of them might have been doing some cooking, because the Cuisinette outlet had been cemented up. It was a filthy place. Nobody'd been let in to clean and none of those louts was doing any." He sighed. "I had to take Verona away from that, just as I had to take her mother away from whatever was coming after her . . . it came anyway."

"When you heard of her death you were in Singapore
. . . and you left for Toronto—"

"Right away. I'd already been posted to Khagodis and
was due to leave in eight days. I knew those trials here
would stir things up, but it was a promotion and I needed
to get away from my thoughts and take Vronni away from
hers. I called in all my markers to cut red tape and we were
both at Moonlift Port on time."

"And your secretary?"

"Oh, I'd told Hammadi to go straight to—" He
stopped, then went on slowly, "I *thought* I'd told Hammadi
to go to Moonlift from Singapore, no use dragging him with
me. I did tell him. Hammadi was my secretary. I did tell
you about him."

"Yes you did. You stayed there on the Moon . . . ?"

"A day and a night. We had SleepLets, those pay-as-
you-sleep boxes where you can't stand up and have to crawl
in."

"And during that day?"

"A big lot of waiting-rooms, that was all, with the usual
chairs, food and game machines and line-ups to get at them.
I was worried because I expected to see Hammadi at Moonbase in our portroom at the ninety-seventh gate. The rooms
were very crowded, everybody who'd been waiting to go
offworld for the last year had come up in those lifts. So I
kept looking around for him. . . ." He stopped in the act of
folding his arms; his eyes had gone a little glassy.

"Yes?" Tharma prodded him very carefully, as if he
might bleed at a touch.

"Well, of course I eventually found him, actually he
found me. I'd been really worried, because Hawksworth
was usually so prom—" He blinked and shook his head.
Sweat had sprung out over it and his face. Visibly he pulled

himself away from his fear. "What happened?" he asked.
"Between waiting for Hammadi and meeting Hawksworth? God damn it, you know what happened!"

Tharma held up her hand, and a shaft of sunlight beyond the window pushed through cloud and made her pearl
nails translucent. "Not completely," she said. "I want to
find out from you."

The door opened that moment and Heth came in shep-
herding Brandsma, who was glowering and rubbing at his
bruised neck. "Have you ever seen this fellow before, Bullivant?"

"Of course." Bullivant felt some relief at seeing an
Earther he knew. "He's Councillor Brandsma. Hullo,
Brandsma! I met him when I was waiting for Hawksw—I
mean waiting for Hammadi." He let himself down from
the table and took a step forward. He held his hand out.
"Don't you remember me, Brandsma? You seem to be in
difficulty, are you all right?"

"Don't you touch me!" Brandsma jerked away from
Heth's grasp with a twist of his shoulder, and backed away
from the hand Bullivant had offered. "I never saw you in
my life!"

Bullivant pulled back. "What—" He turned to Tharma.
"What's this now? Some damn trick again?"

"No, Ambassador," Tharma said. "The councillor is
not eager to see anyone he knows right now. Was that meeting your first?"

"Yes—I'd never heard of him before."

"That's a lie! We never met!"

"Don't answer this man, Bullivant, answer me. How
did you meet him?"

"He just came up and congratulated me on being named
Ambassador—said he'd seen me on the trivvy—and we

shook hands. What's wrong with you, Brandsma? Of
course we've met!"

"You're out of your mind, goddam you! I never was
anywhere near you!"

"I—" Bullivant faltered for a moment. But he had gone
too far. "No. It was you I saw. You told me your name. If
it is your name. I never heard of you otherwise, and I don't
know what you're a councillor of."

"I never saw you!"

Bullivant turned to Tharma. "I tell you, Tharma, we
did shake hands, he had his hand out and I had to be civil,"
he lifted his right hand in an imitative gesture, "we talked
for a while." He looked at the hand he was gesturing with
and saw that it was clenched in a tight fist, fingers wrapping
thumb. He opened it like a flower. "A little cut here, healed
now, right at the base of my fourth finger . . ." He felt it
with his thumb. "He had a ring, I remember it was a bit
rough and scratched me. I thought at the time it was a jewel,
a diamond maybe, turned the wrong way."

He looked up again, at Tharma and the Lyhhrt, but
neither of them wore a particular expression, and even Heth
seemed to be watching him in a dream. He said, "I might
be making this up"—Brandsma lifted his head—"but I'm
not. You've been calling me a liar when I haven't even ac-
cused you of anything, I only said that I met you. But I
know, it's on record, it's known to people on Earth, that
my secretary was a man named Hammadi, and in the few
minutes when I was talking to you he became a man named
Hawksworth, the man who did his best to destroy my
daughter. I don't remember it all, maybe I never will. But
I remember you, Brandsma, too well." He said to Tharma,
"This man's still only a man I met in a waiting room. I

couldn't prove that he did everything I think he did. If I knew that for certain I'd be ready to kill him."

"There are people waiting in line to kill him," the Lyhhrt said. "You can see that by the bruises on his throat. Tharma will keep holding him because he caused a violent disturbance in a public place last night. In a little while we will let the one designated Hawksworth have a look at him."

Tharma added, "You will also want to know that the man calling himself Hawksworth is Herbert Ambrose, a man born on your Moon, one we know about for certain. He was hired on the Moon to take the name of Hawksworth, and was waiting for you there, while he was being trained as secretary and hypnotist by an even better one than Brandsma. He was a quick study—"

"He fooled me."

"Not as badly as he fooled himself. He expected great rewards but there are none. He was likely the one who influenced you to make those fearful threats. Remove this one, Heth. We will send him with Ambrose to the Endless Valley Holding Station where there is nowhere to commit crime. We'll decide about the woman later."

Brandsma turned brick red and yelled at the Lyhhrt, "You fuckless bastard, why did you save me?"

"I also did my utmost to save the Ix," the Lyhhrt said.

When Brandsma had gone, Bullivant said wonderingly, "If he'd just said, oh hullo, Bullivant, how're you doing, as I did to him, nothing would have happened—I'd never have remembered."

"I am not so sure of that!" The Lyhhrt now recalled that Bullivant knew nothing of Brandsma's terrible battle with the Ix. "He was very much shaken. If the Ix had not tried to kill him, and I had not saved him, you would not have remembered. Whatever might have happened, your mind is free now."

For one brief flash, Bullivant saw himself back on the Moon standing in the portroom at the ninety-seventh gate, shaking hands with Brandsma and murmuring, *Thank you, glad to have met you,* and Brandsma replying, *Yes, well, we'll be traveling together and there's something you know very well, Bullivant, it's that your secretary Hawksworth will be here in just a few minutes, he'd never be late, he's been such a trustworthy fellow, your wife always thought so, for over this past ten years, he'll tell you a few things to do and say,* and on and on, himself nodding, saying, *Certainly, nobody more trustworthy, yes, my wife always thought so, yes, I'll say whatever he wants....* And from Brandsma the last word, *Good-bye now, you never met me and don't know me.*

The moment passed quickly, with the flavor of a dream. Tharma did not seem to be aware of any of this.

Bullivant looked at the Lyhhrt. *Maybe there was a little poison in that ring of Brandsma's; I wouldn't like to think I was such a gull as to swallow everything whole ... "My wife always said"—Dear God!* But he would never ask the Lyhhrt. He didn't want to know. He said, "Yes, I'm free of those delusions, but I'm still an ordinary fellow who'd— oh, as an adventure—married a woman that was, in a way, an illusion that's part of an elaborate charade, and I still don't know who she was really, or who her daughter, my daughter, is."

Tharma considered for a moment and said to the Lyhhrt, "You will tell, will you, Representative?" It was not quite a request.

The Lyhhrt said aloud, "I will tell."

Tharma said, "Then I'll see you later, Bullivant, and we will put together a statement."

Bullivant looked at the Lyhhrt questioningly, and he replied, "Sit down in this chair, Ambassador."

The sky cleared and the room flooded with heat while the coolers surged to battle it. The noise sealed Bullivant's memory of this place forever. The Lyhhrt placed himself in a folding chair like Bullivant's. "I promised that you would know everything," the Lyhhrt said, and he began very carefully to tell Bullivant all he had learned from Hasso the Master of Archives, about his wife Darya's agony and the mystery of his daughter Verona's birth, and why the Ix had wanted her. . . .

The Lyhhrt said in finishing, "They meant to terrorize her in the same way as your wife was terrorized. They had been doing that for the Zamos family for generations, to keep the inheritance and authority intact. They might have had her raped, though we doubt it—more likely intended to implant an embryo, though they did not, but we don't know where the embryos are, or if there are any here."

Bullivant found it hard to breathe. "Did they engineer my coming here?"

"No. It was merely convenient for everything to take place here. The Ix were already entrenched here doing their best to disrupt the trials. On your world the police were investigating your wife's death. If your daughter had been kidnapped there the investigation would have gone much further and deeper and the publicity spread much wider. It would have been dangerous to Zamos, Star*Systems or whatever else they call themselves. On this world her kidnapping was only one among a great many other distractions. No matter what might have happened, or what still may, you were acting freely, and you brought your daughter here only because you cared for her and wanted her with you."

"My daughter. My wife's sister." Bullivant shook his head. "Yet somehow I feel I've always known all this but couldn't reach it."

"That is because your mind was blocked by experts. There will still be a great many questions that can never be answered."

Including: *What will happen now?* And: *Did you love me, Darya, ever?* But Bullivant had all the answers he could bear. "Yes, and the terrorists have succeeded," he said. "My wife and Evarny dead, my daughter wounded, and the trials have been postponed."

The Lyhhrt rose. "Whatever can be put to rights will be. Your daughter is safe and soon you can begin to take up your work as ambassador. I/we will not trouble you anymore." He left Bullivant to his lonely thoughts and shut the door.

He found Tharma back in her office. The tea-carrier had refilled her bowl and was flavoring the tea with her usual choice of spices. She had her midday meal, a slab of cold myth-ox on a trencher of bread, lying before her, and was about to devour it. He stepped away. "I will come back later."

"Aki! But stay! No hurry; the bread is already stale and I hate myth-ox, but they are all we drudges can buy at the Official Kitchen in this place. You were going to say—"

The tea-carrier backed out, and the Lyhhrt said, "Yes, you know I was going to say it: I/we are not functioning properly as Galactic Federation Officers, and as you have said before we are drawing the fire of the Ix down on the innocent."

Tharma put out her tongue and bit it lightly in agreement and did not ask when they would be leaving.

The Lyhhrt said, "The charges against Brandsma are not serious enough to satisfy me, but I have no authority to investigate or, of course, to esp, and I/we are grateful for as much latitude as you have given us. I can still do you one small favor. Here," he probed his thorax, where his fingers disappeared for an instant as if into a pool of water, and came out holding a tiny spool, "is a list of those people who were meeting when the Ix was killed in the arcade. I suspect they are members of Star*Systems, and even that they were trying to rid themselves of the Ix. Terrorism has not been doing them much good as well as being too expensive. When you find them Ned Gattes can identify them—he saw them more than once that night. You will get a few useful scraps from that."

"Thank you," Tharma said. This was the longest speech she had ever heard from a Lyhhrt.

"I learned these things from Brandsma when." The Lyhhrt stopped and forced himself to go on. "When I became angry." He was stuttering. "When I might have. Hurt him."

Tharma looked down on his smallness. Of course he had never tried to match her size. It would have been a waste of good materials. But of the other smallness, the important one, she did not know what to say, and said it anyway. "It's not I who's sending you away. I've had word from my superiors . . ."

The Lyhhrt said very quietly, "I was aware of that."

He had opened his vulnerability to her, his shame, and again his guilt, and she had nothing to give in return. She said, "Without your help we would have lost that child, and many others as well."

"Yes," he said, and raised his hand in the only kind of

human gesture Lyhhrt ever made. When he passed through the doorway his mind was already so far away that he might have left the world entirely.

But he went out of his way to make one more call.

Keremer received him in her small exquisite office. Her face was ravaged, and she did not trouble to hide what she felt. "Yes, Ambassador." Her skin was dull and grayish.

As well as he could, Gold gave her the privacy she had not asked for and stepped back from the abyss of her sorrow. "That one who seduced your La'or and—delivered her to the Ix—has been put safely away."

"Safe from me, is he? I nearly had him down there, I would have wrung the truth out of him!"

"Other species find Pinxin attractive, and some Pinxin are attracted. You cannot help that."

"He would not have found anyone attractive after I dealt with him. We live best among our own."

"Granted, but even if you never left your world or traded with other worlds you would be found, as we/selves were found, and forced to work with others. It is how matters go in this age."

"Yes. But for me, I will go home and never love again." As he moved to go she cried, "You!" and then shut her mouth at the futility of making a Lyhhrt understand.

"You have children," the Lyhhrt said. "It is not worth taking your hate home to them." He turned away from her bitter face.

Bronze was waiting for him at the commscreens. He did not need to be told that Bronze had persuaded a very unwilling Ned to take Palma back down into the Arcade. No one now wanted either to use her or punish her. Bronze said, :*WorldGov Office and the Galactic Federation Office on Moon Two have called. You must speak to them.*:

:Yes. It is ending.: He called both offices at once, and looked at the old man with rattling dry wattles on the one screen and the tailwhacking young woman on the other. They both had the same message for him.

"We have asked your Representative from Lyhhr to recall you."

"Yes." After all, the Lyhhrt had invited him/them/selves here, to collect the monkeys and then search for Spartakos. He had hold of them, but they were not doing him any good. The world had commandeered him to save the child, and he had just managed to do that. He had treated the murderous fighting-woman. He had saved Brandsma and killed the Ix. Eh. They did not balance on his scale. He had done something for Bullivant quite unmeasurable, even to his delicate calculators. Two days' work. "I/we are leaving. I will tell Lyhhr. All Lyhhrt will be off this world within one thirtyday."

:All two of us,: Bronze said.

"We are grateful of course," the two Khagodi said, almost in chorus.

Gold signed off. *:I wonder if they will not try to come to an accommodation with the Ix.:*

:That younger one certainly not.:

:She is on the Moon. They will not bother her there and she can afford to be brave. That other . . .:

:Simply collapsing?—that is not be like what we know of Khagodi.:

:Khagodi have not been like what we knew for some time. They have been demoralized by discovering how many of their landsmen have worked for Zamos.: He added, *:And Lyhhrt hired many of them to do Zamos's work.:*

Gold had never before in his life referred to their people as *Lyhhrt* rather than *I/we.* Bronze twitched and rattled for a moment, and then ventured, *:(They are not the only ones demoralized.):* Very faintly. A whisper of thought.

Gold said, *:The more we try to heal the more we wound.:*

Bronze did not reply to this, and Gold went on, as if the reference to *Lyhhrt* had not taken place. *:Also every one of the Khagodi in the armed forces is too heavy to pilot or crew a flying fighting-machine, and every one of their Kylkladi pilots is a mercenary. Sending us away is very much like leaving themselves naked . . . but then there are only two of us.:* They considered this for a long while.

Bronze could not resist the obvious: *:And it is their world.:*

F I V E *

Attack

The Ix held her down under chitinous claws and implanted her with monstrous eggs that contained myriads. They invaded her eyes, her breath with their flashing and stinging, they took away her voice. Her mind screamed, her skull rang with the echoes, and she wrenched herself awake. She lay trembling in the bunk that was not so comfortable as it was supposed to be. A cramp hit her, she found the lamp button, pulled herself out of bed and staggered to the lavatory. A dot of blood told her that she had begun to menstruate, and she burst into tears. Almost she had forgotten what it was to be a girl in her midteens, a perfectly ordinary girl descended from . . .

She groped about in her cosmetics kit to find the sloughing pill and, shivering in the cool air, waited the few painful moments until it worked and her uterus had shucked off its layers of blood. She caught a red-eyed glance of herself in the tiny mirror.

You are Verona Bullivant. What a strange name.

Mother? Father? They were shadows. Last night, Skerow had held her hands. Those scaly ones were much warmer than her own. "There are losses, child. There are losses."

Skerow had wakened hours earlier from a light sleep in which, she thought, all the dreams she had ever dreamed were mingled. Having struggled out of her bed and let its waters run off her skin over the drain, she dragged her mind away from Hasso's sorrows and the painful feelings of the child, rubbing herself with kerm oil out of an alabaster flagon as her mother had done in old age so that her skin would not fall into those awful dry wattles that on some old people actually rustled when they moved. She glanced uneasily at the mirror: *Quite trim still, Skerow!* She needn't worry yet. Then laughed at herself for this vanity, when all was in ruins around her, and still as always observing herself as she observed the rest of the world.

She laughed again and picked up her studies of fomb shingles and sluice-gate controls. After an hour Ksath brought in her bowl of yagha and the glauber slice with soured curd that began her day. Her mind strayed to her poems, at the same time was clouded by yesterday's encounter with the Ix, and quite beyond her control it encapsulated itself into the form of the seh:

> *enemies*
> *come*
> *bearing their sorrows*

She noted this down in her daybook's keypad, wishing she were home in her desert house scratching it into one of the little clay tablets she used there, to be baked in her library kiln or crushed back into dust when she grew frustrated with it. But here she was. Wistfully thinking of the Equatorial poets, whose endless epics were so free and vigorous. . . .

And Hasso's mild presence wakened and lay alongside her.

:I don't want to be a damned old archive, Hasso!:

Prudently, Hasso withdrew.

Then the child awoke, grasping for handholds.

Skerow said, *:Ksath, I will have another cup of yagha or some of that good tea you brew, just bring it into the dayroom. Verona and I will eat there with Hasso.:*

Verona climbed on what she thought of as her high-chair, and sat blinking doubtfully at the imitation bacon-and-eggs omelette that did not look so different from the soured curd Hasso was now eating. The plates were the same: thick ceramic in bubbly green glaze, and out of place among technological wonders.

This morning the air was as cold as Skerow liked it and Verona had put on the red luxleather tunic lined with zaxwul that Bullivant had bought for her in consolation or as peace-offering when he found her in Toronto; it limited her movement and made her feel even more awkward. She could not pull her mind away from dread. "My father was a monster and he murdered my mother."

"But you are not truly the daughter of only that one

man and one woman, Verona!" Hasso said earnestly. "Your mother and father, no—your original progenitors—were ancestors who bequeathed you some of their hereditary material, there were armies of genetic engineers who guided and shaped it in different ways, and those workers may have been monsters too but they dared not make clones of their embryos or someone would have suspected what they were doing. There were a great many refresher genes brought into the line." He whispered, as well as an air-gulper can, "I know their archives, you see."

"You will certainly not become any kind of monster," Skerow said firmly.

Verona thought that either Skerow or Hasso was powerful enough to battle any kind of monster. "The one in the metal suit, the Lyhhrt, said that I was very important. What did it mean?"

Hasso said very slowly, "I think, that evidence of your ... difficulties and your mother's would be important in the prosecution of ... the family business."

"My mother couldn't bear seeing anything about Zamos on the trivvy. Now I understand why. . . . I don't want to end up like her scared of my own shadow or just a piece of evidence stuck somewhere with guards watching out for people trying to kill me for nothing." She had been truly imprisoned. *I've never had a friend or gone to a real school.* The trivvy had been her school, and she had made imaginary friends with the people she saw there. *I don't think I'd know how to be a friend. Let alone a monster. I'm here in Weird Wonderland right now. On the dark side of the mirror.*

"More tea?" Skerow asked, kindly and carefully ignoring the outburst like an unruly child's great-aunt. Then she took her hand off the urn grip. "You pour it for the child, Hasso. Ewskis wants to speak to me."

Dreytha guided Skerow down the five steps into the Communications Room, the most spacious in the smugglers' hideout, and the most heavily fortified. Eight comm-screens lined the walls, looking out over the sea, searching the skies, the mountains, the shadows of the desert rocks. Below them were nearly enough banks of instruments for an astronaut's deck. Ewskis's head was wound with microphones and earpieces that fitted on his helmet. "Madame, GalFed Satellite reports a craft on the ground twelve hundred siguu due northeast of here, a Bri'ak dinghy of the kind used by Ix."

Skerow held her breath for a moment, then said, "That scout yesterday . . . perhaps the one she came here in."

"It appeared suddenly only an hour ago—it may have been hypnoformed. You can only just see it now, not a very good resolution. . . ." She strained her eyes at the screen, in the satellite's view looking down from above, and could just see the dull shape, crouching among the shadows of rocks and scrub in the wilderness along the ocean's edge.

"There is, they think, an Ix standing or lying a few siguu away, just over there"—he pointed to a black dot, "that they thought was a dead body, but now it appears to be moving slightly. Maybe she's wounded—"

Our scuffle, she thought, *two kinds of blood.*

"The satellite's moving away now. In a moment we'll connect with the Geological Surv—*ek!* here is another! Flying at low altitude just beyond to the northeast, and Satellite reports it has no markings, no type they can identify and certainly no leave to land here! They have alerted Sector Base Four. . . ."

"That one is much larger," Skerow murmured. Her helmet was in her shoulder pocket and she unfolded it. "Do you think it could be a—"

"Still coming!"

"—rescue ship?" Ewskis's helmet was massive, but she could see the tilt of his head as the heavy dark image drew up to and hovered just northeast of the smaller ones below, drifted off the edge of the screen and gradually reappeared when the GeoSat image locked in. Nothing moved for a long moment. Then there was an explosion and the fragments of what had been on the ground below burst out and upward like a sun's rays. Another moment of stillness, and the stone vaults rang in a hollow echo.

"I hardly think so, Justice Skerow," Ewskis said quietly. "They seem to—eh—desert their wounded. How easily she found this place that we assumed was so out of the way and well-fortified! If they had rescued her she would have given away our position here. And if they have an esp aboard she may have done it."

The ship remained motionless, blurring darkly on the screen and trembling a little in the heated air above the explosion.

"We are armed and armored well enough for a security force, but we cannot bring that ship down!"

He and Skerow stood hypnotized by the one stationary satellite image though the other screens were dancing with movement. Dreytha had come down to see what was happening, but went back up again quickly to keep the others calm. The bigger ship moved over the exploded fragments as if it were eating them and continued on a steady course southwest, toward Smuggler's Gap.

Skerow thought she should have felt the mass of the dark ship passing over, but there was nothing until the bombs fell, *crump crump* with almost no pause between them. The walls shuddered, roaring with deep echoes. The lights flickered, blinked and came on again. The noise faded, and Dreytha said, *:We haven't been hit,:* but no one wanted to move. Half a clockfall passed before they stirred themselves.

Ewskis said, "That attack came from the southwest, after the ship passed overhead." He forced the quaver out of his voice. "It's not easily maneuverable, so likely it is gone now, but I don't know whether it missed by accident or on purpose. . . . The Base Four Squad will take care of it, if they reach here in time—if they come!"

"It was a warship," Skerow said. "Not even hypnoformed, and a warship." They all considered this for a moment, and she added, "It seems that they did have an esp aboard. I would put a few pistabat on a bet that those Ix will send one or two dinghies back to see what they have stirred up. We have to think of getting out of here."

"Where do you think you may go, madam?" Ewskis was by now thoroughly overwrought; he was a Security man, not a warrior. "There is nowhere on this world that is safe! Even in Endless Valley or as far down as you may go in the Screaming Demons Chasm, the Ix can follow us in their fighting-machines!"

"Ewskis, if we stay here they will have us where we stand."

Before he could answer a great crunching from above sent the walls shaking, and an explosion and terrific pounding rang from the end of the hallway where Skerow had yesterday opened a door too many. Skerow pulled off her helmet and saw through Ksath's eyes that the door had been blown in and the black sparkling shapes were beyond it.

:The Ix! The Ix!: Ewskis cried wordlessly, *:Dreytha!*

Ksath!: a crossbow had appeared in his hands, and Skerow thought its sparkling arrows must be poisoned.

Dreytha had already grabbed her gel gun from its rack and was shooting firestars to explode the first of the swarming Ix. The air stank of explosive chemicals. Ewskis leaped up the stairs to help her and Ksath pulled at the other three, *:Hurry! Come quickly!:* leading them across the room between commdecks to a corner where two sections of the wall slid aside and became a door.

It opened on a stone piling with mooring rings and a stairway that was green with moss, much like the one through the doorway Skerow had found and regretted finding. A thin green light from the lichened walls showed the way down to the narrow rushing stream that ran out to the seashore where Verona's helicopter had landed, only yesterday. There was a skiff moored at the foot of it. Smugglers made sure that there were ways to escape.

Skerow paused on the top step and clutched at the railing. "But Ewskis!"

:He will defend himself!: Ksath pushed her forward almost roughly and she climbed down.

Verona found the stairs steep and broad, but went down fast anyway, with Hasso skittering after. She heard the hiss and whack of arrows and flamers with every step, the blasts from Ix weapons and the awful voices of the wounded in agony made her shiver. At the foot of the steps Ksath picked her up like a baby, lifted her over the boat's rail and set her down inside.

The skiff looked like Noah's Ark to her, out of the old woodcuts from a museum, it was deep and had a peaked roof like that old one, too. But this roof was made of steel plates, camouflage-painted on top in wavy blue and green lines, and lined with wood underneath. It was dark inside and huge, like so much else on Khagodis. She couldn't see much over the railing, and the sliver of sky just visible was dull.

"Hurry, Verona, over there!" Ksath was directing her to the odd-shaped benches, and Hasso and Skerow were actually sitting on them. After a moment she saw that they were less for resting on than for supporting the Khagodi's hips and tails while they used the huge pedals. There were paddle-wheel blades stowed beneath them with other supplies. She wondered how the tiny crew was going to pedal the big skiff upstream.

Ksath flipped the mooring line loose and stepped in beside her. "No, child, we are not going to use pedals, those are only for emergencies," Ksath said. She used one of her many keys to unlock the engine, then took hold of the tiller and started it. It caught without sound, and the boat began to move slowly in its stony channel.

Flight

The fight was still raging, and Verona realized that not all the noise was coming from the building they had escaped. There were screaming engines and blasts of gunfire in the sky over the rocky dome, she could see a swelling smoke cloud. For an instant, in a flash of Hasso's mind she glimpsed, through the eyes of a Kylkladi pilot flying a narrow hawk-winged fighter, a crammed and awkward battle scene where aircraft dived through the sky to smash at each other. The Base Four Squad that Ewskis was hoping for had come.

Skerow cried desperately, "Ek-ekki, Ewskis! what have

I done?" *Opening that door at the end of the hallway.* Ksath reached back quickly to pat her shoulder.

"Put on your helmet quickly, Skerow! We may have eavesdroppers. Hasso, you've lost yours—here it is!" She gave her attention to the rocky banks of the stream, and everyone put on helmets. Then she said, "Once the Ix found her way to that landing the damage was done. They would have bombed it and broken in no matter whether you opened the door or not. You, dems'l, do you have oxygen?"

"Yes." Verona found her voice very small in the dark space echoing with terrible sounds. Since her kidnapping she always kept oxycaps crammed in the pockets of whatever she was wearing. There were some in the pockets of her leather tunic, but Verona did not want to count them.

The fearsome noises diminished as the boat pulled further upstream. "This damned old bucket has no radio," Ksath said, "and all I have on me is the local comm. But silence is safer now." Perhaps she caught Skerow's line of thought in spite of the impervious helmets. "I used to work on the river barges for many years before I became good old Ossta's housekeeper, Skerow dear. It was a life of ease and plenty for me with her then, but I am glad I trained for this one."

"By Saint Gresskow's Seven Bastards, Ksath!" Skerow cried. "If we come out of this alive I will make your life easy as long as you have it!" Ksath merely clucked and kept an eye out for the looming wall of stone to starboard.

Verona, almost incommunicado because of the helmets, took in only the barest skeleton of this conversation. Hasso, still breathing hard from his exertions, managed to gulp some air and ask, "Where are we going?"

"Let me see. . . ." Ksath had taken the chartbook from a shelf and was riffling its greasy pages as she spoke.

"Twenty thousand siguu to the northwest is the Fog Hills Automatic Pumping Station, nobody there and not much use to us, but halfway, about four hours in this current, is a deserted landing, my map says, maybe used for loading by those smugglers . . . we cannot go to sea in this boat, and there is no other way to go but upstream. What do you think about that landing?"

"Smugglers know it too well," Hasso said. "And there is bound to be some official monitoring Fog Hills no matter how automatic it is. If we have enough food and fuel we can reach it."

"We have food—we may not enjoy eating it, but it is food—and plenty of fuel too. Look outside for us, Hasso, and see what's up."

Hasso slowly crawled astern and pushed his own head and shoulders over the side beyond the roof of the ark.

A volcano sent up its smoke column to the southwest, and the sun, in the fourth quarter of the morning, just before zenith, was swathed in red veils of cloud. "Nothing southeast but a bit of cloud somewhat darker. It might be smoke, the sky is otherwise empty."

He dared take off his helmet, glad to be rid of it if only for a moment. The mild breeze refreshed his skin and he saw himself from a new direction through the eyes of a greater thouk heading south to winter in the Great Equatorial River Valley. In the broadwing's eyes he saw his tiny figure waving up at himself. Regretfully he pulled in his head. "There are dim murmurs a great many siguu away from all directions, but I don't dare intrude among them. And otherwise only the thumbokh herders and the thouk that feed on small raketto."

"Then let us push for Fog Hills. There is no other choice."

"Yes there is," Skerow said, "there is another choice."

"What do you mean, Skerow?"

"I want to go home, Ksath! I have been driven out and exiled for seven years only because I was out of the country when that damned alien ship was found and dug up in my township. A cart with a yoke of thumbokh could take me home in a day, and I want home!"

"There are plenty of thumbokh in the fields, Skerow, but we need a cart that will carry all of us, a road, a better map than the one I have—"

"—and they will not let me in when I reach the border, yes! yes! In the last seven years I have thought of so many reasons why I cannot go home, but now we are fugitives and deserve protection under my country's laws, and I must find a way!" She was near tears of anger and frustration. "You think I am a crazy old woman."

"Goodmother," Hasso said quietly, "we have no thumbokh carts to carry us home, and until we find one let us keep going toward Fog Hills where we can call for help."

Skerow forced herself into silence.

As the sun made its way down from zenith the land became flatter and less rocky, the river widened and slowed, and the skiff rode faster upstream. Desert wilderness gave way to fields of scrub and herbage where one of the herdsmen predicted by Hasso leaned on a thick crook and surveyed a score of thumbokh. Once Ksath moored the boat to a stone outcropping while she stirred up a meal of Vertebrate/Nutrient/Omniv/O/Fe/Cu and brewed some tea in an old pot on the tiny gas stove.

After another hour the boat slipped quietly past the landing that looked so inviting, a path to safety and peace. Verona suddenly realized how very long the day was on this world, and fell asleep against the bulkhead.

The *ping!* of her oxycap woke her, and she replaced it with a sense of dread. Her body was racked and cold from pressing against hard ridged wood. Even the new kind of caps did not last more than four or five hours.

The river had narrowed again and the sun was lower; it hung below the canopy of the boat and shone in slantwise. She got up and stood on the seat to pull herself up over the bulwark and look out. Over the stone banks there were grand severe mountains to the northwest, capped by puffy clouds, and Verona hoped they were the Fog Hills. Something else was different. "I smell smoke," she said, turning her head toward Hasso and forgetting that the helmet had made her incommunicado.

Hasso looked at her, at a loss for the word. She could not think of the *lingua*, but sniffed. After an instant Hasso drew a long breath through his gill slits. "That is smoke," he said.

Ksath gulped air, swallowed and muttered, "Best to cut the engine and let us drift now."

Before she could touch the switch there was a movement in the sky and a thump on the steel-plated roof, then another and another. Three pairs of heavy blue legs swung under the eaves, three helmeted Varvani with thick slab faces dropped into the boat. One was armed with a crossbow, one with a flamer, and the third with a rifle that looked to Skerow like the one that had killed Evarny just four days ago.

Verona cried out into an eerie silence. Skerow, Hasso, Ksath, muffled by their detested helmets, were paralyzed.

The Varvani with the crossbow, a woman, said in *lingua*, "Remove the helmets and leave them here." Someone outside was dragging at the boat's painter, and the boat lurched but the Varvani did not.

"Who are you!" Skerow cried, finding voice now.

"Nobody you'll want to know too well, Justice Skerow," the woman said. "We have a stepladder for you, and you can hop out and join the crew. We want you too, little one." A gesture translated the words.

Verona removed her helmet and tried to pull herself away from her fear. She had never heard of Varvani, and to her these were large blue strangers of whom the female had one big double-teated breast bulging out of her tunic. She crept forward and the Varvani woman plucked her up out of the ark and onto a stone platform set in the riverbank. She smelled the smoke more strongly now, and saw that the Varvani had built a fire in a small clearing among the scrub, and while they waited had been roasting meat on a spit for their supper. It was the source of the smell, the first of the evening's offshore winds had brought it to her.

A pair of thumbokh were grazing in a patch of weeds a few siguu from the fire, and a cart stood nearby. Hasso felt Skerow's eyes bursting with tears and watched her carefully, but she did not speak, nor let a thought escape her.

The Varvani herded their four captives toward the heavy dray, dragging the stepladder along with them. "Get on, get on." While the four were clambering up they hooked battery lights to the wagon poles and dragged the ladder aboard. The sun had fallen into a bed of cloud and darkness was rising.

"Where are we going?" Skerow cried despairingly.

"To a place you've never dreamed of, Justice," the riflewoman said, climbing up front to whip the thumbokh while the other two Varvani found footholds on the wheel hubs to jump onto the platform and shove themselves among their prey.

After half an hour of travel the land began to fold into

a series of combes, blind valleys that gathered darkness into themselves, and it was into one of these that the Varvani whipped their great beasts.

Neither Verona nor any of the Khagodi could see anything in the darkness ahead; the moons were hidden behind a cloudy sky, and the lantern gave no more light to this depth than a firefly. The wagon was not following a road or even a beaten path, and sometimes the hooves of the animals stumbled over rocks. Verona did not have time to think, she was so occupied in bracing herself against the bumps that the heavy Varvani and Khagodi could ignore.

Eventually there was a glimmer of light beyond the dark line of the hillside, and the path of the dray swerved into a deeper fold of the valley's depth past the flank of the hill. Ahead a formless flickering shape brightened until someone the riders could not see parted a great curtain of nettings laced with twigs, and the shape became flaring torches, cook-fires, battery lamps and bulbs hanging from wires.

All of these lit up a city of tents and huts made of packing cases, scrap lumber and old weathered canvas tarps. Scores of Khagodi and a double score offworlders of six or seven species were moving among them unloading supplies out of crates, packing up others, making dinner in the thin cold air, boiling stews in steaming pots and roasting fowls and great smoke-reeking ribbed flanks on spits over the fires. In the tents were small figures crouching at low tables and Khagodi squatting at high ones.

The three Varvani summoned the Khagodi from the cart with their weapons and hoicked down Verona with a grab under her arm like a rag doll. They prodded her with the others toward one of the tents, a huge tarp hung from part of the framework of ropes and struts that formed the hutch city. An old and shriveled Khagodi was crouching in its entrance on a padded wooden platform set over a sleeping bath dug out of the soil. He stared at them and the four clung together, though there was no shelter among their bodies.

Skerow recognized him and pulled herself erect. A very old man, *Older than I,* she thought. *Much older. He seemed the same age long ago.* Never a big man, Karbow Blood-Eye had now shrunk so greatly that the wattles of his skin rattled with every breath. Its colors had not faded but intensified into patchy blots of red, green and blue. His impervious helmet was a cage of copper filigree studded with brilliant jewels and so massive that he could hardly move his jaws. *Always so damned suspicious, weren't you, Karbow? I wonder if you ever even take it off now. I wonder if you can.* Like some Khagodi men he had an eye that squirted blood when he was angry or excited, and his was particularly inflamed now.

Skerow had never known a blood-eyed man with any good intent toward her. She wrapped her mind in all of its defenses.

There was a little Bengtvadi woman with a shaved and tattooed head perching on a stool next to him and whispering in his ear. His private esp most likely, Skerow thought. He said, "I see that you have recognized me, Justice Skerow," belching the words out and gulping awkwardly.

Meeting Karbow Blood-Eye

The last time she had seen him was from the judge's lectern where he stood before her waiting to be sentenced to long hard time in the ore-processing sheds deep in the platinum mines for smuggling Zamos's embryos to Ix and slavers. His eye had spat blood at her then. She said carefully, "There are plenty of worlds where everybody knows you, Karbow Blood-Eye. What riches d'you think you will get from me?"

Zzt, zzt! The Bengtvadi hummed at his ear like an insect. Karbow gulped air and spat it snorting. "Perhaps I will make you love me. You never know."

Skerow did not move or speak; she and Karbow stared at each other for a moment. As a young girl, and for a short time, she had thought him a romantic figure. Karbow drew up his shoulders and looked away.

"And I suppose this other one here," he pointed to Ksath, "is one of those busybodies that scuttled about the courts."

"I was a bargee on the Great Equatorial River in your high days, Karbow, and I knew of you then too," Ksath said boldly.

"Much good may it do you! You can do our errands here until your steam evaporates." Turning his big head to stare at Verona. In her scarlet coat and under the glaring light there was no shadow for her to pull into. "This bit of an alien here is the little miss that her father is going to pay a great deal of gold for if he wants her alive—"

Verona burst out, "Never! He'll never—" Hasso put his hand firmly on her shoulder, and then his arm around her defensively. The Varvani who was lifting a thick fist lowered it.

"Idiot!" Karbow curled his tiny wrinkled hand into a miniature fist and shook it at the Varvani. "She's worth nothing if you crack her skull! Little miss, if your father won't pay for you I will sell you to a trader or to the Ix.

You are every bit as exotic as a Pinxid to the trade I deal in and there is no way I will lose money on you!" And his faded graying eyes at last rested on Hasso. "Now. The gimpy runt who calls himself a master of archives."

Hasso pulled up his shoulders and waited for the blow.

Karbow dipped his head toward the Bengtvadi woman as she buzzed in his ear, "I have my own experts among the archives, Evarny's son, and they tell me that from the time when you were born on Saint Skathe's Feastday your mother wanted to expose you in the outlands and would not look at you for ten hallows' nights because of that twisted leg, even though you were the only living clutch-mate."

Skerow stared at Karbow, and then at Hasso. She did not know Hasso's secrets, and could not see how the Bengt-vadi would have learned them. Then it occurred to her (she shielded the thought very tightly) that Karbow's esp was being fed this information—or lie.

Hasso murmured, "My mother was too old to care for children by then, you see." The darkness was thick now beyond the bowl of fires and smoky warmth in the valley but the stars still blazed brightly in the thin clear air above. Verona and the three Khagodi huddled together, numbed by fear and chill.

Karbow regarded Hasso with livened interest. It was past his sleeptime, and his gulps of air became more strained, but he nodded as the Bengtvadi kept buzzing. "You have spirit, young Hasso. I admire that, and I can make use of it. You may limp among others, on the outside, but here now, among us, you may be the equal, of everyone else! You can tell us all of the world's secrets, yes, and we can use, a man like you, young Hasso! What d'you say?"

"Me? You want me?"

Karbow thrust his head forward. "Yes! There are riches here, endless riches for your secrets! Say now!" He wept a tear of blood.

Hasso's eyes darted through smoke, watering and trying not to take too much note of the grimy scullions and greasy pots of Karbow's empire. "How can I say without thinking!"

"Ingrate!" Karbow spat a mouthful of air and gulped more. "You are in luck that I want sleep now." He raised his hand and the nearest Varvani cuffed Hasso on the side of the head. "Do or be dead! You have until tomorrow!"

The Varvani woman with the bow and arrow grabbed up Verona, who kicked and scratched reflexively; she had not much outrage left. Skerow and Hasso, full of outrage, reached for her, but the Varvani snarled in her thick snorkeling voice, "Be quiet! I will not harm her!"

Ksath and Hasso pulled Skerow away. :*They need her, Skerow, they cannot hurt her.*:

:*Need her for what?*: Skerow closed her bitter mouth.

She, along with Hasso and Ksath, found herself delivered into one of the hutches built from the sides of packing cases on a framework of wooden struts and old galvanized pipes. It was backed up against the hillside, windowless, and guarded at the doorway by a Khagodi woman who was one of the tallest Skerow had ever seen. She was filled with despair. :*What are we going to do, Hasso? I cannot let you be killed! Perhaps you ought to take Karbow's—*:

"Do not think it, Goodmother! Not a thought!"

"I cannot sense the child, Hasso, can you?"

"I have not got coordinates yet among all these people, and I dare not go too rashly."

"Who would have believed that there were so many felons on this world!"

"Most of them are here, dear Goodmother. We have truly fallen into the grokkl-nest." He could sense the grok-kli, surely enough, hissing and writhing around him. "And I must not become one of them!"

"Hasso! Did your mother really do that terrible thing?"

Hasso gave Skerow a smile that was less humble than usual. "My mother also told me one thousand times how grateful she was not to have lost me after all. Karbow wanted very much to bait us, and I let him have that crumb so he would not think up something worse."

"This is worse enough." There was no sleeping bath here, even as rough a one as Karbow had, and no bench or table either. The plank floor had a square opening in one corner for the spit-hole; the cold air kept the smell down somewhat. In the dim light Skerow was just able to see a few mattresses made of old sacks; when she touched one of them it crackled with dead leaves. A larger hump in another corner resolved itself into an old Khagodi herdsman sleeping off a drunk.

He was without a helmet, and Ksath hissed, "That's one of them that we were seeing in the fields. He's no prisoner!"

"No, he's not." Hasso spoke sadly. "I imagine he was well connected by radio and reporting us to Karbow as we went by. He was surely wearing a helmet then." Hasso was most crestfallen. With all of his care to scour the country-side without leaving a thought-trace he had missed this one. *Filthy villain!* He suppressed an impulse to kick at the old hump crouching on knees and elbows with his tail swagged around his rump and his rough breath squealing through one gill-slit.

Skerow could not suppress the thought: *Eki, he had thumbokh and a cart and I was a day away from home! No no, Skerow! Everyone will think you are mad!* Before she could think any more thoughts like this their guard sent three bowls and a ladle skittering along the floor and banged down a basin and a jug. There was herb tea in the jug and chunks of meat with boiled winter-bracket in the basin, she could smell it.

Ksath dealt out this food and Skerow forced herself to take her share. She did not want to look too closely at what was in the bowl, but found it to be chunks of fresh field zysst well flavored by the winter-bracket, and was surprised to find herself eating heartily. She had had little appetite in the days since Evarny was killed and she herself forced out of her home in Burning Mountain. Now her body had responded without asking her opinion.

But tomorrow, Hasso. He said tomorrow. That dreadful choice! But Hasso was wrapped in thought or dream, and Skerow did not press him. Her full stomach calmed her enough to let her reach out toward Verona. *I will not hurt her,* the Varvani woman had said—but the Varvani was not the one she feared. As she reached she sensed the guardian minds and fields of white noise erected around her.

Her strength was so blunted by weariness that she was forced to leave the task. Perhaps Hasso . . . Even fear and despair had been muffled. She crouched down near Ksath on the crackling leaf-bed that was too symbolic of her feelings, and sank into sleep undeterred by the bugs that crawled over and under her, only once stung back to near consciousness by a terrible thought that did not have time to articulate itself before sleep swept over her again.

It was not tomorrow that worried Hasso but now. The thought that did not surface in Skerow became clearly and completely articulate in his mind, and he shielded it very carefully before he dared consider it in all its complexity:

The Ix attacked the hideaway at Smuggler's Gap. They must have known that we were staying there, known who we were, whether from that one woman that Skerow ran into, or earlier. That's not so strange, there's no reason why they shouldn't have esps and other spies. But they did their best to kill us all. All. Not only two troublesome Khagodi, Skerow and myself, but Verona Bullivant, who is so valuable to Zamos's heirs. They meant to kill her. Not to pick her up and deliver her to the Zamos people. They came in a warship, with bombs and artillery. Is it possible that the Ix have somehow become the enemies of that miserable Family? If that is so, no Ix would give Karbow Blood-Eye any gold for Verona! No, they will—

No! His mind went surging outward toward her, running like mercury through the mazes that parted them.

And found nothing of her but a shadow.

No matter how he lost himself among the minds Verona was not there. The Varvani who had carried her off was helmeted and unreachable, the Bengtvadi esp and her cohorts would be alert for his signals. He sensed the echo of one cry of terror, but there was not the horrid wrench of death that all Khagodi knew too much of in their naked lives. Her mind had been muffled, not in a whitewalled room because there would not be one among these shacks, but by a helmet. Alive, so far. He was half sure of this. He pushed at the door, but it would not give, then beat on it with his fists, but there was no answer. The guard was gone.

✳　✳　✳

The Varvani woman half-carried, half-dragged Verona among the flapping tents and grease-spattering fires where no one blinked an eye at either of them, then stopped at the doorway of a small hut in the shadow of the hill and shoved her through. As she stumbled on the plank floor the woman set her upright and grabbed her around the shoulders, pinning her arms while she dug into the pouch slung under her arm. Just as Verona heard the internal *ping!* that warned of her oxycap's last half hour she felt something being pulled over her head and thought she had reached the end of everything, but after a moment recognized the mesh of an impervious helmet that fitted her tightly down to the eyebrows and locked under the ear with three clicks.

The oxycap pinged again and Verona, thinking the socket would be blocked by the helmet, cried out in panic, "No! No!" scratching at the woman's arms, but the Varvani bunted her away. While she was scrambling to keep balance her jailer grubbed in the pouch and tossed something to or at her. Verona stared at it in the dim light and picked it up. It was an oxycap; she felt back of her ear for the socket and found that place clear. But she was incommunicado again. Hasso, Skerow, Bullivant—the man who once was her father when she thought she had one—no one would ever find her.

The Varvani woman took up her post in the doorway. She filled it from transom to floor with the big arch of her bald head, broad shoulders and heavy thighs and legs, and Verona could only see flickers from outside, but some light filtered in through cracks and places where the walls did not meet the ceiling. She clawed at the helmet, and just managed to straighten her braid and ease the pressure of the metal knots on her skin. She might well be imprisoned in this damned thing forever.

She was alone, again. In the last few hours, hardly more than a day, she had been thrust among strangers who had made themselves her friends, and then been wrenched from them. She stared at the leaf-mattresses and the bugs crawling in and out of them. There were no benches or seats of any kind, so she knelt down and waited squatting on her heels, without knowing what for, not knowing how to fight this situation or against whom. Her six days on Khagodis felt like half of her life. Eventually her oxycap gave its last *ping!* and she changed it.

After a while she too was offered a jug and a bowl. The herb tea, that tasted like sarsaparilla, was the same that she had drunk with Skerow in the morning so far gone, and she sampled the meat because it had been stewed and was probably safe, but did not find it tasty, and wondered if eating was better than starving. Without answering herself, she ate. The Varvani collected the bowl and jug, and closed the door, barring it from the outside, Verona heard the thud. Locked in. She eyed the leaf-beds and their bugs, but was so tired that she lay down on one of them anyway, and the bugs did not find her tasty either.

As she was drifting into the depths of sleep the door was unbarred she thought, someone pushed in, some stumbling on the floor, some shouting, or snarling, faint through thickly clotted sleep, "You let me out! My friends will kill you!"

Talking English. I'm dreaming. She slept on.

Ping! Sleeping in this thinner air she knew she'd wake up after four or five hours. The network of the helmet was digging into her scalp, and there was a long night still to go in this place. Drowsily she changed caps rather than waiting another half hour for the last gasp, and shoved the unexpired cap back into her pocket. She opened one eye a slit.

The air of the place, leaves and wood, something like a manger in a Holiday crèche. A dark shape lay still on the other leaf-sack .

Dead or sleeping. Thin, a woman or adolescent wrapped in dark cloth. The oxycap's *ping!* would not wake her, being a resonance against the user's bone, barely audible to others. The noises outside had ebbed a little, the fires dimmed, but the flashes of light, torches and jittering lamps, still winked in through the slits.

She saw the glitter of a helmet on the other head, the crescent of a face. An open eye.

A staring eye. Dead? No, after what seemed an immoderately long time the eye blinked.

Verona pushed away her unease. *Maybe she does speak English . . . but I don't think I want to—*

Drifting off to sleep . . . a sting in the nostril and a point of white flash pitch-black deep in her brain. She opened her eyes wider, closed them again, bit her lip to keep from screaming. Her hand stung pins and needles under the dermflex that covered the bloody asterisk on her palm. *Silly little girl, did you think I was one of them?*

The head rose up, an arm lifted. The mad eye blinked.

"You!" the acolyte said. The sequins on her shoulder glittered faintly, red, green and white in a torch's flare, and her jeweled helmet flashed. *I am not yet worthy to be called one of them.*

The Last One

"You got away," Verona whispered.

The other was up on one knee now, eyes wide enough

to show, even in this dimness, their glassy whites. "You noticed. You noticed I got away . . . when they left. No-where to go when my Lords left. For my safety, they said. *We'll leave you here in these hills, go save yourself.* I climbed them up and down. I wasn't yet worthy of reward, of dying for my Lords. You see." Lips pulled back snarling from white pointed teeth in that so white face. "And it's your fault, you caused all this! If you weren't here none of it would have happened! My Lords would let me love them if you hadn't come here and made them take you and bring you to us! And then you ran away and wouldn't let them plant the egg! We were happy before you came here, we adored and my Lords were gracious on us and you drove my Lords away and killed us and—"

"You did it to me," Verona whispered, her hand was stinging hotly. "You did it to others, I didn't do anything to you!" But there was no arguing, She recognized the other side of the unreason she had tried to staunch in her mother's night thoughts, and began to rise and back away. "You're crazy. They drove you crazy."

The Ix-worshipper was snarling, "Little miss suckling Ambassador's daughter, little lamb, we wouldn't hurt you! One more little cut, this time your face?"

Half-risen, Verona saw the sliver of light that flicked once on the knife as the acolyte launched herself. She began to crouch into a squat, thinking to snatch at the mattress and shield herself, but it was only a loose bag of leaves and air, she had no shield or weapon and her right hand was weakened by the asterisk that had slashed into its muscles. Nowhere to duck away from this. She tried to guard her face by the crook of that arm, her terror mixed with anger that she was to die locked into this pit.

Then in an instant of delay the toe of the woman's boot

tipped into a crack of the floorboards and she had to regain
balance by putting a foot forward just short of where she
had aimed herself, and the tip of the knife caught in Verona's helmet along her jaw. While the acolyte took one
short step back withdrawing her arm to free the knife Verona twisted away, and when she madly surged forward
again to drive it home her head came down under Verona's
jaw and blasted the breath out of her.

Verona fell backward and her head rapped the floor,
she gasped sucking air, did not know where the knife had
gone, saw in a flash that the blade had glanced scratching
off her left shoulder and picked up a stitch of her leather
jacket over her breast, with the point sticking out, a triangle
of steel. She did not feel that head-bang or the cuts on her
shoulder and cheekbone, her chin was huddled into the
fleecy neck of the jacket, she was getting her breath back in
shallow gulps and her whole soul was devoted to keeping
that knife in its sheath of red luxleather and the acolyte's
driving hand trapped around its hilt between their bodies.
Anything to keep the fine edge of that knife away from the
thin skin of her neck.

Hints of the Ix pheromone made her ears ring and her
tongue prickle, but her mind was clear enough. The acolyte's free hand was clawing for her eyes, she knocked it
away, wrapped her arms and legs around the squirming
body on top of her while the madwoman howled her muffled rage, and held on for love of life. The long-nailed fingers kept reaching, and when they reached her mouth she
opened it wide and bit them hard.

But she was still on her back, trapped in this position
like a turtle, only worse. There was still a sharp knife between herself and the acolyte. She had no freedom to move.
Only to let go. After a moment of furious thought she made

the only move, let go limbs and teeth, and gave the acolyte one savage push away from her, rolling to the right with all her strength so that she would be free to grab the knife hand in both of hers. Her right shoulder was holding down the woman's left arm now, and she pried the numbed fingers of the right hand off the hilt, gave the hand a wrenching twist, jerked the knife free and flung it to the corner of the room.

Verona was dragging long breaths into her squeezed ribs and her shins were sore from kicks, but she had an advantage now, her one weapon, being half-a-head longer in body and three or four kilos heavier in weight than the acolyte, and after a few more kicks and scuffles was on top of her, yelling and drumming her fists on that hateful face.

The woman's nose burst out in blood and she gaped like a fish in air, with the blood running from her nostrils across her cheeks like a grotesque mustache. Verona stopped her pounding and stared at her clenched fists, panting. How could she be doing this? *Little miss . . .*

What she would have done next she never had to ask herself, because the world exploded then.

An Exit

The first bomb blew the door in and the top edge scraped her bootheel and raised a huge cloud of dust as it slammed down. She fell flat on top of the acolyte from the shock and rolled over slowly, coughing. From outside came hideous screams, and a voice inside her mind howled, *Ix! Ix!* Not so much a voice as a thought, and she felt the helmet's grip around her neck loosening, it had broken one of the times her head banged on the floor, and she grabbed it off and flung it away—then wished she had kept it because of the bursting flares, crashing, and agony, *THE FIRES! PUT OUT THE FIRES!* more bombs in the distance, limbs flicked off, one slice, and blood-jets, *SAVE ME I'M DY—*

She clapped her hands to her ears, but this did not stop the horrible maddening clamor. She pulled herself to her knees and then to her feet, staggering, the acolyte stirred beside her and Verona grabbed her by the arm and yelled, "The Ix are attacking! Got to get out!"

"No! No!" The acolyte pulled away, screeching. "My Lords! My Lords have come! Take me, my Lords!"

"They won't help you, they're killing you!"

"Kill you!"

Verona left her flailing about the floor for her knife and ran out into chaos among Khagodi loading sacks into wagons then running away from bursting shrapnel and splintering boards, thumbokh bellowing and Varvani whipping them, a rising howl, aloud or in her mind, *THE IX ARE MY FRIENDS! MY FRIENDS!* That one she recognized: old Karbow had fought his way out of the helmet and the hissing Bengtvadi was dead. She could not see the Ixi ship hovering in the smoke of the night sky, only the churning terror of Karbow's tiny world. The next cluster of bombs fell among the surrounding hills with dull echoing booms, and the one after that not twenty meters away, it sent clods of dirt raining on her.

Frantic to get out of this hell she felt her way in the darkness, stumbled between two of the huts and behind them where they backed into sharply rising hills, and scrabbled along their flanks. Once a back wall canted over as she was passing. She shrieked and fell to her knees; the top edge of the fiberboard slab came to rest on the slope above her and she crawled under with her teeth chattering, and kept going that way, praying that no one had esped her. Karbow would not want to leave her alive now.

:*VERONA!*: The word spun into her ear like a silver arrow.

The noisy heads fell silent around her instantly, and one mind she would have loved and known anywhere opened itself. "Hasso?" she whispered.

:*Alive! Alive! I knew you must be alive! Verona:*—urgent now—:*pay attention, dear one, come along as you have been doing, and carefully, ever so carefully, there is no one to stop you back there in the darkness and you will know our cabin, it is seven or eight away from where you are now. We are barred in here, Verona, and you must come open the door. The bombs are slacking off now, and if any of these grokkli that are left alive notice us we will be killed—but come CAREFULLY!*:

:*Verona?*: The mind was Skerow's now. :*Is that the young dems'l?*:

:*Yes, Goodmother, she is coming!*:

:*Come quickly, good one-strong-hearted child!*:

"Yes, yes, I will!" Not sure how to think these thoughts in silence, keeping her voice to a whisper when she wanted to scream, she kept crawling, even more fearfully now, because there was some hope. Bombs fell again, flinging dirt that bounced off the slope and buried her feet so that she had to kick them free. Skerow and Hasso covered her with their minds so that she did not hear Karbow's curses of pain and despair, nor those of the other terrified and wounded souls who wanted to get far away out of that place and give up lives of crime if they were only left to live.

A mind-whisper from Hasso. :*The Ix are gone.*:

No one noticed Verona as she crept round the hut

where the lives of Skerow and Hasso were pulsing, the only one as small as herself was the dead Bengtvadi—and the acolyte, who had finally crawled out of the badly-shared prison and been swept up in a rush for exits. There were not many faithful henchmen to tend Karbow. Most had streamed out to find safer valleys. The cries and their echoes were fading away.

The wooden bar was at shoulder height, and Verona dragged at it, remembering how she had pulled at the wheel-latch of the great stone door to give Hawksworth his dream of escape.

The door creaked open and she was enveloped in the arms of Skerow and Ksath. "Good child, you are safe!"

Safe as could be for the moment. Verona glanced back fearfully at the landscape of black shapes under gray starless dawn. The only other light came from a few dying embers from hearth fires or the lazy licking flames charring the beams of the ramshackle city.

"They are dead, run away, deserted," Skerow whispered. "Let us take that villainous old man"—the old herdsman was crouched whimpering in a corner—"and there is still one cart with a thumbokh tangled in the bushes over there—"

"Skerow dear . . ." Ksath murmured.

"Eki, Goodmother," Hasso said a bit sadly, "the Base Four Squad has finally found us—only seventeen hours late—you can even hear their engines now, and I think that no matter how much we weigh they will find a way to take us with them."

Skerow listened for a moment, sighed and swallowed her tears because she was only one day away from home by cart and thumbokh, and even that one day was too far away.

SIX * *Life Times*

Lyhhrt, Khagodi and Ix

The Ix appeared suddenly in the tri-V holocube during the WorldGov Assembly session while the assembled representatives were watching a presentation by the WorldTrade Organization on the export of fomb shingles to Pinaxer, and other matters Skerow had been wrestling with, that now must be attended to without her.

"—not to forfeit our contract," the sententious voice was saying, "we must be ready to ship three hundred and seventy thousand kogga of class one fomb, two hundred and—"

The trivvy went *zzt!* first, then to black-and-white sparkles and after that became a terrarium of black-grained fog with zips of white lightning going up and down as if it were a very ancient film. Three Ix rose up from the depths of this chaos and the sparks and black spatters seemed to be part of the pheromone atmosphere that always went with them.

The Chairman, who had good control of herself and the Assembly, had a bellyful of air ready and cracklingly addressed the block of swirling darkness. "Explain this!" She spoke in *lingua*, not the Old Vineland language in which affairs were conducted at WorldGov assemblies.

"We are declaring war on this world Khagodis!" The three seemed to speak at once, but one voice emerged.

"That is preposterous," the Chairman said quietly. "You have never declared yourselves or spoken to us in any way until now. You are an entity unknown to us. Who are you?"

"You know we are the world Iyax! You know that you have been harboring those Lyhhrt who have deserted and betrayed us in our greatest need! Murdering us!"

The Khagodi stared at these images, and in unison removed their impervious helmets.

:*These murderers of Evarny! What does this mean!*:
:*irrational*:
:*stopping the trials for*:
:*nothing, no help—*:

"You have no rights on this world," the assembly leader said aloud.

:*No no, your honorable! not to argue*:
:*discuss*:
:*or expostulate with the irrational!*:

"What do you want?" the Assembly Speaker said plainly and cleanly.

Flickering and bespattered with streaks of light the three Ix boomed, "We want the Lyhhrt! Their ship, their bodies and their goods! If we do not have them we will have yours!"

"The Lyhhrt ambassadors have been called home," the Speaker said quickly. "They are not ours to give or keep." She touched a button on her lectern and a messenger was on his way to call Tharma.

"They are with you. We do not want them to go to their home but to come to ours on our ship *Ygszu.* You have one day."

"You are not the world Iyax but a ship's crew." Khagodi knew well enough that the Ix ship had been in orbit just beyond the mega-siguu limit. But Khagodis, the home of that heavy hard-walking people, had never been a spacefaring world. Their ships were designed by Lyhhrt and manned by Kylkladi. They had no forces but tactical ones, and no way of driving off the Ix ship except by calling for help from other worlds, and even if they were willing to do this had no time for it. "You do not have rights within this orbit or permission to land in any country on this world. Your threats are empty." She raised a hand to signal transmission shutdown.

"Wait!" Two of the Ix faded away with all of the sparks to leave one Ix of cracklingly black chitin against a white background. "Look!"

The Ix was replaced by a landscape, but the voice went on. "Some of you do not know that region, but your maps call it Smuggler's Gap. Your friends the Lyhhrt chose to hide your Chief Justice Skerow and the alien called the Little Miss in that place. Your Law's two dearest treasures, the Judge and the evidence."

There were a few who recognized the sheer cliff whose rocky dome had been half cut away by the sea, but even they had not known of the iron doors set in the rugged wall. Then the view moved slightly aside and the bombs fell. Rock splinters sheared off and flew everywhere. Every one of the Khagodi felt the throbbing veins in the heads of all the others. They could not speak.

Then the dinghy was landing and unloading its forces, twenty-five Ix armed with the guns that the Lyhhrt had also designed. "You will find little trace of them left there. Perhaps you will recognize us now," the Ix said. "You will give us the Lyhhrt and their ship or there will be more bombs, and more and more."

The Leader of the Assembly swallowed hard and cried out, "No! Never would we deliver our friends and allies to their enemies! For shame! No two-hearted citizen of this world would allow this!" Frightened as they were, for this rare moment the assembly had become single-minded.

The Ix, never having reckoned with the pride of Khagodi in their own morality, seemed taken aback, but not much or for long. "That is all you have to say? We warn you!"

"Absolutely!"

"You have made your terrible choice, and so be it! Now—"

"You need not do any more violence to this world." In the holocube, blocking the view of the devastation, the gold Lyhhrt's head rose up as it had risen before Ned Gattes's eyes in the Great Equatorial River. "I/we will deliver our bodies and our ship and goods to that ship *Ygszu* within one half day of this hour."

"We cannot let you do such a thing!" the Assembly Leader said desperately.

But the Ix's voice overrode her. "You will serve us for as long as we demand? Say that you will!"

"We swear that we will be at your disposal."

The three Ix reappeared in the tank for one spinning

moment before it went smoky black and the Khagodi were
left to decide whether they wanted to go on discussing shingles.

Passion

"Skerow. . . ." Gold Lyhhrt spoke aloud. "That child." He
wanted to say no more, but he said it. "There was no mistake possible that we failed to make. The more we worked
to restore, the more we destroyed."

:*As I have pointed out, we ought to have fissioned,*:
Bronze Lyhhrt said.

:*It was already too late for that. The Ix would surely
like to breed us.*:

They had been watching the Ix transmission on their
own tri-V, as had everyone else on the world who owned
one. They had been alerted by Tharma first, and afterward
they had refused her pleas to reconsider their decision, to
allow armed guards inside their offices, or to open their
doors to anyone, though there was a troop of peacemen
stationed outside around the building.

Ned had earlier been sent to escort Palma to the Arcade;
there was nowhere else on the world where she could find
work, and the Lyhhrt did not want to leave her to the mercy
of the Endless Valley Holding Station. The monkeys were
in the quarters the Khagodi had provided for them, and no
one else was with the Lyhhrt now but Spartakos, who was
standing in a corner with his afferents turned down. A servant, not a slave, Spartakos would not be one of the gifts
brought to the Ix.

Gold and Bronze looked at each other across the great distance they had drifted.

Bronze said, *:We have more than enough hormone.:*

:Let us see what we can do, then,: Gold said. He shut off the frantic signals coming from the Assembly as well as Tharma's calls, leaving a signal open to the Ix to assure them of Lyhhrt presence; then adjusted dials and pressed buttons on the worktable.

The wall plates that the Lyhhrt had built into the apartment now stripped and stacked themselves, the shelves and cabinets elongated and clustered themselves, and the racks of vials and jars holding nutrients and hormones moved out of the cupboards to the worktable with its banked instruments.

Gold and Bronze stepped forward so that their workshells faced each other across its surface. Bronze took two gold baskets from a drawer in the worktable and set them down. Both Lyhhrt pressed studs in their necks to open the abdomens of their workshells and reached in to bring out the glastex globes holding their bodies, and the uninhabited shells, acting as robots, set them into the baskets. Holding a tiny remote in one pseudopod, Bronze directed his workshell to unplug both globes and pour himself and his nutrient into the one with Gold.

The Lyhhrt, floating together as creatures in the same sea, activated their light receptors and contemplated each other. They touched pseudopods tentatively, as if to confirm that they were really together in the same space. For they had after all developed minds of their own, as Lyhhrt on their home world never did, and this unhealthy independence was what made their work offworld so dangerous, and sometimes made Lyhhrt dangerous too.

They touched pseudopods again, and once more. They

moved around each other in contact and after one revolution brought their undersides facing, then unscrolled as if two cowry shells had been able to open, join inner surfaces and seal their edges. They centered themselves for a moment and then the flower-shaped genitals in their centers opened petals and clasped like two hands with interlaced fingers.

Their union was a white-hot exquisite half-agony of rapture. It lasted a long slow moment, a life's experience.

Bronze's robot workshell filled their common globe with liquid nutrient and they separated slowly and floated in this for one more moment of rest/in/prayer. Then the bronze hands poured one Lyhhrt into the unoccupied globe, sealed it and placed it in the gold workshell; it would not have mattered which shell. Neither Lyhhrt was the same entity now.

The Lyhhrt in gold went about stacking shelf and wall units on wheeled platforms and sending them into the apartment's private elevator. The multiarmed brass workshell came from its repair closet to accompany the materials to the roof hangar and build them into the flier. The roof activity was hypnoformed to invisibility and the Khagodi standing guard duty there did not wonder why there was an area they could not patrol.

An hour passed in which the Lyhhrt did not communicate. The one in the globe rested there, and at the end of the hour a capsule emerged from its genital opening. The Lyhhrt received this into three pseudopods and held it against his body while his mate in gold prepared a quarter-sized globe with nutrients and hormones.

For the next hour neither of the Lyhhrt moved, the one standing in the gold shell, the other floating in the globe holding the capsule to his body. When this hour had passed, the Lyhhrt in gold removed the capsule in an iridium-plated dipper and decanted it gently into the small globe. The bronze robot placed the Lyhhrt's gobe inside its body and the two parents spent a few moments contemplating the embryo; it had extruded cilia with which it was navigating its surroundings not out of curiosity but to stimulate its fissioning cells and neural ganglions.

The Lyhhrt in bronze sealed this small globe into what Ned Gattes might think of as a gold Easter egg and tapped one more button on the worktable. Spartakos stepped forward to face him in three strides and stood, unawakened.

The Lyhhrt touched parts of the robot's gleaming body and an opening appeared in his upper right torso just below where Ned Gattes would have had a nipple. The Lyhhrt went on touching the body until its waist thickened slightly to make room and the opening enlarged to his satisfaction. He picked up the gold egg and set it in where it fitted sweetly, nested among the platinum, iridium, and vanadium steel of Spartakos's workings.

A few more touches, and the opening closed like an iris without a seam or dimple. The Lyhhrt said, "Wake up, Spartakos."

"Here I am, Makers," Spartakos said in his warm hearty voice.

"Spartakos, remove from your memory all references to: Zamos, Goldyne, Interworld Trade Consortium, Interworld Court, Star*Systems, brothel, escort service . . ." A long list.

When it was finished, Spartakos said, "That's done, Makers. What now?"

"We are leaving, but we cannot take you with us."

"Can I never work for you again?"

"You will work for others of us. You will keep yourself

safe and stay with Ned Gattes for now. He is enough of a coward not to lead you into danger." The Lyhhrt had not meant to say this aloud, and his companion made a startled movement.

Spartakos said unreproachfully, "If my friend Ned Gattes was such a coward I would not have chosen him for a friend, and he would not have come here to certain danger. He tried his best to save one of your people when we were in the Labyrinth on Shen Four. You did not take all of those memories from me."

"No, we did not," the Lyhhrt said. "And yes, he is our best, our only choice, brave or coward. Now go and bring us the monkeys, Spartakos. We must erase their memories too—some of them. Go through the galleries upstairs. No one will notice you."

This took one more hour, and there were three more hours before the Lyhhrt ship would be cleared for flight.

:*Second last thing,*: the Lyhhrt in bronze said, and reached for the flagon of fissioning hormone. :*It is a chance.*:

Death in Orbit

No one noticed the Lyhhrt flier move off the roof in the early evening. It passed with a whirling of leaves, a ripple in the deepening blue of the sky just clear of the late-afternoon rains. One hour later, at the Vineland Spaceport in Lightning Tree City, it nested into its shuttle, and the shuttle whispered into space, out toward orbit and into the ship that rode there, the Lyhhrt body in which they had come. Gold and Bronze were parts of one mind now.

The orbiting ships they joined were all friendly or neutral—the Ix ship hove to well beyond the zone limit—and for a brief while the Lyhhrt in their licensed path traveled in parallel with the *Zarandu* and the *Aleksandr Nevskii.* Both were still unloading and clearing to take on new passengers who had been waiting for years. If they had looked the Lyhhrt could have seen those ships as moving lights in the black sky. They did not look or communicate.

At its exit node the Lyhhrt ship skimmed off the zone at a tangent toward the orbit where the Ixi vessel lay. The Lyhhrt watched it rising in the well of the viewer, its shape a sphere of wrought-iron darkness glowing dully in the light of Khagodis's sun. With its spiked armaments and its thorny tangle of shuttle bays it seemed to the Lyhhrt like the universe as created by the Anti-Force of their theology, the Great Demon.

They knew it by the millimeter: Lyhhrt had designed and created it to Ix specifications, and the Ix had planned to make it the first of thousands that would swarm the depths of space. By itself it was still terrifying, even to its makers.

The hours of freedom slid like oil, but the Lyhhrt waited in a wide orbit until the last of the Ix's warships and shuttlecraft had berthed. Then their narrow coppery-dark ship moved in slowly, and in the viewing well the Lyhhrt saw bay doors opening in the spherical ship like the small eyes of a great beast. The planet Khagodis moved into the way of the sun and the swing of the Lyhhrt ship brought its nightside briefly into the viewing well, the width of the desert lands flaring with volcanoes like tiny red blossoms, and then with the next turn everything became dark.

Like a seed stalk, the outer surface of the Lyhhrt ship sheared away in eight parts and drifted around the circumference of the great metallic sphere while the Lyhhrt's now thinner main body moved toward the bay doors. The eight parts, four plastial robots controlled by four newly fissioned Lyhhrt in casings of the same shape, were as dark and unreflective as the Ixi ship. Their small jet streams evaporated at once and they nested among the frameworks of the *Ygszu*'s shuttle berths, opaque to antennas and spy-eyes, and set to work.

The bay doors gaped, the Lyhhrt slipped into their darkness and the steel plates boomed behind them. Hours belonged to the Ix now. Let them think so until the work was done.

The Lyhhrt did not try to see what was happening while the conveyor belt carried their ship into the reception chamber. It went lumberingly; the Ix were used to deeper gravity than Khagodi or Lyhhrt. When it stopped the ship unfolded itself and before the Lyhhrt could move there were Ix swarming over them.

"Take them! Hold them! Don't let them move!"

The Lyhhrt knew all of the Ixi languages well enough after one hundred and twenty-nine years. They also knew all of the pheromones; though they were not affected by them their instruments had always sensed them; surrounded by Ix the Lyhhrt recognized the smells of greed and fear. Like most other peoples the Ix had always felt a little fear in the presence of Lyhhrt; it had only made the Ix more brutal.

There were nine of the Ix around the Lyhhrt ship in the reception chamber. This was a structure shaped like the interior of a hive or anthill with groined arches leading to other chambers. The joints of the arches held flame-shaped lamps with trembling filaments that cast a greenish white light. The room was lined and floored with hexagons of marbled ceramyx, and the steps of the Ix resounded in it. The Lyhhrt felt the vibrations of the gravitors beneath the floor and behind the walls. All of the Ix had impervious shields.

One of them cried, "Is this all of your ship and goods? You have not brought everything as you swore you would!"

"Everything of ours is with you."

(Softly rising and falling by their jet streams, the Lyhhrt fission brothers and their robots out in space began to garland the Ix ship with links of explosive cable.)

"That robot, for instance?"

"The robot is registered as a World Citizen by Galactic Federation. If you were to tamper with it, it would self-destruct," the Lyhhrt in gold said. This was true; the Lyhhrt had made sure of it. "We'll build you twenty if you want them."

The Ix backed away from the Lyhhrt and stood looking. "This little ship cannot be all you have!"

"What are you arguing for?" another Ix cried. "We have their ship and its instruments and their robotic work casings, and if we cannot use them we have their bodies."

"They are lying." One of the Ix had not spoken or moved up greedily with the others, and now stepped forward. "I sense there are many things your Lyhhrt have not told you."

The Lyhhrt examined this one through a flash aperture of the mind and realized why it was standing apart. It was not an Ix at all, but a Lyhhrt in a workshell that resembled the Ix. An Ix acolyte like those Solthree women.

:*Renegade!*: the Lyhhrt in gold said.

:*You may call it that.*: No more access to that mind.

The Ix workshell was a marvel of metal and polymer

with its bristles and glaring eyes. Its metal girdle was set
with precious jewels, not cheap ones, and the black surface
was embedded with slivers of diamond, sapphire and ruby.
Like any other Lyhhrt, the acolyte could not help orna-
menting himself even though it meant nothing to the Ix; he
knew that.

"One thing they have not told you is that this other
Lyhhrt in bronze is less than half-grown! It is a child, I
know it!"

"What do you mean?"

"These are not all of the Lyhhrt! They have fissioned!"

(With gold fingers terminating in screwdrivers the
young Lyhhrt lifted the plates of the hull away and set in
the explosives.)

"Is this what comes of trusting Lyhhrt? WHERE ARE
THEY!"

"Let's take them both apart, and their ship too!"

Hemmed in by Ix on all sides, the Lyhhrt in gold faced
the Lyhhrt in Ix clothing. Lyhhrt cut off from their people
became strange, and every Lyhhrt who served Galactic Federation understood how it happened.

Gold Lyhhrt knew that the acolyte would be a fiercer
enemy than any Ix but was still a being halfway between,
a link.

"Cannot we talk, as people of the same kind?"

"Where are those others of you!" The Ix thumped at
them with their fists and shook guns at them. The acolyte
said nothing.

"Is there nothing else for you to say to us than this?
We have kept our part of the bargain!" the Lyhhrt cried.

(One more moment, now.)

The acolyte spoke, finally, in contempt. "Here's a
Lyhhrt pleading. A frightened one."

"We swore to be at your disposal, and here we are! Don't destroy us, let us work for you the way we do for others in the Galaxy! We are willing to build what you want, do as you wish, devote ourselves to you—only let us not be slaves! Let us do this for you!" The Ix stood as if deaf and blind.

"Take them both apart," the Lyhhrt-as-Ix said.

:No!: For one savage moment Lyhhrt and acolyte forced at each other's minds, but they were equals.

(*:Finished,:* said the four young Lyhhrt, setting the last switch.)

The Lyhhrt in gold sensed and saw as intensely as anything he had seen and known in his life and that of his ancestors: the eight Ix, the acolyte, the copper-hulled ship, the tiles lining the reception chamber, the throbbing of the gravitors—

One of the Ix said finally, "These Lyhhrt are tricksters as well as murderers, and none of them are going to do us any good. I say destroy them and let's get on with what we were doing down there, teach those Khagodi a real lesson."

"Men, women, children, embryos and eggs," the Lyhhrt whispered, truly pleading. "Let us, let us work for you!"

"You are mad." The Ix raised her gun.

"Finished," the Lyhhrt said.

Two Khagodi astronomers in the observatory on Five Winds Mesa saw the flare of implosion, a lantern being lit in the dark southern sky, lasting a moment, burning out.

SEVEN *

The Depth

Though siesta time had run out an hour earlier, the Old City of Burning Mountain was deserted. As he sweated his way across the burning white stones of the market Ned Gattes did not know that Skerow and Verona had fallen into the hands of Karbow Blood-Eye, or that Bullivant was mourning his loss and wrestling with facts he had not really wanted to learn. Ned was sorry he had learned that Brandsma was responsible for his badly repaired jaw. He had no way to get even.

Palma Ruiz was keeping well to his northeast, and there was no one else to fight with. The souvenir stands were bagged and chained, and the great stone mill wheel was still.

Ned paused at the lip of the Arcade, unwilling to start descending the filthy steps. "You sure you want to go down here?"

"Why not? It's where I always worked before I hired

on with Brandsma. What do you need to come along for? This is my ground."

"I'm being paid for it." Lyhhrt would know whether he'd obeyed orders.

"Then just keep off me! I'll never clip a swag with you on my tail!" She flicked down the steps like a fox going to earth, with a last glitter of sun on her splint before darkness took her.

Ned followed reluctantly. The steps were Khagodi-sized and took three paces each. On the broad side of the spiral they were wide enough for a Kylkladi woman with ruffled and dirt-edged feathers to make a bed on; likely she had been fighting or flame-tossing on some bally platform all night before her media customers left to cover the Great Excavation. She had a half-burned dopestick screwed into one nostril, but it had gone out after she fell asleep.

Further down was a curled-up Bengtvadi with the look of a crewman who had spent all his pay and would crawl away soon to board his shuttle with a burning headache. He smelled of jhat and his breath bubbled in the hot thick air. The peacemen did not bother to sweep the sleepers away; most of their force had been called in for emergency crowd control during the trials and now had gone back to more boring duties. The jittering lights and fancy signs had been turned off, and the bare glaring filaments left to light the place stripped it of its orgiastic excitement and left it merely dull and shabby.

Ned half ran to keep up with Palma, stumbling on the rough cobbles. He was tired of her and of hanging around doing useless things in this sweaty city and alien world. The tunnel was so empty now that footfalls and voices rang against the tile walls. More than half the bally platforms were unoccupied. A couple of performers were swallowing

flames and juggling glass bubbles for three or four customers who were sparing of their coins. Out of the corner of
his eye Ned saw the Varvani and the O'e woman, crouched
together not quite performing some act that no one was
interested in watching. He went quicker to avoid their seeing him, because he had no help for them. One of the loud-
speakers crackled and began to spit the music of some other
world, adding to the echoes. In the arenas two awkward
Khagodi were making a show of whacking at each other
with their spiked tails; the crystal gates of the brothels were
locked shut and the empty gaming rooms smelled only of
last night's dope.

Suddenly Palma turned down a narrow arching hallway
faced with ancient stones and raised her fist at a battered
wooden door.

Ned ran following. "Wait!"

"Too late for anything you want, pommy!"

Her gesture made him think she still might have a knife
somewhere on her, and he stood back with his empty hands
out and wide. "What I want's for you to stay away from
Brandsma, for God's sake, that's all! Go someplace where
nobody knows you and if somebody does, run like hell."

She looked at him, calm and cold as when he'd first seen
her. "I've been told that before, and you can shut up, too!"
She drummed the door with the butt of her fist. "Hey, let
me in, it's Palma!" The door opened and she was gone with
a slam.

Ned wandered back out into the echoes, and uneasiness
dropped on him like a wet sack. He had been shucked off,
and the Lyhhrt had no more for him to do than go off on
fools' errands. *What've I done? Shifted the monkeys from
one cage to another. Took Spartakos away from people who
needed him more than the Lyhhrt did.*

He hung around for a few moments near the arenas where the Khagodi fighters had given up and gone home, and a Kylkladi handler was raking the sand; bought a beer at a stand near the skambi rooms, took a salt pill with it and socketed in a fresh oxycap. He noticed a flickering and found his attention picked at by a newsstrip streaming above a doorway.

Among the betting results in Khagodi cuneiform and symbo*lingua* there was a flash with a familiar name: *Skerow*. Ned stared. WORLD COURT JUDGE SKEROW AND ALIEN CHILD MISSING AFTER IX ATTACK˙.........˙LYHHRT EMBASSY OFFICIALS SACRIFICE SELVES TO IX IN BID TO STOP FURTHER DESTRUCTION . . .

Sweat ran down his sides. Skerow, the Lyhhrt, and that frightened little girl—all gone?

And what about Spartakos and the monkeys? And the secrets the Lyhhrt had stored in them . . . were they gone with the Lyhhrt, too? *Everything they tried to do, all I tried to do—wiped out?*

And where are you, Ned Gattes? Trapped here without any GalFed contact. *Christ, how am I going to get home?* He took a last gulp and tossed the empty squeezer in a cycler bin, his mind racing to no purpose. He wanted to be out of there, turned back and headed for the side cone. Getting that feeling again, of being a center of attention. That gray-feathered Kylklad sweeping up between the games machines was probably not one of the conspirators who had killed the Ix last night—only last night! The old Khagodi pushing a wagon filled with bottles was not the pearl-sprayed old man who had paused to gape at the dancing women on their bally platform.

Ned ducked into an alcove to catch his breath and find out if anyone actually was following him. A tall woman

passed by, walking quickly, and he dared to put his head
out and stare after her. Woman with reddish hair, white skin
that goes with redheads, where from? Very few Earthers
were left in Burning Mountain after the media cleared out.
He connected Red-hair with a different red, crimson, a
woman wrapped in something red. Velvet. Coming in
through the gate along with Pearlskin and Grayfeathers.
Streaming out of that room where the Ix had been killed,
face a white half-moon, mouth open.

She was one of them. The Lyhhrt would want to know
about—no, there were no Lyhhrt, no one to report to now
but Tharma, his only connection on this world and the only
one who could give him any help. He followed the woman,
thinking he ought to be running in the opposite direction.

The red-haired woman turned abruptly down the narrow hallway where Ned had left Palma, and Ned backed
against the tunnel wall to keep track of her, squatting
among rusty pipes and antique generators. He wondered if
she had been following Palma, or had come looking for her
because she couldn't find Brandsma.

Both women came out of the hallway quickly, and
turned toward the lateral cone exit, Red-hair with her hand
on Palma's shoulder, Palma animated, showing the splint
and making a face, Red-hair nodding gravely. Ned followed
cautiously, keeping to the shadows of the rough walls. He
thought the woman hadn't seen him, couldn't be esping
him, there was nothing in the set of her shoulders, her relaxed self-confidence, to show she was aware of anyone but
Palma Ruiz. No one passed them except one old Khagodi
weighed down by a heavy toolbox, and all were walking
soundlessly on thick xyrene soles; the Arcade's noises ech-
oed from far away. Ned had no weapon of any kind, not
even those old cracked knucks.

The tunnel was very narrow now, very near the stairs going down through the side cone. "—Shorter this way." Red-hair's murmur was carried by the air current rising from below, and the two women scrambled along over the last rough pavements and began to go down the stairs, three, four, five steps, quickly now; no one else but Ned was near them.

Everything ran in quicktime then: at the same moment that the red-haired woman gripped Palma's arm hard with one hand, and pulled the little gun from her belt with the other, Ned ran forward, down three steps, and she caught his movement from the corner of her eye.

Ned shouted, "Get down! Get down!" Palma twisted, gaping while Red-hair coolly shot her through the breast-bone and swung the gun aiming at Ned in one movement. He saw it clearly: a tiny Zepp Dart that killed in ten horrible seconds.

Red-hair jerked back from Ned's chopping fist, her fingers flicked the gun's lock and tightened on the stud. Palma, in her last convulsive moment, grabbed at her leg. The gun hand jerked away, the stud clicked—a sliver of sound went *tzung!* past Ned's ear—and Red-hair, pulled off balance, fell back against the railing on her shoulder and the gun flew out of her hand and skittered down the steps. She kicked Palma away with one swing of her boot, and Ned helplessly watched Palma's body thrashing down the stairs while Red-hair followed scrambling for her gun.

Quicktime ended when her fingers touched it. Ned climbed up and ran.

Back through the twisted gut of the tunnel, pounding on cobbled floors past rings, dealers, brothels, ballies, and up the stairs over snorting bodies, breath panting thickly— not that she was following, she'd have gone out through the side cone if she wasn't stupid and he didn't think she was. But she'd seen him now, and she'd know everybody connected with Zamos.

"Heyo, mister!"

Spartakos's friends, the O'e and the Varvani, were leaning against a bagged-up market stand in the hot late-afternoon sun, waiting for him. He grunted. Someone had been watching.

The Varvani raised a fist and Ned ducked. "I am not going to hurt you," the Varvani said, "you gave me money, but I want to know where that iron one is who works with us! Without him all we can do is fuck and anybody can do that! First you come and then he goes and now we have no money."

He looked so mournful with the O'e woman wrapped around him like an ivy that Ned swallowed down on all his other thoughts and feelings. "I didn't take him away from you! The people who made him are gone and I don't know what they did with him."

"We want to come with you and find out!"

"To see the police?"

"Yes!"

The Varvani was big and hefty. Ned thought that having him for an ally instead of an enemy was not a bad idea—not that he'd be much help against Red-hair and her zap. He sighed. "Let's get going then, I've had enough of hanging around here."

The Lyhhrt had taken all of their marvels with them, and the apartment had been left with its bare walls and two dusty sunken sleeping basins. There was no furniture now except for a lectern that Tharma had brought in for her casebooks, and her battery lamp produced the only light to break the shadows of evening. She was muttering into the audio and looking weary.

"Ned Gattes, is it?" She raised a hand to her eyes. "I can't see much in this damned dull light, but it's cooler here than the broom closet I've been working in."

She pulled out the comm's ear-button and scratched her gill-slit. "Come in, Ned Gattes." She looked at him thoughtfully, but before she could say anything the comm chimed and she replaced the button in her gill-slit. She listened a moment and swallowed hard at air. "Good! Good! That damned old villain belongs in a cage!" Then, "Unharmed?" A long moment. "As well as can be . . . heh! I understand!" She signed off and turned back to Ned. "Judge Skerow and the girl have been found. Somewhat battered but safe. A great relief."

Ned took a long breath. "Oh. That's good." *I've been here these damned, what? six days? Haven't done anything that works—who'll pay my way back?* But . . . "I'm glad of that, at least."

Tharma gave him her rather too careful attention again. Of course she would be deeply into his mind. Ned sighed, and thought of twenty-eight different things he could have done to save Palma.

"No, I don't believe you could," Tharma said.

"I wanted to, I tried," Ned said, swallowing

"You'd better tell me all of it."

"I thought you'd have esped me enough to know it."

"Rummaging around in anyone's mind is no pleasure, Gattes, and I would rather not do it unless it is necessary."

Ned told her all he could remember and more than he wanted to.

"And you are sure you had seen her before, this woman?"

"Twice, coming in through the Old City gate with Brandsma and Palma, and afterwards out of that room with the dead Ix."

"You say red hair?" Tharma touched the red logo on the comm with her pearl nail.

"No, it's—" Ned ran a hand through his own hair, of a color no one had been able to find a better name for than dirty blond. "Um, like orange, no, you don't know oranges either. Rust."

"Both times when you saw her her hair was covered by a red garment, in real red."

"She had a bony face! Cheekbones, jaw, nose!" Forced to look up at her massive head, Ned felt like a schoolboy.

"I'm no enemy of yours, Ned Gattes. I want only to find out properly." Tharma pushed her open casebook toward Ned. She had called up an old and crackly holo portrait of an auburn-haired woman with steely eyes and full brightly reddened lips. "This is seven or eight years old, but there are not that many rust-haired aliens in this district." She tapped keys to rectify the flesh tones and rotated the holo to show the lines of brow and cheekbone.

"That's her," Ned said.

"Yes. We knew her very well. A rare natural Impervious. No one here can esp her. Lyhhrt might, but there are none. Her name is Anna Ellesmere and she has a hearty taste for more than death. Once she drove a red-hot iron bar into an old man's eye."

Ned gulped. "She was ready enough to kill me."

"We have been looking for her in connection with the Ix in the Arcade." Tharma closed her casebook and the holo whisked away. "A pity." *That you could not rid us of her.*

"Why would she want to kill Palma?"

"She is a specialist in cleanup operations. By now everyone knows that the Lyhhrt are dead and the Ix are gone; Palma must have told her that we have Brandsma and whatever operation that was planned here has collapsed. She has cleaned up Palma and I suppose we must put an extra watch on Brandsma, that wretch." Tharma was silent for a moment.

"They're really gone, the Lyhhrt?"

"Yes, they have blown themselves up in the Ix ship, we all of us down here felt it when ... and their evidence is gone. Sainted Skathe alone knows when the trials will reconvene. Palma.... Not even the Lyhhrt could help her, and none of their good deeds seems written down to survive."

"Yeh, and Lady Red-hair will be coming after me now!"

"Not if we find her first—and at any rate you were not intending to stay long on this world, were you, Ned Gattes?"

"I guess not." *Damned if I know how I'm gonna get off it, that's all.*

"You did everything the Lyhhrt asked, and helped save that child as well. We don't have the means to reward you or protect you as well as you deserve, but you have the friends who came with you, and—Spartakos!"

"Yes, Officer Tharma, here I am!" Spartakos stepped gleaming out of the dark corner behind her.

"Spartakos!" Ned cried. "I thought you'd gone with the—"

"No, my friend Ned." Spartakos said in his wonderful warm voice. "My Makers have told me I must stay with you!"

"Me?"

Tharma tapped the lectern with her nails. "This, eh'm, Spartakos—you do know him?"

"Yeh—" Ned struggled to talk sense. "Of course. I've known him for years. He saved my life more than once."

"Then I suppose I can call him a person, because he seems to have World Citizen documentation—Spartakos claims that the Lyhhrt, his makers, have instructed him to stay with you and go wherever you choose to go."

Ned swallowed.

"This is not right with you?"

"I didn't know about choices. But if he said it they did it."

"And will you take responsibility for him?"

"If it means protecting *him* I'm not so sure, but he can come along with me if that's what he was told, and if I can figure out where I'm going."

"And also those creatures, the monkeys."

"Monkeys!" Ned yelled.

Spartakos stepped forward quickly. "I have money for us, good friend Ned, and I have passports."

Tharma stepped back to let Ned splutter his way out of this one if he could. Ned Gattes plus Spartakos plus monkeys? And with their Arcade friends a wonderful variety of beings. Neither she nor they could do anything more to destroy Zamos, except that she was left to chop off the last of that serpent's heads on this world.

She switched off her lamp and with a swag of her heavy tail shooed them all out of the dark apartment, then went off to tell Bullivant that his daughter was safe. Yes. The world had been rescued from the Ix, and with their one great ship destroyed they would not visit again for some while; Bullivant's soul had been restored to him, and so his child would be.

Sergeant Ned

Ned and Co. stood outside on the street in the late sunlight, among the vendors selling jukaru in clay bottles and coin machines full of salt pills and antihistamine patches. The monkeys were climbing all over Ned and Spartakos to keep their feet from the burning pavement.

«*Where! Where are we going!*» Aark buzzed.

"We are going home," Spartakos said.

«*Where is that?*» Aark slapped at Spartakos's thighs but the robot did not seem to notice.

"I don't know. Where is home, Ned?"

Ned's hair stood on end. He stared at Spartakos and swallowed. "On Fthel Four, I guess. Where I live."

The paddle-wheel barge gently slapped its way down the Great Equatorial River, perhaps the same barge Ned had come up in, or the same as made no difference. Fly-buses were faster, but Ned was nervous about anything that flew in Khagodi airspace. The late evening sky was deep even at the horizon in the thin air, and the two white moons left rippling trails on the water.

There were no tumbling schoolchildren on this journey and few people on the barge now. Aark had led the macaques searching every cranny of the old wooden boat and found nothing, but Red-hair could have been black-haired, bald, brown-eyed, feathered, could have had sense enough to take the fly-bus, or delegated her task to some other killer. No one was stalking here, and no one had noticed the nine monkeys moving in the shadows, but Ned still felt exposed; he did not have the Lyhhrt's ability to turn the eyes of others away from themselves.

Spartakos had done something to his surface that made it dull, but he was still very visible. The Lyhhrt had relieved the macaques of half the telemetry on their heads and the crowns had dwindled to coronets, but to Ned they were the same exobi animals who spoke with the help of machines, and still looked like bearers of secret records. Like Spartakos. The O'e and her Varvani protector, crouching a little away from the others and clinging together out of a common fear that Ned shared, were two more exotic species. They had names now: he was Embi, his woman Yeya.

"My Makers' records have been removed from us," Spartakos said suddenly.

"Yeh," Ned said, "and will Zamos's people know that? Will they care?" He could not shake a feeling that Spartakos had not only changed himself but had also been changed somehow. "Spartakos, why did the Lyhhrt tell you to stay with me?"

"They said that I would be safer with you, Ned-Gattes."

"Eh, and I thought you were supposed to be my protection! Safer from what?"

"From being tampered with. My Makers said: YOU WILL KEEP YOURSELF SAFE AND STAY WITH NED GATTES FOR NOW. Of course if I am tampered with I will not be safe and I will self-destruct."

Ned recoiled slightly. "I hope you don't do it around me! Did your makers plant a bomb inside you?"

"Of course not, Ned. They would never do an action that was harmful to others." *Like blowing up the Ixi ship, Spartakos?* "No, I would simply disintegrate." He went on, "I need not self-destruct if I don't wish to, but I have the ability."

Number one, keep yourself safe. Number two, stay with Ned Gattes for now . . . yeh, and number three?

Ned watched the macaques crawling all over Spartakos, trying to groom his metal surface without success while he sat like Buddha with his legs folded and his hands on his knees. Buddha. There was definitely something different about Spartakos, not in speech or manner but in body, something that moved away from the superhuman ideal. Thicker. He could not stop himself from trying to pinpoint it, or explain it. It not only suggested that there were still secrets, but declared that there were. Whatever they were, he could only be thankful that they did not include a bomb.

No use thinking about it. Ned's mind had blanked at the thought of taking a Varvani, an O'e, a robot and nine monkeys home to Zella. But it was Spartakos to whom the Lyhhrt had given the orders along with the cashbook and the passports. The arrangements for shifting all those species offworld had taken ten more long hot days in Equatorial Khagodis.

Ned knew he was an NCO by nature, not a general; somehow fate had promoted him to lead that bunch into safety. *But not to draw down the fire on Zella and the children.* He couldn't go home, not yet.

He looked out toward the banks of the river where a great fire had been built on a stone piling; lines of Khagodi were marching around it and its flames were reflected in the rippling waves. The smoke was fragrant with spices, and he thought of burning ghats and pyres. The Lyhhrt and one hundred and twenty-nine years of their records had died in their own kind of pyre, and nothing was left of them but a robot, nine monkeys and a wad of money. Thank God for the money. Where to find safety with it?

Two days later aboard the same *Zarandu* he had arrived on six days earlier, he dropped into the long cold sleep combing his mind for safe places in the cities and valleys of his world.

Fthel IV: *Scudder's Inn*

First thing when he woke he thought of Manador. No, first thing he thought he was home in bed with Zella, *so goood, Zel!* Then he woke up to Citizen Spartakos, Aark, Tcha, Ki-Ki, Skee, and the rest of the macaques, and the Varvani/O'e couple. There was rehydrating and after that there would be exercise. He lay in the cage/coffin/bed with the IV flooding him and thought: *Manador will find me one of those "safe" places she keeps for pugs who get off on the wrong side.*

Eh, maybe there's somebody just waiting for me to make that call on some line that can be tapped . . . no, I've got to do all of this myself. No calls for help. *Can't even call Zella . . . Christ, Zel, how'm I getting out of this?*

When the mech disengaged him and he stood up to feel the familiar dizziness and tingling in his limbs, the escape line buzzed at the moment he was about to pull its button from his ear. The mech supported him while he listened.

GATTES EDMUND OUT OF BURNING MOUNTAIN IN-TERWORLD DISTRICT KHAGODIS, a metallic voice said.

Ned swallowed. "Here."

WILL YOU COME SOONEST TO TIER SEVENTY-THREE
PLATFORM FOUR EIGHT-FIVE AND IDENTIFY PASSENGER
YOUR DISTRICT.

"What—" But the line was dead.

What passenger? Ramps, lifts and streamways took him
on rubbery legs to Tier 73 and a railed platform where a
Bengtvadi and two mechs were waiting for him. So was
Spartakos. The landing was surrounded by vast banks of
drawers that rose spiraling to cathedral heights.

The Bengtvadi said, "You are one of two Solthrees who
embarked from Burning Mountain. The other, we regret,
has died en route."

Solthree. Relief for Ned: not one of his company anyway.

The Bengtvadi touched a keypad on his list, a drawer
opened and slid out. "Her DNA was not compatible with
that of the person listed in her berth on the manifest. This—
eh, being," indicating Spartakos, "has a name for the person
here but cannot give a background. Can you?"

Her hair was black and chopped short now, her lips
pale. Ned stared at the white pinched face, its jaw and
cheekbones, and sharp nose. "What did she die of?"

"Most likely from having a DNA structure not listed
in our manifest. We fit environment to individual with extreme care, and have never lost more than one in a hundred
thousand passengers. There are no signs either of homicide
or of malfunction in her capsule. You do know her?"

"Her name was Anna Ellesmere. She was wanted in a
lot of places for murder and other things." No signs of
homicide did not mean anything. Ned wondered if some
relay-racer had decided to clean up Ellesmere.

The Bengtvadi bowed his head in disappointment.

"Yes. That name matches the one given by your companion here. I presume the fact of her background means you will not take responsibility for her body."

"I damned well will not!"

Spartakos followed Ned down to the Exerciser. "Why were you here, Spartakos? You're no Solthree."

"ShipMaster Computer informed me and I came."

Ned turned and looked at him. "And you knew her. I thought your makers had relieved you of your records."

From somewhere in his body Spartakos produced a tiny wreath of red hair, such as a woman might pull from a comb and wind around her finger, and held it between his calipered forefinger and thumb. "I have saved this specimen for many years. There are some things my Makers wished me to keep and remember."

In his new-dog days Ned had been too easily drawn into a quick-rich bunco that left him holding the dripping bag, and Manador had found him a Shangri La, more like Devil's Island, where he hunkered shivering for a thirtyday until the whirlwind blew off. Now too many of the people who had been running the place were closely connected to former Zamos establishments, and it was no refuge.

Feeling vastly lonely, he sat draped with monkeys, in the darkest and grimiest of the spaceport bars, sharing a plate of tacos with Yeya and trying to plumb his mind for other items on Manador's list, while the monkeys fought over the mixed nuts and Embi dug into a bowl of very crunchy food that looked like gravel. Spartakos was simply sitting there in sculpture mode, and finally Ned asked him,

"You ever hear of a hideout called Scudder's Inn?"

"If I ever did I have forgotten it, Ned."

"It's the only one I can remember, so let's go there."

On Fthel IV, maps of the State of Bonzador called the tropical sink of trees and brush in its southeast corner Garden Vale, though no one had ever planted anything there. Its weeds and insects were so noxious that not even environmentalists had a good word for it. The attempts of its first colonists to promote Garden Vale as an exotic resort failed early, and the hotel built in a rush of enthusiasm was soon sold cheap at the first offer.

Scudder's Inn was out of the way, for those who wanted to stay out of the way, a broad and awkward spread of sweeping red tile roofs and adobe walls thick with clumps of old ivy. Most of the rooms opened on the flagstone courtyard, and some of them may have been luxurious, but Ned had bought the cheapest. Its sleeping alcoves were dusty and the floor was cracked cement.

The only luggage was Ned's duffel and a case of power cells for Spartakos; these and some mattresses for the bunks were brought in on a cart drawn by a bossuk, a mutated ox—no expensive robotic carts here—and it had a small head with a flattish face and features that looked almost, in a dim light, human. This disturbed Ned. He thought if it could speak with that lipped mouth it might scream. "Zamos," he muttered.

"Zamos, Ned?" Spartakos turned his gleaming head, but his face was robot-blank.

Ned shook his own head. "Thought they might be selling off their leftover monsters." He wondered how a slave, even a robot one, could ever forget Zamos. The beast made no sound, but that night in his dreams Ned heard its helpless bellow.

Next day he came out near noon after the long sleep he always needed to warm his bones after sending them through space, and stood watching the inner courtyard from the colonnade that lined it. The air was hot and thick.

The corners of the yard were drifting with endlessly falling leaves from trees and brush; a draggled Kylklad and an emaciated Bengtvadi were sweeping them with straw besoms. A quarter of the enclosure was taken up with five or six market stalls where lodgers could buy slabs of meat and root vegetables, and three great braziers where cooks were grilling the meats and roasting the vegetables on the beds of coals.

In another corner a corps of Brazilian machete fighters were warming up in a dance with batons, *crick-crack!* stamping their feet and insulting each other while their old buck-toothed priestess danced around them chanting in a shrill voice. There were ten of them, all men of medium height and with shaven heads. They might have worked on Shen IV when Ned was there, but most likely those had come later. He ran them through the mugbook of his memory and came up zero.

Spartakos had come out for a look, and the monkeys first clustered around him and then climbed the walls of the buildings into the swags of ivy, rubbing the leaves and twigs between their fingers, ducking in and out to play hide-and-seek. The richer oxygen of Fthel IV did not seem to bother them, and Ned wondered what other ways the Lyhhrt had changed them.

A whiff of dope and stale sweat made him notice that there was someone else standing three or four meters away from him, leaning on the balustrade smoking, the dopestick stuck on his lower lip. An Earther in denims and a rough straw hat, his stringy blond hair roughly cut to match. His face was weathered, and his wrists and hands gnarled.

The dope smoker was saying, "Eh, there's that robot, same as I saw on Shen Four, ainit?"

He'd come from somewhere else with that dialect. Ned couldn't tell where, but he twigged this place wasn't the backwater he'd believed. "How would I know?"

"Ehh, you'd know." The smoker screwed up his face as if he was going to tip Ned the wink. His eyes were whitish gray. "Used to give all them speeches, regular o-rator, all about being a slave?"

"Yeh?" Ned wondered what this customer had been doing on Shen IV.

"Thinks e's human e does, eh?"

"GalFed does. They made him a World Cit." Ned thought he must have been Security. He had the look of all the other bokos Ned remembered there. Probably was here too.

"Some nerve he's got calling himself human."

"Why don't you go tell him that? I don't own him." Ned glanced at the three O'e women dashing across the courtyard loaded with shaggy towels and bricks of soap. Then he watched Spartakos.

Spartakos's diamond eyes were following them, and Ned stared at him. There was something even stranger about Spartakos now. It could not have been said that his forehead wrinkled and his brows drew together, but there was a still intensity about him in the midst of all the noise of yelling and cracking batons, as if he were trying to remember, or decide. Something. Following that look, Ned saw that the O'e were wearing neck chains with silver asterisk pendants. The heavy air suddenly lost its ability to warm Ned.

One of the three women tripped on a rough stone and her soap and towels flew out of her arms and landed in the courtyard's dirt. The smoker was over the rail into the courtyard with a one-handed jump, screaming, "You goddam stupid bitch!" The O'e stood as if she had turned to stone with fear, shrinking back with her thin hands held up to protect her face, the towels and soap in a heap in front of her on the dirty stones.

The smoker's hand grasped her shoulder hard enough to crunch stone, and she cried out. The punch he aimed at her face was stopped by Spartakos's gold hand reaching out from nowhere to grasp the rawboned fist. Reeling himself in by that stretched-out arm Spartakos put himself between the woman and the attacker in one easy flow and said, "Stop that." Then he let go.

The attacker yelled out, beginning with "What you—" and ending in incoherent gabble, and shoved at Spartakos with all his fury. In an instant he pulled back screaming, the palm of his hand blood red. The red imprint of a hand rested on Spartakos's chest for a moment until the blood dripped off and left the gleaming chrome. Ned saw, or thought he saw the flattening of the minuscule scales, ten thousand razor edges, that had seemed so smooth a surface. "Spartakos, for God's sake!"

Three women watching from the upper gallery screamed, "Oh my god!" almost in unison while two men yelled, "Hey, what—" The machete fighters had stopped clacking their batons and were staring. The man with the bloody hand ran off howling, "I'll get you! I'll get you!"

Spartakos gave his attention only to picking up towels and soap. Ned noticed Yeya slipping a knife back into her boot and hurrying to comfort the other O'e women. The watchers in the galleries were moving away—the spectacle they had gathered for was over—and the market tenders had backed behind their stalls. Ned climbed over the railing and called again, "Spartakos!" He was suddenly very wary of that machine person. And of Scudder's, the place that had stopped being safe.

Spartakos looked up as if he were awakening and said, "I must apologize to that man." He carefully offered the linens to the woman who had dropped them.

"No, no!" Ned said.

"But I harmed that man. Everyone will be angry with me."

"Stay with me."

"Everyone believes that I am violent now."

The machete dancers were muttering, some laughing: "Go on, iron man, do it again!" They were not fearful of Spartakos. Most of them had seen or heard of him at one arena or the other.

Ned did not wait to see what Spartakos would do next. "Spartakos—"

"Perhaps it was good to be violent, if it was to save myself," Spartakos said. "I need not listen to you. My Makers never said that I must." Ned thought those makers had pushed one button too many.

They were standing alone in the center of the courtyard as if it had been cleared for them, in the eerie calm that was bound to be broken very soon. Yeya hovered nearby, and the monkeys were climbing down from the walls and chimneys. Spartakos was standing very close to Ned, who forced himself not to recoil. The thought flicked his mind like a knifepoint: *How did Ellesmere die, really?* He said very quietly, "Your makers told you to keep yourself safe and stay with me for now."

"Now need not be forever," Spartakos said in his new affectless voice.

"There are at least seventy-five citizens here who have guns that shoot projectiles, and can smash you. And me. And Yeya and Aark and—"

"I understand, Ned," Spartakos said in his normal voice, as if Ned had finally found the right button.

"Call in Aark and the rest of the troop and stay with them inside our room. Keep out of sight and safe. I'm going to those stalls and get some food for the rest of us because we're leaving here tonight. I'll take Tcha with me, she'll tell me if anything's wrong." *When everything's wrong.* The silence around him was thick as the air: forces being gathered, he thought.

"Yes, Ned. Whatever you say." By the time Spartakos spoke the last word his signals had already brought the monkeys running, and they were crawling up his back. He walked off with them riding his shoulders and holding his hands. Tcha peacefully hung on to a fold of Ned's pants leg, turning her head this way and that with a sharp-eyed stare at everyone who was carefully not staring at her. Ned, looking down at her for a moment, noticed that flesh and skin were beginning to fill in and cover the metal plates in her skull, and that at the peak of it there was a solar array no bigger or brighter than an old Khagodi pistaba of tarnished silver. The Lyhhrt had provided power for the macaques.

Praying for the posse to hold off for a quarter hour, he went over where the cooks were grilling meats. The fighters were cooling down nearby, hunkered in a shaded corner behind market stands, some of them eating and others blowing blue powder into each other's nostrils through thin reed tubes.

One of the fighters, a brown-faced man sunburned black, said, "I saw that Spartakos once, but I never hear of him doing anything like that. You think he's gone *maluco*?"

"He gets upset when anybody comes down on the O'e."

"I got nothin against them."

"That chukker in the hat, is he Security?"

"What passes for it here."

Ned bought a bowl of mixed grill with a jug of the local pinqa and squatted beside them, pouring himself a cup. "Know anybody here?"

"Not this trip. We knew about you and Machine Man on Shen Four," the sunburned man said. "After the place got cleaned up we earned less—"

Ned looked at him sidelong.

"—but they didn't make us give all those kickbacks and we kept more of it, so I owe you one, the way it comes out."

"Eh, any way to get out of here in a hurry?"

"Over the wall is all I know. Find a tree to climb there, you better be really fast."

"Thanks." He gulped pinqa and let Tcha watch for trouble, remembering all he had forgotten about Spartakos—how he had wondered who was programming those rousing speeches on Shen IV, how they had forced him to see that the O'e had been created to be slaves of Zamos. Created by guilt-stricken Lyhhrt who had made Spartakos to be their evangelist against Zamos when they had no other way of rebelling without breaking their oath.

He did not know how free Spartakos was, or how much

memory the Lyhhrt had taken from him. But one look at the O'e had brought out the evangelist, and when attacked he had defended himself. Very roughly. Whether he would have attacked Ned—better not think of it. But the Lyhhrt had given him the ability to self-destruct. And changed his shape. And given him to Ned.

They said I would be safer with you.

Safer from what?

From being tampered with.

Why would anybody want to tamper with Spartakos? Why change his shape?

It's obvious. It has to be he's carrying something, that's the only reason, something really valuable. Why didn't I realize—they could have hypnotized—no, they just thought I wasn't smart enough, Lyhhrt are like that.

What were they hiding?

Not their records, they wouldn't take them out of his memory, roll them up, and stuff them somewhere else in his body; that doesn't make sense. Then what? Something else . . . the only other thing, isn't it? one of them? A Lyhhrt— they're smuggling a Lyhhrt!

«Ned-Ned!» Tcha was pulling at his pants leg.

"Eh?" Ned jumped up. "What is it?"

«That one Spark is talking to all those other ones.»

"Other which?"

«Like Yeya.»

"The O'e!" Tcha jumped to his shoulder and Ned picked up the food and walked deliberately. In a glance he was conscious of the tableau across the courtyard: Spartakos at the railing in front of the doorway of their room with a half-circle of O'e before him, pointing and stretching his arms like a prophet in stained glass.

"Oh my god, Spartakos!" Across the yard along the

wall opposite was a quick-walking posse of Straw-hat and two other Security men with a rifle and stunners, and a straggle of followers he took no time to count. It occurred to Ned that though he had seen no impervious helmets here that did not mean there were no telepaths. He didn't know who those men were, or what their connection with the Lyhhrt was, but they were sure of his. "Tcha! Everybody into the room fast, fast!"

Tcha signaled, and there was a mad scramble in the doorway, monkeys buzzing, shooing away the O'e, Yeya protesting, Embi standing scratching his head. Ned slowed to quickstep now, dodging fighters and tourists, who made no move to catch him but were only standing there with vacant greedy looks, and reached destination with a twenty step margin. "Hurry! Inside!"

"What is doing!" Yeya cried. "I want to help them."

"You can't do it now! Spartakos!" He dared not even raise a hand. Spartakos backed in, suddenly stiff-legged as a clay golem, arms straight out rigidly semaphoring. Ned did not have time to stare at this apparition, but pulled in Embi by the shirttail and barred the door.

"Maybe they just want to talk," Ned said. "But break that window and get out, all of you! It's forest out there, you can scatter!" The monkeys went at it with the enameled cups from the washstand, and the thick glass fell in chunks.

Outside, several fists pounded on the door, voices yelled, "Don't knock, break it, dickheads!" and kicks came thick and fast.

«NO!» Spartakos stood rigid and said in a deep zinging robot's voice. «NO! NO!» Then rising, tolling like a bell, *«NO!»*

Ned snarled through his teeth, "Spartakos! Get out!"

The robot had become a machine he did not know anymore. But he could not stop staring.

Baby Rockabye

"No! This is wrong! It is impossible!" Spartakos said in his most melodious organ voice, which somehow expressed true despair, and while the blows and kicks were cracking the door, knocking dust out of the old planks, he raised his hands to his breast in the shape of a gold basket. A dimple appeared in the chrome where the nipple might have been if the Lyhhrt had felt it belonged, became deeper, opened, and set the gold egg, nested in his body so carefully, into his hands. "Too soon!" Spartakos said in real agony.

A hideous mental shriek burst huge and resonant with waves and echoes. :WHAT! WHAT!: Screaming its message: uncontrolled Lyhhrt. Ned saw stars and for one long moment there was absolute silence. *Oh my God, it's a baby, it's a baby Lyhhrt!*

Then the voices outside yelled, "They've got a Lyhhrt in there! Get them!"

A blast blew a hole in the door and exploded into the ceiling, showering dust and splinters. The monkeys, brains bound to instruments that deafened them to the telepathic surge, had pulled out the cords that lashed the cots to their frames and looped them into the framework of the window, each with a handhold. In another crash of splinters and dust they jerked it free.

"Now get—" Ned's yell froze in his throat. Everyone was gaping at the gold egg, now unfolding—trying to unfold—what looked like tiny legs. *:LET GO!:* it mind-screamed. A hundred other voices were screaming outside.

"Spartakos!"

"Stop. Stop." Spartakos was paralyzed, his fingers almost flowing into each other, trying to contain the egg.

But Aark leaped up on Spartakos's shoulders, buzzing, «*Give me, Spark, Give me!*» He plucked the egg from Spartakos's opening hands. "Yi yi!" he yipped, all the other macaques gathered around him and they leaped through the opened window as if they were one.

"Free!" Spartakos cried, and went out of the window in a flow of chrome and gold.

The next great rain of blows and kicks against the door split its bottom timbers, and Ned knew that another couple of slams would break it down. He pulled at Embi and Yeya who had been trying so hard to shrink into a corner he had almost forgotten them. "Come on, for God's sake, we're on the ground floor!" He shoved at Yeya and thumped on Embi's back, and they went out somehow.

But when he got his head over the sill he saw that he was not quite on the ground floor. From the stucco wall the land slid into a shallow bowl crammed with spine bushes. "Oh Christ!"

But no one had fallen into it that he could see, and a voice above his right shoulder cried, "Up here!" Twisting, he found Embi, squatting on an overhang where the red tiled roof sloped over a buttress, and offering his hand.

The door crashed down—"Got 'em!"—and Ned grabbed at Embi's hand. Something struck his left heel as his foot went over the sill but he had no time to look, and scrambled up and over the peak of the roof. Then he fell on his face, bruising his nose, and slid down toward the eaves trough. Something stopped him, but he could not feel what. He twisted to look back, saw that Embi and Yeya had gripped his ankle and leg as he slid, and realized with horror that his foot was numb. He could see where a dart had lanced into his boot, just grazing the heel.

Neither Embi nor Yeya dared rise up to get better purchase on him because of all the darts, bullets and other missiles coming at them. Spartakos had disappeared, but every once in a while Ned could see one or other of the macaques dancing over the tiles, tossing the gold-encased infant to another, pursued by one or other of the thugs.

He managed to pull himself crablike along the roof peak and over to the top of a dormer window where he rested for a moment. He dragged his foot up over the other knee to reach the dart and push it through in the direction it had hit. When the point appeared, he plucked it away with a hard yank. He was grateful then not to feel anything. "Come up!" Embi yelled, his earnest blue face creased with effort. "I can't reach you!"

Ned's foot was still twisted up over the other leg and he couldn't get himself untangled. "Shit! My foot's hurt and I'm stuck. You go!" He spilled tears with the effort of trying to turn over on the bruising tiles so he could free his good foot.

Down below in the courtyard, tourists, fighters and hawkers were milling about laughing, pointing and shouting encouragement to the hunters.

"Hey!" Ned looked up and saw a blue-jawed face rising over the ridge, and then two bony-fingered hands aiming a rifle. He observed with terrible clarity the black curling hairs on their backs. There was only one way out of this and that was falling down into the courtyard, and he thought that was an even worse way of dying. A tree that might have broken his fall was two meters beyond his reach.

While he was thinking all of this in a small calculator in a distant part of his mind, one of his flailing hands found a loose tile and flung it with a skill he had almost forgotten. The heavy tile hit Blue-jaw's forehead with a *thok*, the rifle blasted, and Ned crouched there, twisted over the dormer's roof on his hip and one elbow, hair plastered to his forehead, panting, wondering where he had been hit.

"Hey, Wingo, it's over there!" another voice yelled. "Go get it!" Silence. "Wingo?" But Wingo had gone down somewhere beyond the wall.

Ned let himself lie there breathless for a count of ten, realized that he'd not been hit, then pulled his breath back into his body and pushed his feet over the edge of the dormer roof. He saw some blood seeping from the seams of his boot, but there was still plenty of feeling—mostly bruises—in his knee. He had a quick esp flash of jumping macaques, a silent howl of terror from the baby Lyhhrt, and nothing. They had escaped, or else the Lyhhrt had learned in a hurry how to shield itself. The tree by the wall hid him somewhat from the courtyard and no one down there was looking up.

"Now where's Wingo?" No one answered

"Get the esps! Where the hell are they?"

"Sigman took one of your darts and Marisa's dead drunk."

"Then kick her awake!" The voices diminished.

Ned twisted over onto his belly and looked downward. There were only two storeys below him at this edge of the roof, and a pair of casement windows hung open just below. He heard a loud snore and thought he could try to climb down using the casements as supports and get through the dormer window. It was dangerous, but there was no other way to go anywhere with his dead foot.

He maneuvered himself so that he could put some weight on one of the opened windows with his left hand, hoping desperately that it would not swing him away or collapse. It held. He eased himself down with his right hand catching the eaves trough, hooking his right leg over the sill before that could collapse. He pulled up his left knee so his numbed foot wouldn't catch, managed to grab the sides of the window frame inside and plant himself on the sill.

He sat there just long enough to let terror wash over him again for being stupid enough to fling himself into a room where there might be screamers or guns waiting for him. Then let himself down onto the floor on his good foot.

The snorer was a strong-looking heavyset woman sitting in a cane chair with her body twisted so that her arms and head rested on the table beside her. Her skin was deep Hispanic gold and her hair a smooth black coil at the back of her neck. She was wearing a sleeveless gray cotton dress and her feet were bare and set to either side of a ceramic jug with a glass stopper. He noticed a heavy, very modern lock on the door behind her: this person was not one who could be burst in on.

Ned found a chair like hers just in front of him and sat down in it. The woman was dreaming of a yellow field in a blue sky, herself in a red dress. His awareness of this seemed so natural to Ned that it was only with real effort that he could force himself to think straight. This woman, unconsciously broadcasting, must be the dead-drunk esp that Security had been yelling about. Someone who wanted to be somewhere else. Like himself. He turned away from her dream to rest himself and then he saw the flickering, and jumped.

Monster Dreams

Coming in from the light of a bright sky he had not noticed the narrow bed in the dim corner and the long body of an ancient man, skeleton with skin, lying in it. The color had long ebbed from his ashy skin, and he could have come from any Earther country. The flickering had come from a hypno-eye, set in an eye socket that seemed too big for it. It was powerfully intense but not aimed, only randomly flickering, the natural other eye beside it closed under its fan-fold lid.

The living skeleton was wearing a white tryclon under-suit, his feet were knots of bones and his right arm was a miracle of gold and platinum wires and ribbings, its joints jeweled with diamonds, sapphires and rubies. Lyhhrt work. *The Lyhhrt do our clean work* came into Ned's mind unaccountably. The mouth was a closed slit and there was a breathing tube in the throat. The wall to his left was a panel of sensors that showed a life dimly pulsing.

The old man's dreams were full of blood and fire, they plunged their way into the esp woman's dream, her yellow field burst into flames, the blue sky blackened with smoke, the girl in the red dress shrieked in agony as his fire took her.

The esp woman whimpered and twisted in her sleep. Good enough reason to stay drunk. Ned shivered. He angled to look out of the window and saw the courtyard as untroubled as it had been that morning, fighters lounging,

hawkers calling out wares, guests laughing. The sun stood
halfway between noon and evening. The Lyhhrt, and all the
rest of the company, must be out there somewhere, but he
heard and felt nothing. He was in the mind of the ESP.

Now the girl in the burning field was running, could
not get out. The ancient cyborg loomed up in her blasted
sky and built lattices with fleshly hands, seeded them with
embryos of every being that lived and grew heads, hands
and feet. His jeweled hand twitched, his hypno-eye flickered.

The dream swelled, burst again with fire, and ebbed
smoldering. The esp coughed, licked her lips and said without waking, "I have done everything and there's nothing
else, nothing but to die now, all gods must die, the eggs
have broken, there's nothing to be done." The old man's
cyber arm rose slightly and clenched its too sharp fingers.
The esp, not speaking for herself in that heavily slurred
voice, went on dreaming of fields and sky.

Ned sensed with a start that he had been on the edge of
falling asleep, no, had been asleep, because the sky had
deepened. He pulled himself out of the tangle of thoughts
and dreams, aware that his foot had begun tingling unpleas-
antly. Also that a lamp had been lit and the woman was
looking at him, quietly and without fear. Her eyes were
red-rimmed.

"I—"

"Go quickly now, mister." Her voice was a little thick
but very steady. "I think this one will not wake again, there
will be great upset in this place and I cannot shield you any
longer, I have to leave. The servants' stair is at your right
hand."

"Who is he?" Ned had to know this.

"He is the owner. Hurry now."

His heel hurt like the devil but he found that he could stand on both feet. He nodded and limped out of the room without looking at the cyborg, still half in a dream, found the stairway to his right, felt his way down its dim coil. At the bottom he heard running footsteps from above and a noise like the lick of a wave on the shore and glanced back to see the hot glow of fire on the walls. He hoped she had found an escape. There was none for him up there. He opened the door to the courtyard.

The place was full and noisy. Across the quadrangle the fighters were stamping and clacking with batons, priestess ululating and guests yelling *Ole!* as if they were at a bull-fight. Ned saw the tree he had not been able to reach, and crept into its shadow, but had no way to reach the wall unseen.

The lights went out. The audience said, "Ooh!" and there was no other sound except the *klak-klok* of the batons that suddenly became the deep *clish-clash* of machetes, with great sparks like lightning flashes going *white! white! white!*

Ned pushed pain and nightmares out of his mind and ran straight for them. He knew that the dancers did not whack about indiscriminately but worked in careful lines, and if he stayed at the edges of their formation he would be where no one wanted to follow. Hardly noticed in the darkness here, he found one space to slip between them, perhaps it had been left for him. He didn't stop to think about that, or question how he knew there was that particular tree by the wall, draped with strangler vines for him to climb.

With one leg over, he heard screams that were not from pleasure and took the last glance back at Scudder's Inn. The fire had burst out of the window and was cracking the tiles above, and the roof was beginning to cave in.

He went over the wall, too far gone to worry about falling into a spine bush, felt himself passing through a bubble-like film of static and hissing, and found when he fell into a clump of spineless bushes at the base of the wall that the bubble had been an insect repellent, because he was immediately attacked by a thousand wings and stingers. He brushed them off his face and found it covered with flakes of dried blood. It had spilled from his nose when he fell, up on the roof.

The moon was not much of a lantern on Fthel IV, but the stars were thick in this sector and he had the light of eleven other worlds to guide him. He was pleased to find a narrow but clear path ahead; he had obviously not been the first to leave Scudder's Inn by this route. No one came after him.

He followed the path, limping along on his sore heel and still-tingling leg. After a while he heard a chuffing sound, and a rusty old landcar puttered up to meet him. He knew it carried no enemies by his sense of the Lyhhrt's telepathy, and he was not surprised to find Spartakos in the front seat, with the Lyhhrt egg grasping his shoulder with tiny claws, the monkeys hanging from the steel framework, all nine of them, and Embi and Yeya asleep on the back seat, clasped in each other's arms.

Ned had little breath, and did not know what to say except, "How did you get hold of this um, vehicle?"

"I asked it to come," Spartakos said. "My Makers' child wants to be with his own kind and deliver their records, but I made him wait." This baby was probably the only Lyhhrt Spartakos could ever control.

Ned climbed in, not surprised that the egg held records after all as well as a Lyhhrt. "I thought you'd gone where you'd be safe."

"We are safe," Spartakos said. "I would never leave without you. I knew you would escape."

"Eh, did you. Now where we going?" The car seemed to be dashing out in a direction Ned was sure was wrong.

«It is we who are going,» Aark said.

"You?"

«Yes, we are free now and have all discussed it.»

«This is a good place,» Tcha said, waving an arm at the spiny and insect-ridden wilderness under the moon, worlds and stars. *«No one else wants it, we can live in it without bothering anyone; we will make sure no one else sees us or tries to force us to do anything»*—anything to do with scalpels and dissection, Ned was thinking—*«and we are able to breed now. You have brought us home.»* This was a long speech for a macaque, and none of the others found anything in it to disagree with. So when the landcar stopped at last in a particularly vile thicket, Ned without elaborate words gave his good-byes to Aark, Tcha, Skee, Ki-Ki, Mei, Bola, Floy, Liu and Til. They disappeared immediately.

:I want we/us/my/selves,: the baby Lyhhrt whined.

"Let's go find them," Ned said, and fell asleep.

Homing

In the Embassy apartment Tom Bullivant sat by Verona's bed for one long twenty-eight-stad Khagodi day, watching her sleep, having food brought to him by attendants who were not robot valets, and not eating much. He looked at the brown scab lines on her cheek, and at her hair, gone wild as if she had grown a mane. There was nothing of his wife in her face, certainly not the fear. She had come down the airbus gangway and fallen into his arms first, and then fallen asleep.

The ugly music box and Skerow's miniature terrarium were on a shelf beside the bed. Corpsman Ewskis, one arm in a plasmix cast, had recovered them, along with Sergeant Dreytha's body, and they were the only undamaged objects left in Smuggler's Gap. Skerow had given Verona the terrarium as a souvenir of whatever she wanted to remember.

He waited there. *We're going home. God damn it, I'll make one for us somewhere!*

Tharma gratefully went back to her own office in the city of Burning Mountain, and gave Evarny's old apartment to Skerow and Hasso so that they could recuperate and be debriefed.

"Of course you will have your father's house, Hasso," was the first thing Skerow said when they woke. "I will clear my belongings out of it as soon as possible."

"I have his house in the Spine Hills to live in, Goodmother. You needn't disturb yourself."

"No. I am going home," Skerow said in a voice of iron. *:I will break the law if necessary, to get home.:*

Hasso wisely shut off his mind and folded his tongue.

All too near Skerow's house in the Pearlstone Hills, the alien ship crouched in the pit of its excavation. Forged of substance much like plastial, it was shaped like a titanic clamshell rather than that hoped-for Egg, and stained dark rusty orange by eons spent buried in the rock. During the seven years since the quake it had been gradually and finally excavated. Its great arching entrance was choked with rubble and its entry ramp cracked with age.

At sunrise, thousands of political and media giants and would-be giants gathered in a huge temporary amphitheater built by Khagodi loggers—no Kylkladi bowers here!— along with selected citizens and schoolchildren as well as representatives of all major Khagodi religions: Digger, Inheritor, Watcher and Hatchling.

Four heavy iron robots collected the rubble from the ramp and entrance and loaded it into hoppers. Three tri-V camera robots with silver sides and bulging eyes stepped in on grasshopper feet. No life had been detected inside, no world-eaters were expected.

The ship waited.

Beside it a broad platform had been drawn up and holograms, projected by the cameras, began to build on it. The bulkheads of the ship were lined throughout with glassy cases reinforced with vanadium steel struts. Almost all of the more than eight thousand held an animal, some in liquid, some in murky gases, most in unknown atmospheres.

Eyelids half-closed, a great heap of fur and tusks might merely be asleep. "An Opothrux," Kmanir the Pirigosian zoologist whistled through his ivory mouth. A writhing of shimmering color twisted diagonally for what seemed half a kilometer. "Eki! There is our great-grandfather!" Seffa, Chief Priest of Khagodi Skywatchers, huffed after a great intake of air. "Oh no, it's an Allosaurus!" Greta Holmquist, an exopaleoanthropologist, cried. On and on the witnesses named them, the Lesser Known Thouk with its wide wings spread, the Oboloniskop wrapped in its feathers, the glistening Pahiyepitran, and a thousand others they had never seen nor could imagine. A half-score of cases were smashed and empty, as if their occupants had dissolved and evaporated. Of the ship's inhabitants there was no sign except dust. They had not had the foresight to seal themselves in glass cases.

A great sigh swept the audience like a communal racial memory, and they lingered there enthralled in a silence no one wanted to break.

Finally, in a very deep voice, Kmanir said, "It is the Tower of AdaBaniZep."

"Noah's Ark," said Greta Holmquist. "One more great mystery without Noah."

Within a quarter year the ship was moved by huge hoists to an unclaimed spread of desert with its huge mesas of gray-pink stone, and this was named a World District so that no country could annex it. Many scholars and schools of study began to gather in it.

All barriers removed, Skerow did not need to commit a crime in order to go home. The State had protected her house from burglars and vandals, and her sister Tikrow had tried to save her garden. Her library of vellum and papyrus volumes was safe, as was her kiln, and only a few of the clay tablets she scribbled on in cuneiform had crumbled to dust.

Hasso accepted Evarny's house in Burning Mountain because the city had become an interworld center and he had access to electronic archives and the best minds among many other authorities and experts. He and Skerow visited each other twice a year at GreenWreath Festivals.

The rule of Law inched its way forward again, and on many worlds the Justice System rebuilt its case in the Interworld Trade Consortium prosecutions with the evidence Ned Gattes and Spartakos had rescued along with the infant Lyhhrt.

Waiting to testify, Skerow rested in her desert home with Ksath, and dreamed, strangely, of Burning Mountain, set on its branch of the Great Equatorial River, where she had experienced her greatest dangers and deepest pleasures,

> *that great River soothes*
> *my parching*
> *thirst . . .*

One day she picked up a fresh clay tablet and her stylus and began to consider how she might use those experiences in her poems, perhaps even learn to write in the looping cadences of the Riverine poets—

> *finding myself stilled here after long absences*
> *in the deep lands of a green world strange to me*
> *where the sun falls sharp as the fruit of a swaying*
> *ebbeb from its twisted stem to pull the night with it—*

"Ek, this is dreadful stuff! But perhaps a beginning . . ."

"So goood, Zel!" That's how Ned woke, finally.

"Happy, lover?" She ran her hand over that jaw of his.

"Absolutely."

"Now you can tell me if you met any of those dangerous women!" Zella scanned his carved-up face as if it were
a map.

"Did I ever! The only one wanted to fuck me was the
one who'd just tried to kill me!"

"You've got the scars to prove it all right," Zella snig-
gered and then was all over him again. Nothing was different except that the children were half a centimeter taller.

On the way home in the airbus, Spartakos had said,
"The child of my Makers tells me that you were afraid I
might kill you."

"I didn't let myself think that," Ned said. Spartakos had
never made the least sign of a threat to him. He put Ellesmere out of his mind and said, "Will you stay with me and
Zella?"

"Certainly, until I am sent for."

The Lyhhrt did not send for Spartakos. Ned was per-
plexed at this, but Spartakos said, "They have no more use
for me, Ned, but I will not be useless." He spent half his
time performing with Embi and Yeya at Dusky Dell's bar,
and they improved her business so much she had to apply
for an Entertainer's License for them. In the other half of
his time, Spartakos gathered O'e around him, dealt out ser-
mons on freedom and found them work and medical treatment. "It is these ones who have a use for me."

One autumn day a brilliantly glittering Lyhhrt came
calling. He drew a few stares even from citizens who had
gotten used to Spartakos, and a long one from Ned.

Ned found something like Cupid in curlicued gold and
platinum, with a little potbelly and a navel that held a ruby,
chubby hands and feet with fat-creases, a half-score of dim-
ples filled with sapphire, topaz and emerald, altogether a
parody of lust and mildly repulsive.

In a twittering voice the Lyhhrt said, "I am a very young Lyhhrt, you know, and there aren't very many of that kind."

After a moment, Ned caught on. "Oh," he cried, "you're the Baby!" The flavor of this mind took him immediately back to that long day at Scudder's Inn.

"Child of my Makers!" Spartakos said. "Have you come to stay with us, child?"

"Not at all. I want to be admired by as many fools as possible before I am too old to enjoy this stupid stuff."

"Well, then, why have you come?"

"Ned Gattes, we believed you were foolish and cowardly but our opinion of you has improved since you saved me, and we have a little work for you in one of our consulates. No great distances, only the other side of the world."

"Not hanging off the edge of any roof?"

"Not at all. Only ground floo—I see. You are making humor."

"I've paid my debt to you and you won't use me again. No thanks."

In the long run, Ned thought, the Lyhhrt had really wanted only to get a good look at Spartakos. He got this, then walked away, and Ned did not expect ever to see him again, or hear from the world Lyhhr whether their Cosmic Spirit was ever eased by the outcome of all their agony.

Tom Bullivant made a home in Toronto and married a woman who loved him dearly. Verona welcomed her and basked in her warmth but could not call her mother.

One summer day during her years as a law student a greeting showed up on her monitor with a route trace that scrolled three screens long.

Then Hasso popped up on the screen wearing a red sash and a gold tassel, saying, "Dear Verona, I miss you so much and I so long to see you, but, eki! it is not as easy as wishing. I am a Master of Archives now, my dear, the Learned Hasso, and none happier than I, for I have traced it out, Verona, I have traced it all out!" Huge gulp of air, then, "All of that whole villainous family—no, no!"—as if he could see Verona shrinking where she sat in her cubicle— "I don't mean to frighten you, good child, but there are people like yourself, there is a wonderful woman who lives right around the corner from you, and her whole life would have meaning if she could only see you in your youth and strength! I will print out all the information for you in your very own English! Don't be afraid, child, please let her know you. Skerow sends love and I love you, and we miss you. Good-bye, dear child!"

Verona looked at the name, Darya Ndombele, and at the address, not far away, and at the miniature terrarium, emblem of a land that was so very far away, off and on for the next three weeks. Sometimes shivers of terror would break out over her. But all these years she had also missed Skerow's benevolence, Hasso's comforting and powerful presence. After a few more deep breaths she took the bullet train to London, Ontario, a helicab to Chatham, and a hoverbus where she got off at the end of an avenue lined with gnarled fruit trees, and walked a long way to a big old brick house with a veranda halfway around it.

On the veranda was a thin, old, and very black woman with pure white hair, wearing a white lace dress, who said just as Verona was putting her foot on the first step, "I have no daughters, dear, and my sons have made lives for themselves." She raised her right hand with its violent star. "I've searched for one of us survivors all my life and I am so happy to have found you at last."